Reac
Touchstone (1: Th

"A brilliant teenage tin both intelligent and action-packed. Leads to a climax that takes your breath away…"

"A really cool concept that rattles along like an express train. It's never too long before something interesting happens, so it's turn, turn, turn. Ideal for mobile devices like Kindle…"

"The story makes for an interesting, enjoyable and easy read, and opens the reader's eyes to a time in Moseley long forgotten. It draws your attention to details of how the area was 100 years ago: the beautiful old buildings, the steam tram, how the Village green was actually green…"

"An extremely riveting short book that I didn't want to end and would have loved the book to be longer…"

"I enjoyed this book. I have read a few time travel books but this one really got to me. I thought it was going to be a typical teenage romance but it certainly wasn't. I had to buy the second book and can't wait for the third. Absolutely gripping…"

"I was rapt up in the story, couldn't put it down. As the old saying goes *always leave them wanting more*, just like the old Dr Who series, a cliff hanger leaving you wanting to buy the next instalment."

Touchstone (2: Family at War) [1940]

"Although the Touchstone books may have been written for a younger audience, I assure you; if you are a true fan of timeslip reads these will not disappoint! Each went by far too fast and I find myself waiting in anticipation for the next instalment. Rachel and Danny, along with the characters they meet on their 'journeys' are real, likable and completely caught up in the craziness that's so drastically changed their lives. Delightfully, Andy Conway has a unique way of throwing in twists and turns when least expected. For the price, you won't be better entertained, and soon, you too will be as hooked as I am."

"A very good short book that kept me riveted through the whole story — I never wanted it to end."

"Brings home to one what life must have been like on the Home Front, in cities suffering nightly air raids. Doesn't flinch from the true horrors of the Blitz, nor the petty squabbles amid the rubble…"

Touchstone (3: All the Time in the World) [1966]

"As per the previous two in this series, it is an interesting concept and is developing the story nicely with obviously more time eras to come with all the central characters and now this new introduction of some sort of monitoring team. Who are they? What is their function? I'll need to keep reading the series now I'm hooked."

"I've read all three of the *Touchstone* stories now and each brings the period, in this case the sixties, to life. By concentrating on one area of the world, Moseley, Andy Conway has given it a depth and realism. He turned my preconceptions of the swinging sixties upside down a couple of times. They are easy reads certainly. Roll on 1959 (the next episode)."

"I really enjoyed Touchstone 1 and 2 so much that today while in Birmingham I went to Moseley village to see if the place were real. Thank you for writing the books…"

Touchstone (4: Station at the End of Time) [1959]

"A cracking, spooky read with some great twists… oozes atmosphere, reminiscent of old TV shows like Sapphire and Steel or the Twilight Zone.

"As ever, it's a cracking read which never really stops for breath, exactly like the freight train bearing down on the protagonist's grandmother.

"Touchstone 4 also comes with a bonus short story which is a real head-wrecker. Worth the price for that alone."

"This was a good read, enjoyed the whole series."

"Just read Touchstone 1-4 in one sitting. Unfortunately, I have now time-travelled up to your writing speed. This novella-at-a-time e-publishing with print sets of multiple instalments goes back full circle to Dickens: serialisation in the ephemeral media, followed later by consolidation in permanent record. Looking forward to Touchstone 5."

TOUCHSTONE: 5. LET'S FALL IN LOVE FOR THE LAST TIME

The first two parts of *Touchstone* were originally published as part of Andy Conway's challenge to publish 11 titles before 11 November 2011. He has continued to publish fiction under a variety of pen names since then. His first feature film, *Arjun & Alison*, a campus revenge thriller, was released in 2013. He teaches screenwriting at Birmingham City University and runs the Shooting People Screenwriters Network bulletin, which goes out to 11,000 writers every weekday.

Read more at www.andyconway.net

Also by Andy Conway

Novels
Train Can't Bring Me Home
The Budapest Breakfast Club
The Striker's Fear of the Open Goal
Lovers in Paris

Novellas
The Girl with the Bomb Inside
The Very Thought of You

Touchstone series
Touchstone 1: The Sins of the Fathers [1912]
Touchstone 2: Family at War [1940]
Touchstone 3: All the Time in the World [1966]
Touchstone 4: Station at the End of Time [1959]

Shorts
Meet Me in Montmartre
Ghosts on the Moor

Andy Conway

Touchstone 5. Let's Fall in Love for the Last Time

WALLBANK

This is a work of fiction.
Names, characters, places, and incidents either are the product of the author's imagination or are used fictitiously, and any resemblance to any persons, living or dead, business establishments, events, or locales is entirely coincidental.

This paperback edition 2013
1

First published in Great Britain by
Wallbank Books 2013
Copyright © Andy Conway 2013
The right of Andy Conway to be identified as the author of this work has been asserted by him in accordance with the Copyright, Designs and patent Act, 1988 © Andy Conway 2013.

ISBN-13: 978-1493711604
ISBN-10: 1493711601

All rights reserved. No part of this publication may be reproduced, stored in a retrieval system, or transmitted in any form or by any means, electronic, mechanical, photocopying, recording or otherwise without the prior written permission of the publishers.

This book may not be lent, hired out, resold or otherwise disposed of by any way of trade in any form of binding or cover other than that in which it is published, without the prior consent of the publishers.

Cover design by Simon Moody at Wallbank Art, based on original Touchstone cover design by Pete Bradbury at Digit64
Cover models: Sallyanne Moss and Martyn Nelson

To Richard Matheson

ACKNOWLEDGEMENTS

Thanks must go, as always, to Lorna Rose, David Wake, Jonathan Turner and James Donaghy, whose input made me go the extra mile.

Pete Grafton's remarkable book *'You, You & You! (The People Out of Step with World War II)* has long been a favourite of mine and I found myself delving into it once more to reacquaint myself with its opening chapter. The numerous accounts of the appalling and cynical actions of the CPGB, particularly over the battle of Cable Street, have been transferred from that book to my imagined world of Moseley in 1934. While I accept that the CPGB did much good work during the 1930s, it is overshadowed by the betrayals of Stalin, which directly created the disaster of Germany, and it is this that has informed the political backdrop of *Touchstone 5: Let's Fall in Love for the Last Time*. A restored version of the original full text is now being published online by Pete Grafton at http://youyouandyourestored.wordpress.com.

Likewise with the portrayal of Benny Orphan, who, though he bears a superficial resemblance to Al Bowlly, is entirely a fictional creation, not least in that Al Bowlly, by every account of the day, was a thoroughly decent chap. I know of no entertainer of the 1930s who staged a nightly raffle in the manner of Benny Orphan and must stress again that it is entirely a fictional invention of my own.

One real person who appears in the story is Anthony Pratt, a keen pianist who lived in my own neighbourhood of Kings Heath, and who would later go on to invent the board game *Cluedo*. I know of no evening when he stood in for a jazz pianist, nor that he ever played with a visiting swing band, but I couldn't resist giving him a chance to star in this fiction and hope that it is viewed entirely as the affectionate portrait it was meant to be.

As usual, profuse thanks go to Sallyanne Moss, Martyn Nelson, Claire McKinney and Stuart Smith for their sterling help staging the cover photograph.

Touchstone

5. Let's Fall in Love for the Last Time...

TOUCHSTONE 5 - FAMILY TREE

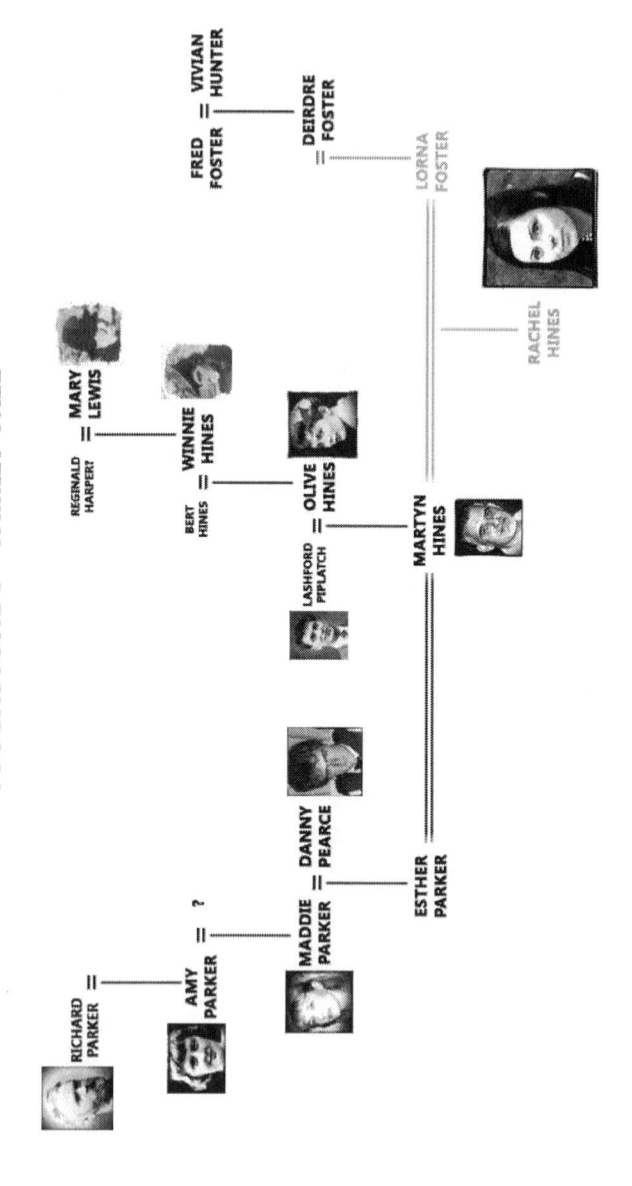

REGINALD HARPER? = MARY LEWIS

BERT HINES = WINNIE HINES

LASHFORD PIPLATCH = OLIVE HINES

FRED FOSTER = VIVIAN HUNTER

= DEIRDRE FOSTER

MARTYN HINES = LORNA FOSTER

RACHEL HINES

RICHARD PARKER = AMY PARKER

= ? MADDIE PARKER

DANNY PEARCE = ESTHER PARKER

— 1 —

Henryk Kertész heard the wail of a train and the hiss of steam, and felt a terrible sense of foreboding. A premonition of death.

He paused as he entered the station and wondered why he should feel this so strongly. He was not a superstitious man. Even though he attended synagogue in the city, he wasn't really a believer, and regarded it as merely a social event through which he could keep in touch with other Jews.

The station was a grand arch of steel and glass and rather busy for a Sunday, men in overcoats and trilbies, woolen scarves, their leather shoes shining; women in cloche hats and their skirts swirling daringly mid-calf even in this cold.

A newspaper vendor kept guard over a small snowdrift of headlines about Hitler.

Henryk shuddered and tried to shake off the feeling. Why would the wail of a train and the hiss of steam, two harmless sounds he heard almost every day, fill him with such dread? The English had a phrase for it: *someone has walked over your grave*; and in German it was *Death walked over my grave*.

He plodded on and went through the barrier, flashing his ticket stub at the uniformed man — again the sense of dread — and that was when he saw the gang of Blackshirts.

They looked eerily futuristic in their buttoned up black shirts with no ties. The men all cheekbones and moustaches; the women all blonde curls and pale venom.

He scurried on past them, staring at the floor, hoping to avoid their gaze.

'Curtis!'

He flinched, carried on walking.

'Henry Curtis!'

He stopped and turned. The entire gang was looking his way, a gaggle of blue-eyed malice. One of the girls had called him. He saw her now and it took him a few moments of vacant staring before he recognised her.

'It's you! Jew Henry! The big clever dick!'

The men stepped forward to flank her, their fists whitening. One of them snarled, 'Do you know this Jew boy?'

She was gleeful with spite. 'I went to school with him! Jew Henry, the school swot!'

Henry found himself laughing and tried to stop himself. It was a dangerous thing to do; to laugh at a gang of Blackshirts. They tended to want to be taken seriously and frowned on being ridiculed, especially by young Jewish men.

The bruisers accompanying his ex-school friend stiffened some more and their fists became even whiter.

Henry was sure that he could handle any one of them — one on one — in a fair fight. But Blackshirts didn't really play like that. It would be him against ten of them, and although he might dish out at least three bloody noses, he would very quickly disappear under the boots of the other seven, no doubt with the girls joining in.

Henry raised his hat and bowed.

'Good day to you, Julie Hickman. Still the same charming girl, I see.'

Her grin of malice soured with hate.

'Watch your mouth, Jew boy!'

The men stepped forward and he ducked as one threw a punch at him. He scooted back. They sprang forward.

'Your days are over, Jew!' she shouted.

He decided to dispense with dignity, turning and running full pelt for his platform.

The Blackshirts chased him. All of them. Including the women.

He knew that if he didn't catch the train, he would suffer the beating of his life. But other passengers were running for the platform too, turning and wondering what all the commotion was behind them.

The train was leaving.

He pushed through, their fists punching empty air behind his head. At least one of them kicked him and he staggered momentarily, his backside stinging. *Do not fall. If you fall they will be on you.*

A whistle.

He pounded for the train already pulling out. His hand gripped the brass handle, turned it, pulled the door open, a jump and he was riding the train.

A hand grabbed at his sleeve and he turned to see one of the Blackshirts running alongside him. Henry knew that if he fell now, they would have him, the entire gang of them running alongside.

He shook him off and kicked out.

The Blackshirt crumpled, his mouth exploding teeth and blood. Two of his friends tripped over him. The rest stopped and shook their fists, spitting their hate.

Julie Hickman shouted after him, 'Adolf Hitler is coming for you! Oswald Mosley is coming for you!'

Her hateful face shrank as the train pulled out of New Street station, through the cluster of Birmingham city centre, and he didn't get his breath back until it pulled into peaceful, quiet Moseley.

— 2 —

The pain was unbearable. Her whole body felt like it had been used as a football. But she was smiling.

'Can you stand up, madam?'

Rachel grinned into his face, even though she could see it was disturbing him. Of course it was: he had never met her before, even though she'd met him many times, through different decades that were still to come.

He was Charlie, the man who had been there for her — a safe embrace in the Hell she'd been living since she'd been lost; Charlie, the dashing lieutenant in 1940 who'd kissed her right here by this gravestone as he sent her back to 2012; Charlie, the sharp-suited, bespectacled, sports car driving 50-year-old businessman who'd 'sort of proposed' to her in 1966; Charlie, the overcoat-clad matinee idol who'd embraced her for a brief moment in 1959 — a nightmare 1959 that might have been all in her head. A 1959 that had almost destroyed her.

She had escaped it somehow and emerged here, back in the graveyard at St Mary's church, Moseley. And she knew exactly what this was: she was meeting Charlie for the very first time, in 1934.

This was the time when she would persuade him to help her in all the subsequent years. She knew it because he'd told her about it in 1940.

'Are you quite sure you haven't been attacked? Was it those bloody Blackshirts?'

'I don't know what you mean.'

She let him pull her gently to her feet, staggering against him. He held her firmly, but not as strongly as future Charlie would. Had.

'They've been busy locally,' he said. 'Unfortunately, the place name seems to have attracted them.'

He looked at her now and stopped, as if he recognised her. Could he possibly recognise her?

'What is it?' she asked.

'I don't know,' he said. 'Just a strange... Quite peculiar. Almost as if someone walked over my grave.' He dismissed it with a tight smile. 'I suppose that's what you get for walking through a graveyard.'

'Why are you here?' she asked.

She had a sudden desire to know exactly what had made their paths cross. This was their first ever meeting. Why was it Charlie here now and not someone else?

'I don't know,' he said.

That tight, self-deprecating smile again. *He's shy,* she thought.

'I've never actually been here before. I was walking to Moseley and sort of just found myself here. Quite peculiar.' He rubbed his neck. 'Still, good job I did.'

'Yes, thank you,' she said. 'You've saved me.'

'Just what exactly happened?'

'I don't think you'd believe me if I told you.'

He smiled uncertainly and she knew he was already a little bit spooked by her. She let herself wilt in his arms and he tried to steady her. *If you act helpless, he'll want to help you*, she thought.

'Look, we really should get you somewhere safe. The rally's out at Bingley Hall, but there might be a few still around.'

She put her hand to her face, pretending to be dizzy, groggy.

'What rally?'

'Wretched Oswald Mosley. The Blackshirts. There are thousands of the idiots all over Birmingham today.'

'Oh… yes… Blackshirts,' she mumbled. She didn't know what he was talking about specifically, but she'd read about Oswald Mosley and the British Union of Fascists. His surname had made her wince at the irony (Moseley village in her time being the epitome of liberal cool). In history books and old news reels it had seemed unbelievable that a mass movement of Nazis had goose stepped all over Britain in the 1930s. Britain: the country that would face Hitler alone for much of the war that was yet to come.

'Was it them?' he asked.

'Yes,' she lied.

Charlie seethed. 'Those bloody, hateful thugs. Why can't they just live and let live? Promoting hate and envy, when it's the opposite of that that life is all about.'

'The opposite?'

'Love,' he said. 'The opposite of hate.'

He blushed suddenly and she saw the teenage boy he was; ardent, passionate, full of belief. For a brief moment she wondered if she were about to destroy all of that in him.

Charlie looked around wildly and walked her towards the green wrought-iron gate at the rear of the cemetery.

'Come on. Let's go.'

She walked alongside him, occasionally pretending to trip as they edged down the alley and emerged at the village green.

It was fairly similar to Moseley as she'd seen it in 1940, but without the sandbags, the public information posters and people walking here and there with white gas mask boxes bobbing at their waists. It was Moseley in peace time. Moseley before the bombers would come.

She felt a sudden sadness for them all and wanted to warn them: *enjoy this, appreciate this; really* live *this, because it's about to disappear.*

'I live just up there,' he said. 'You can sit there till I call an ambulance.'

She looked up and was surprised that he wasn't pointing at the stucco battlements of the corner house: Charlie's flat above the street in 1940 and 1966, which he'd left to her in 2012.

He wasn't pointing there at all. He was pointing across the street to one of the windows above the shops on Victoria Parade. It was Barrow's Stores now, but she knew the place. It was above what would one day become Mrs Hudson's costume hire store.

— 3 —

Kath Bright dug her iPhone from her pocket and paused on the village green, about to cross the road. The traffic whizzed past, busy even on Sunday. A fleet of middle aged men on a scooter run went by so she decided to check her phone before crossing.

No one was calling her and it wasn't even a text message, just the reminder for the meeting she was about to attend above Mrs Hudson's shop. *I am so Belinda No Mates*, she thought.

She swiped the appointment clear and waited for a gap in the traffic. The shop was closed for the day and her gaze wandered up to the bay window above it. The two-storey flat Mrs Hudson owned, which had become a headquarters for their group. In the upstairs back attic room was a safe in the wall where they could deposit reports from various time zones. It was an awkward but effective method to communicate with each other across the decades.

The traffic thinned and she stepped across the street, walking down the hill to the side of Boots on the corner and turning in to the courtyard at the rear of the shops, up the steel staircase to the flats above.

Mrs Hudson opened the door and smiled kindly, kissing her on both cheeks, ushering her through to the lounge.

Mitch was sitting in the armchair with a blanket across his lap.

'Hello, Kath,' he croaked.

She stopped cold and couldn't hide her shock.

'You look awful.'

'Thanks,' he chuckled.

'I mean it,' said Kath. 'You look at death's door.'

She looked to Mrs Hudson for support.

'Nonsense,' said Mitch, waving a hand towards the coffee table at his side where a pitcher of orange liquid sat. 'Nothing that a few thousand milligrams of Vitamin C won't put right.'

He laughed and coughed and spluttered and sank back into his chair, wheezing.

'Mrs Hudson, he shouldn't be here.'

Mrs Hudson shrugged and sat down and poured a cup of tea for her.

'Mitch is fine, Katherine. He's like this every time he has to do a possession. He was the same after he had to rescue *you* from your Untime episode, if I remember rightly.'

Kath sat across from Mitch and patted his weak hand and blushed a little.

'He'll be right as rain in a couple of days.' The old woman's eyes twinkled with mischief. 'It's only a bit of Time Flu.'

Mitch smiled and Kath gave in to the mood, sipping at her tea and nodding agreement. She was the junior member and had to bow to their experience. But Mitch looked like the uncle she'd visited once on his death bed. His skin had a translucent sheen that you could almost see through, as if he were already fading away from the world. It scared her.

Mitch polished his glasses before tangling them back behind his ears, grunting as if he were lifting weights. He sat back and idly twirled his moustache, curling the edges up into Dali points.

'So,' said Mrs Hudson, tapping her lap for emphasis. 'What do we do about this Rachel Hines girl now we've dragged her out of *her* Untime episode?'

'Do we know where she is?' asked Kath.

They both looked to Mitch. He shook his head.

'Not yet. Not got a fix, I'm afraid. It'll come.'

'She might even be *here*,' said Mrs Hudson. 'Back in the present, where she belongs.'

Kath glanced out of the window across the village green to the rooms above the corner pub, where they knew she lived.

'I could go and call on her,' she said.

Mrs Hudson shook her head. 'Not yet.'

Kath felt a flush of anger. Why was Mrs Hudson constantly holding her back on this?

'But we need her.'

'That remains to be seen.'

'She's more powerful than any of us,' said Kath, looking into her tea cup, aware that her voice was rising with anger. 'If we don't get her on our side, Fenwick will get her on his.'

'That is entirely possible,' said Mrs Hudson. 'And might already have happened.'

Kath shook her head.

'I rescued her from that padded cell. She's not on Fenwick's side at all. I can tell.'

Mrs Hudson surprised her by smiling, leaning forward and patting her on the knee.

'I know, Katherine,' she said sweetly. 'You have faith in her, and believe me, I trust that. And there's a part of you that resents me a little because I'm too cautious and you've made a commitment to this girl.'

'No, I don't think that.'

'It's all right. I understand. I would feel the same if it were me. But it's my job to be sure about who we recruit. It's a matter of security. We know how dangerous Fenwick can be and I have to be totally sure she's not already under his influence. Her closeness to the boy Danny is a real concern.'

Kath nodded. The old woman was right. But it didn't stop her feeling that they were missing a great opportunity. Rachel had skills she'd never seen in anyone, including Mitch and Mrs Hudson.

'And I needn't remind you how dangerous it can be. This meeting would have more than three people present if it wasn't for Fenwick. We all know what happened in 2005.'

Mrs Hudson glanced up at a cluster of framed photographs on the wall. All three of them were there, plus a number of others she'd never seen, and one she'd known briefly who was now wiped out forever: Kieran Fickley.

His face stared out of the frame, like a man imprisoned in time. A real person, who was now nothing but a fossil on a photograph.

'Yes,' she mumbled. 'You're right.'

'No,' sighed Mrs Hudson. 'No one's right or wrong. I'm just a cautious old biddy. And I trust your instincts. You've worked hard to contact this girl. You plucked her right out of Hell, so you know a little bit about her. And you've spent some time with Danny too...'

Kath blushed a little. Here, in this room, serving him his breakfast in 1966, pretending to be the footloose hippy chick, wanting him in her bed.

'... so I think I should pay the respect of trusting your experience on the matter. We'll talk to her. As soon as we find out where the hell she is.'

Mitch let out a strangled gargle and they both turned to him with alarm.

He was shaking, gripped by a seizure, eyes rolling, the Vitamin C drink spilling all over the blanket across his lap.

Kath leaped across to him and took the glass from his spasming hand.

His body stiffened and jerked right and left, his body arching as if a million volts were shooting through him.

'He's having an episode,' shouted Mrs Hudson.

'What do we do?'

Mrs Hudson calmly took his head and eased him down to the floor. She held his head safe as his body writhed, jolting, his heels slamming the carpet.

Kath felt herself panicking. *Don't die, please don't die.*

A fleck of froth speckled from his mouth.

'New... poor... raw...' he croaked.

Kath looked at Mrs Hudson. The old woman was whispering a soothing 'Shhhhhhhh,' to him, as if putting a baby to sleep.

'There... for...'

Therefore? What was he saying?

He sucked a giant gulp of air deep into his lungs and collapsed. She thought for a moment it was his dying breath, but no, his chest rose gently again. He was breathing. His eyes fluttered open.

'Oh God, Mitch. Are you all right?'

He smiled weakly, coughed, winced at the pain.

'My word, that was a bad one,' he croaked.

Mrs Hudson was smiling, as if she'd seen it many times before.

'I know where she is,' he said.

'What?' said Kath. 'You just travelled?'

'It's what I call his episodes, Katherine. Mitch has a talent for seeing things. *Feeling* them, actually. He can lock in on a disturbance, sense it somehow. Like he's a lightning rod.'

'Feels like it too,' he groaned, lifting his head. He sat up and rubbed his neck. 'That was a particularly painful bolt as well.'

Mrs Hudson wrapped the blanket around his shoulders and Kath helped her lift him back into his chair.

'Did you see her?'

'Not her,' he said. 'Someone else. A man. Might be him: Danny. Can't be sure.'

'Where?'

'Thirty-four,' he said. 'Nineteen thirty-four.'

Kath saw Mrs Hudson go pale.

'No,' she said. 'Please, no.'

'What is it?' asked Kath.

Mitch looked to her with surprise also.

'Did you see a dance hall?'

Mitch shook his head. 'No, a door. A house on Newport Road.'

'You're sure?'

'It wasn't a dance hall,' said Mitch. 'But... the strangest thing...'

'What?'

'I could hear music really clearly. As if it were being sung right into my ear. An old tune. A man singing. A crooner.'

He hummed a tune and Mrs Hudson put a hand to her open mouth. Kath had never seen her look scared before.

'What is it?' she asked.

Mrs Hudson stared up at a picture frame on the wall. It contained an old concert bill for someone named Benny Orphan. Her hand dropped to her neck, as if she'd seen her own death.

'He's going after *me* now,' she said.

— 4 —

Danny walked down the stone path towards the rear of the graveyard. It looked like the place had been cleaned. It wasn't so overgrown as it used to be. At least, he thought so. He'd seen it in so many different times now that he could hardly remember that first time.

Fenwick walked ahead, clutching a leather document folder under his arm, an eager spring in his step, as if he were the student, not Danny.

He reached the familiar gravestone that was almost like a stone bench or a baby's cot.

The touchstone.

'So it's not really a time travel portal?'

Fenwick laughed. 'You know that's not true.'

'Well, if we're talking about *experience* as opposed to *theory*, I'd say the opposite.'

He knew more than Fenwick; felt stronger, knew he had outgrown his mentor but was keeping him close, pretending deference, because there were still things Fenwick might say that could be useful to him.

He'd been reading a lot. This was unusual. Despite being a history undergraduate he'd never really been one for reading books. But recently he'd been speed reading a great many. Everything he could find on time travel. Tapping the screen of his Kindle every second and absorbing the books without really reading them. It was astonishing, when he stopped to think about it: he had suddenly developed this new skill of photoreading. Just like his skill for time travel.

Yes, he had outgrown Fenwick. His teacher still seemed gleefully excited by it all, but his smile fell at Danny's irritated tone.

'Look, Danny. I have no talent for this,' he said. 'I can't do what you do. But I've learned from people like you. I understand it a little bit more than you. Despite your undoubted experience.'

Danny pushed his hands into his pockets. 'What people?'

'What do you mean?'

'You said you've learned from people like me. Who else has done this?'

Fenwick grinned, caught out, half laughed at a private thought.

'You don't really think you're the first person to do this?' he laughed.

Danny shrugged. 'I hadn't thought about it.'

'Well, you're not. There have been others. You've met them.'

Danny tried to think. Of course.

'You mean that Mrs Hudson?'

'And a certain gentleman who runs your local junk shop.'

The bloke at Buygones with the silly moustache and waistcoat who drank tea from an Art Deco tea set and ate cucumber sandwiches.

'And,' Fenwick added, 'a certain redhead you spent some time with in 1966?'

Danny looked at him with alarm now. This was something he hadn't known.

'You mean Kath? She was…?'

'I'm surprised you've never recognised her as the girl who works in the Central Library. She's handed you fiche records, Danny.'

He tried to remember the girl at the library. Rachel had accused him of flirting with her, but he couldn't remember her face. Was it really the same girl who'd befriended him in '66?

Rifling through the 1939 edition of Kelly's Directory, pen poised to take notes.

'Hello, did you get your photograph?'

He looked up, startled. A woman. His eyes flitted to her name badge. Kath Bright. He placed her. The librarian who'd helped. Of course, the photograph of Amy and her father that Rachel had handed to him. Only the other morning.

'Yes! Yes, I did. Thank you very much.'

'We don't normally make finds like that, but as I told your girlfriend, this photographer kept an archive of his subjects' names.'

'Oh, she's not my girlfriend…'

'Oh.'

'We're study partners.'

'I see.'

Kath Bright ran her fingers through her hair.

'It's a brilliant photo. Thank you very much for finding it for me.'

'Any time,' she said.

She backed away, bumped into a table behind her, flushed red, walked quickly away.

Danny frowned and then forgot her.

'They're all in Mrs Hudson's bloody cabal,' said Fenwick. 'And there have been others too.' Fenwick reached over and touched the gravestone, his fingers tapping at the exact same place Danny had always touched to pass through into the past. 'You see? Nothing.' Fenwick couldn't hide his bitterness. 'It doesn't work, Danny. I've tried it.'

Danny frowned and tried to work it out.

'I used it to pass through to 1912, the first time. Here. On your field trip. It sent me back there two more times. Then it sent me back to 1940, again I used it twice. Nineteen-sixty-six, again, twice. Each time I went through by touching that gravestone in that exact spot.'

'And what about the last time, Danny? What about 1959?'

Danny floundered. It was more like the bad memory of a trance, as if he'd been hypnotised. It was a far off dream: just a few flashes of images that might tell a much more involved and detailed story if only he could remember more of it.

But he remembered standing on Kings Heath railway station platform in bitter cold. A demonstration at University on a bright sunny day. He had kissed Rachel in the middle of it. Why had he done that? He didn't even fancy her. He was in love with Amy Parker.

'Can you remember using this to get there?' said Fenwick, pointing at the gravestone.

'I can't remember anything.'

There was something else; something behind those few random images flashing inside his head. It was big and dark and terrible and it made him shiver with fear. But he couldn't see it.

Fenwick put an arm around him, patted him on the back.

'Hey, Danny. What you have is a natural talent. It's inside you; not in that gravestone. I envy you so much. I've never travelled. I thought one time I'd managed it — a sensation, nothing more. I can theorise about it, write it up, research it. But you've *been* there. You've walked the streets of the past. You can do anything you want.'

'So I can just think myself back there?'

Fenwick nodded. 'I believe that. But if it helps you to touch that thing, then just do it.'

He wanted to reach out and touch it, as much to escape this conversation as to be in the past.

'Bear in mind,' said Fenwick. 'Whatever you do, Mrs Hudson and her cabal will be trying to stop you. Rachel too.'

'Who died and made her the queen of the time travellers?'

Fenwick laughed and squeezed his shoulder and shrugged him away roughly.

'I know what you want,' he said. 'You want to get back to Amy Parker. It's all you've ever wanted. And what right have they got to stop you doing that? You saved her life. She wouldn't even have lived beyond

1912 if it wasn't for you. In a way, she belongs to you. You belong together.'

Danny nodded. It was sort of true, when he put it like that. He'd saved Amy Parker's life. But the last time he'd seen her she'd shouted hate at him, collapsed and died. An old woman in 1966, accusing him, rejecting him.

He wanted to woo her all over again. Go back and find her before then. Recapture the spark he'd first felt with her. The love he'd seen in her eyes in 1912 and in 1940.

'I miss her,' he said. 'I can't stand how I saw her the last time: an old woman shouting hate at me, telling me to stay away from her daughter. I made her daughter rich.'

'Go back to before then,' said Fenwick. 'You can do what you want.'

Danny stared at the touchstone.

'It's always sent me back so randomly.'

Fenwick shook his head. 'No, no, no. Think about it. What year were we talking about that first morning, minutes before it first sent you back to 1912?'

Danny thought hard. He'd been hungover from a student party and had barely listened as they'd discussed the history of the church.

'You remember? I asked the class when Moseley had become part of the city of Birmingham. Rachel said the correct answer: 1911.'

Danny frowned, not getting it.

'But you gave the wrong answer. You said 1912.'

'Did I?'

Fenwick nodded. 'You said it, and five minutes later you were there. Don't you see?'

Danny wheeled away and rubbed his face suddenly, trying to wake himself up. 'This is crazy. I don't know how to control this!'

'You don't need to. Not yet.'

Fenwick flipped open his leather document holder and delved into one of the pockets. He took out a photograph and held it out.

'Let's try an experiment. What if you knew where she was on a very specific night?'

The photograph seemed to have been taken in the murky interior of a night club or dance hall, but it was unusual in that it was taken from almost behind the singer. A man in a tuxedo was singing into an old fashioned microphone. A crooner. His face was side on. What was interesting about the picture, though, was the group of people you could see in the background. A few audience members, who were right up against the stage, were watching the crooner sing.

One of the women seemed to be a teenage girl in a ball gown with a fur stole over her shoulders, wavy bobbed hair. She was gazing at the crooner as if entranced.

Next to her was an older woman. Not old enough to be her mother, perhaps an older sister. She looked in her mid-thirties, also wearing a ball gown. She was gazing at the crooner too. He must have had a hypnotic effect on women.

Danny could see quite clearly that this older woman was Amy Parker. 'It's her, isn't it? It's Amy.'

Fenwick dug into his document wallet again and pulled out another sheet of paper.

'Now what if I could tell you I know exactly when that photograph was taken. Almost to the hour. And the exact location too.'

He passed Danny the sheet. It was a yellow poster. A concert bill, proclaiming in very large letters: *BENNY ORPHAN* and underneath, in smaller type, *With the syncopated accompaniment of Lester Johnson's Coloured Jazz Orchestra*. It was taking place at the Moseley and Balsall Heath Institute on the night of Saturday the 27th of January 1934 at 8 p.m. One lucky lady could also win the prize of being serenaded on stage by Benny Orphan himself.

Danny looked back at Amy's face with wonder.

'She was there. At this.'

Fenwick nodded and smiled paternally.

A sudden gust of wind nearly took the photo and handbill from Danny's hand. They flapped furiously like captured birds trying to be free, till he shoved them in his pocket and reached out instinctively for the touchstone.

Fenwick gripped his hand, shaking his head.

'Not so fast,' he said. 'You'll want to do some research before you go there.'

— 5 —

Rachel walked with Charlie into the rear yard behind the shops and looked up at the iron staircase to the upstairs flats.

Too many coincidences swarming her brain. The apartment was above Mrs Hudson's shop. The redheaded girl from the library had been staying there in 1966 and she'd had Danny staying with her. Rachel had delivered the letter to him, staggering up the stairs, desperately ill — the letter that had told him Amy Parker was dying in hospital.

And now this. Charlie, her confidante, her protector: he had lived in the same place.

He walked her up the steps to the top, cradling her in case she fell again. Two doors. Perhaps it wasn't the same apartment. Perhaps it was all a coincidence.

Charlie fumbled for his keys and seemed embarrassed.

'Shan't be long. We can call an ambulance from here.'

She propped herself up against the iron banister.

'I'm sure I'll be fine. Once I've got my feet back.'

It was the same door. What did it mean? If Kath Bright and Mrs Hudson were on her side, and they'd rescued her from the station at the end of time, then why had they been harbouring Danny here in 1966?

And what was the connection with Charlie?

'Come in,' he said. 'Bit pokey, I'm afraid, and rather a mess, but…'

He didn't finish, just shrugged and blushed and blustered through into the flat, leading her to the sofa where he let her sink gently into the cushions.

'I'll put the kettle on,' he said, rushing over to a stove in the corner of the room. He filled a tin kettle with water from the sink and lit the gas. Then he took a green glass from a cupboard and filled it with water.

'Here,' he said, offering it to her. 'Have some water while the kettle's on.'

She sipped at it and felt better instantly, the leaden cloud inside her head lifting.

Charlie paced back to the stove, seemed to realise it would be a long time before the kettle boiled, paced back. He dug into his jacket pocket and pulled out a packet of Craven As, lit one, puffed on it nervously, blew out blue smoke, paced again.

He caught Rachel's astonished stare.

'Oh, I'm so sorry, do forgive me.'

He pulled the packet out and offered her one.

'I don't smoke,' she said.

'Oh. All right.' He shuffled, thought about it, seemed puzzled. 'Really? You don't smoke?'

'No.'

He scratched his Brylcreemed head.

'Oh. I've never met a woman who doesn't smoke. May I ask why?'

'Cancer,' she said.

He seemed surprised. 'Really? That's just an old wives' tale, surely?'

He sat in the armchair, crossed his legs, tried to relax, puffed on the cigarette some more.

Rachel stared. This Charlie was so much more boyish than any of the other Charlies she'd met. She wondered for a moment if it was her that had changed him, perhaps changed him for the worse. But no, surely it had been the war: the war that was coming in only five years' time and would turn this boy into a man.

'I say, do you like music?' he said.

He rushed over to a sideboard and pulled out a ten inch disk in a crinkly yellow paper wrapper.

'I have some marvellous new jazz from America. There's a pianist called Teddy Wilson, who's quite breathtaking.'

He placed the heavy disk reverentially onto a wind-up gramophone and cranked the handle. The tinny tinkle of ivory floated across the room like the blue smoke from his cigarette.

His records. Rachel couldn't help smiling. She knew them all; had worked her way through them in the long days alone after he'd given her his other flat across the green.

A woman's voice soared over the music; haunting, familiar.

'That's Billie Holiday,' she said.

Charlie frowned, went over to the gramophone, tried to read the label of the record that was spinning round. He looked back at Rachel with surprise.

'How do you know that?'

Rachel shrugged. 'Billie Holiday's famous. I love her voice. You're the—'

She wanted to tell him she loved Billie Holiday because of Charlie, but she caught the words in her throat.

Charlie stood quite still now, gazing at her as if he wanted to paint her and was memorising every detail.

'What?' she said. She'd never seen Charlie look at her like this. There was something unnerving about it.

'No one knows about Billie Holiday,' he said. 'This arrived last week, and I don't know anyone in this entire city who hears the latest jazz before I do. And *I* didn't know the singer's name.'

She shrugged and tried to laugh it away, but he stared and stared and she knew now that it was fear.

'And another thing,' he said. 'How the hell did you know my name when I've never met you in my life before?'

She held his gaze and wanted to tell him so many things — about the war to come and how he'd already be wealthy by then because of the sports almanac she was going to give him, and a lieutenant, and about the Blitz, and all the dates she'd meet him in his future.

A piercing scream cried out and didn't stop.

She jumped with fear and Charlie walked over to the stove and took the kettle from the hob. He didn't return to interrogating her. He took a teapot, scalded it, scooped in a few teaspoons of tea leaves, poured the hot water in and swirled it around. When he'd finished, he brought it to the little table by the window and laid out two china cups on saucers.

The music ended.

He reached for another disc and set it going. Al Bowlly drifted through a dreamy version of *Time on My Hands*.

She watched him from the sofa. He didn't seem to want her to answer. She watched him pour the tea through a strainer, take a fat bottle of milk from a cupboard that must have been the larder. He didn't look at her till he picked up a sugar cube with tongs.

She shook her head.

He dropped one into his own cup and stirred, brought them both over, held hers out to her, sat opposite again with the teacup on his lap.

She sipped at it: too bitter.

She finally looked up into his expectant face.

'I'm going to tell you some things that you'll find totally crazy,' she said.

He frowned, as if she were speaking a foreign language.

'That you'll find rather odd. All I ask is that you hear me out. Listen to everything. Will you do that for me?'

'How do you know my name?'

'Because we've met before.'

'I've never met you.'

'In the future.'

His eyes widened now. He lifted his cup and sipped. It rattled on the saucer when he put it back. Was his hand shaking?

'I've met you in the future, Charlie. You probably won't believe me, but I'm going to give you a book that will prove it.'

When Charlie spoke he didn't seem surprised or astounded. His tone was light, amused. It seemed he'd already decided she was crazy.

'So give it to me. Let me see this proof.'

'I don't have it with me now. I have to go back and get it.'

'Back where?'

'To 2013.'

Charlie's eyes widened with a new emotion and she realised it was anger. He'd had enough.

The doorbell buzzed. Someone banged a fist at the door.

Charlie kept his eyes on her as he crossed the room, as if she were a dangerous animal.

He opened the door and a man bustled in, flapping his overcoat and peeling off a scarf. He was young, in his twenties, but, like Charlie, and every other young man in the 1930s, he looked twenty years older than he was. He stopped short when he saw her and his face broke into a giant smile. He raised his hat and held out his hand.

'Well, Charlie didn't tell me he had a guest! Good day, madam. Henry Curtis, at your service.'

She smiled up at him and glanced at Charlie, who was glowering behind him.

'Yes,' mumbled Charlie. 'I sort of… er… that is…'

Rachel shook Henry's hand.

'I'm Rachel Hines.'

'Rachel. Good Jewish name. Charlie didn't tell me he had such a beautiful female friend.'

Henry laughed and wagged his finger at him.

Charlie reddened and mumbled 'We were just discussing some music.'

'Oh. You're helping us with the concert?'

Rachel checked Charlie's face, alarm writ large.

'Well, yes I…'

'She was just leaving…'

'Nonsense!' cried Henry. 'You're just in time to hear the news.'

Henry walked over to the window table and poured himself some tea.

'Er… Henry,' said Charlie. 'You know you have a boot print on the back of your coat?'

Henry wheeled round, swept off his overcoat and laughed at the grey outline.

'Ah, I was in town and encountered some of our friends from the British Union of Fascists. They didn't like the cut of my jib.'

'What?' cried Charlie. 'Are you all right?'

'Perfectly. I did what everyone must do when they are hopelessly outnumbered by the forces of darkness. I ran like the clappers.' Henry sipped at his cup of tea and sighed with pleasure. 'But never mind those ogres. I have news about the concert. Good news and bad news.'

Henry sat down at the table and slurped his tea.

'What is it?' said Charlie. 'Don't tell me Orphan's cancelled.'

'No. Benny Orphan's still with us. Unfortunately, he won't be accompanied by Lew Stone's band.'

'What?'

Charlie had forgotten about Rachel now. She watched him totally caught up in his world: the fly on his wall she'd always wanted to be.

'That's a disaster! We've got posters all over Moseley saying it's Benny Orphan and the Lew Stone Orchestra!'

'Yes, that's the bad news,' said Henry. 'But don't worry; here's the good news. I met Louis Szekely this afternoon. That's why I was in town. He told me Fred Herschel in London has a new band he wants to rehearse. He wants to send them out to the provinces to sharpen them up before they get a residency at one of the London clubs.'

'And can they do it? It's this Saturday!'

'We'll call him tomorrow. They're a good band, he says. Jazz men. From Jamaica.'

Charlie raised an eyebrow. 'They're a coloured band?'

'Oh yes,' smiled Henry. 'Should be something to see here in Moseley, eh?'

'Blimey,' said Charlie. 'Imagine that. A coloured jazz band. Here in Moseley.'

'We'll get a new poster printed as soon as it's confirmed,' said Henry. 'Then we have to go round and paste them up over all the old ones. Should only take a day or two.'

'Yes,' grinned Charlie. 'We could do it.'

Rachel felt sudden warmth for him. He was so eager and full of boyish enthusiasm. He seemed to hear her smile, noticed she was in the room again. His smile faded.

'Right. Er, Miss Hines here was just leaving,' he said.

Rachel winced, a dart in her heart. Charlie was chucking her out.

'Yes,' she said. 'I really have to get back.' She stood, reached for her handbag, waved at Henry. 'Lovely to meet you.'

'The pleasure was all mine,' said Henry. 'With bells on.' He stood to attention and clicked his heels, bowing his head.

Charlie ushered her to the door, his hand at the small of her back.

'Thank you for helping me, Charlie,' she whispered as he opened the door for her.

'It was nothing,' he said. 'Goodbye.'

The door closed in her face. Charlie had thrown her out.

— 6 —

Rachel didn't remember walking down the iron steps. She must have sleepwalked her way to the village green because the first thing she remembered after Charlie closing the door in her face was standing outside Boots looking up at the battlement tower of St Mary's church, standing guard over the Bull's Head.

Her eyes fell on the latticed windows above the corner house, which was a pub in 2013 but a tailors now. This was her home, the apartment Charlie had left to her. This was where she had to return.

She had to go back there and get the almanac, then come back here and give it to Charlie. She knew she could because she *had*.

She crossed to the village green and sat on a bench. There seemed to be quite a crowd, people piling off the trams from the city and heading for the church or just promenading. It seemed to be the place to come on Sunday afternoon.

She'd imagined that Charlie might welcome her. That she could stay with him. She must have done more than simply hand him a sports almanac and a list of dates detailing her future visits to him. Something must have passed between them for him to wait for her to appear again during an air raid in 1940.

At the moment, if she handed him a sports almanac from the future and a list of dates she'd return to him, she could only imagine he'd throw them in the bin.

She still felt a little unsteady. Needed to rest a little more. Her spirits had sunken. The thrill of seeing him again had turned to a cloud of gloom that hung over her head and showered acid rain on her.

It was hopeless.

She didn't belong here. She needed to give him what she had to and then return to 2013 and her empty apartment above the pub — the loneliness and nothing but Charlie's record collection for company; wondering how she might one day work out what had happened in the previous hundred years since they'd saved Amy Parker's life that had wiped out Rachel's existence.

It was there somewhere.

But it wasn't here in 1934.

She would find it one day and try to correct it. Or she'd never find it, and have to live the rest of her life as an exile from her own existence.

She put her head in her hands and tried to think herself back to 2013. This was how it was supposed to work, wasn't it? There was no touchstone. *She* was the touchstone. That was what Mitch had told her, and Mrs Hudson, and Kath Bright. *You are so powerful,* Kath had said. *More than any of us.*

But she was still sitting on a cold bench in 1934. She would just have to go to the church yard and touch the stone and hope that it would work. It was all so hopeless.

'You look a little lost, Miss Hines.'

She opened her eyes. A kind smile. A raised hat. It was Henry.

'No,' she said. 'Just preparing myself for the journey home.'

'Have you come a long way?' he asked.

She nodded. 'A very long way.'

'I should apologise for my friend,' he said. 'But I'm not as much of an ass as him, so I really can't.'

She smiled.

'May I?'

He indicated the space next to her. She nodded. He sat down.

'Charlie is a nice man, believe me, but… well, a little bit scared of women.'

'Do you think so?'

'Believe me; I've seen him in action. He's terrible.'

She was laughing now. There was something about Henry Curtis that made her feel instantly more cheerful. He was a nice person to be around.

'You should try with him. He needs a gentle shove sometimes.'

'I don't know,' said Rachel. 'I've got a book for him. I think I'll go home and get it, give it to him and then leave him alone.'

Henry didn't ask about the book, even though he was burning with curiosity, she could tell. It was another nice thing about him: he saw everything, but didn't intrude on your privacy.

'I'll meet him again some day,' she said.

Henry stood up.

'I hope so. He could do with a lady like you around. Give him a boot up the backside.'

He turned around and brushed at the now faded boot print on his overcoat, smiling mischievously. Rachel covered her mouth, laughing.

'It was a pleasure meeting you,' he said, holding out his hand.

She shook and he kissed her fingers.

'Don't leave it too long to see him again,' he said.

He raised his hat and jaunted off.

Rachel gazed up at the church clock. There was nothing to do but give Charlie the almanac and let it all play out from there — let it all play out just like it already had.

She would go and touch the gravestone again. She wasn't ready to think herself back to the present. She pushed herself up off the bench and headed up St Mary's Row.

She would meet Charlie again someday, she knew that. And those days would be happy ones. The problem was: for Charlie those days were all in the future. But for Rachel, they were all in the past, and this was the last time.

— 7 —

The church bell was clanging as Rachel walked through the lychgate on St Mary's Row. Did that mean a service was starting or ending?

There was a crowd of people gathered in their Sunday best by the church entrance. She hoped no one would be in the graveyard at the rear or she would have to wait to perform her disappearing act.

She turned the corner and took the grass instead of the stone path, so no one would hear her footsteps.

It seemed to be empty.

She walked swiftly but softly down to the far end of the graveyard, looking behind every few yards, making sure no one could see her.

There. The touchstone.

But you *are the touchstone. That's what they said. You don't need this.*

It didn't matter. She couldn't sit and meditate for hours and hope she ended up back in 2013. She knew that if she touched that certain spot on the gravestone, it would send her back, just like it always had.

Almost always.

She was ten yards from it and still glancing behind her when a movement made her stop.

The air shimmered around the touchstone ahead of her. Shimmered and folded in on itself and then coughed up the shape of a man.

She ducked behind a tall marble crucifix and peeped through its Celtic ring.

The man was dressed in a baggy blue pin-striped suit, with brown loafers and green tie. He was holding onto his hat and clutching a brown leather suitcase. He glanced around and didn't see her. The wind seemed to be whipping at his trousers, which was strange, because it was quite calm where she stood.

She saw his face and caught her breath.

The man marched down to the wrought-iron gate at the rear of the churchyard, pushed at it. It creaked open. He scooted through and was swallowed by the shadow of the alley.

Rachel felt cold fear run its icy fingers up her neck.

Danny had come to 1934.

— 8 —

Rachel had thought about staying.

If Danny Pearce had come to 1934, whatever the reason, it would probably spell trouble for someone. Usually it had involved him protecting Amy Parker and her ancestors at the expense of Rachel. But this might mean trouble for Charlie.

What if he'd come there now to interfere in some way: wipe out Charlie before he could begin to help her?

She watched him disappear down the alley, heading for the village green, and felt relief that she'd decided to be cautious and take the long walk around. If she'd taken the short cut through the alley, she'd be standing facing him right now.

Should she follow; find out what he was up to?

She stood frozen and tried to think it through. Everything told her to follow Danny and stop him interfering in her past again. But she also had to go back to the present, get the almanac and give it to Charlie.

And that was the only thing she should do.

It didn't matter. Whatever, she had to get the almanac. She might as well do it immediately. She could be back here in 1934 in ten minutes and then warn Charlie about Danny.

If he would ever listen to her.

She marched over the sodden grass to the touchstone, looked around one more time, and reached out.

She yelped as her fingers burned, a ghost whispered in her ear, the church bells became white noise traffic roar and the grass at her feet grew half a yard.

She steadied herself, looked all around.

The grave stones around her had gained decades of moss. The gate was rusted and padlocked. She was back in 2013.

She marched out through the lychgate and onto St Mary's Row, confectioners, watchmakers and milliners replaced by an art gallery, hairdressers, Balti restaurants.

It was no longer a cold January morning at all. It seemed like summer.

She wondered how long she'd been gone as she walked quickly down St Mary's Row and found the unobtrusive door to the flat above the pub.

Her key was on a string around her neck. She was in and scooting up the stairs, as if someone were chasing her.

The apartment was just as she'd left it. One of Charlie's jazz albums laid out by the Dansette. A half-drunk cup of coffee on the table, a crust of green mould floating on it.

She couldn't remember when she'd last been here. She'd found herself back here the day Charlie sort of proposed to her and she was ready to accept and stay with him in 1966. She'd visited the library and researched her maternal grandmother's suicide. After that there was nothing. She'd found herself suddenly in the rest room at Kings Heath station, trapped in her own personal nightmare.

The station at the end of time.

She grabbed the almanac and shoved it in a canvas bag, then looked around for anything else she might take.

She realised she could give Charlie the book, but unless she could tell him something that happened the day she appeared to him, there was a good chance he might throw it away.

But he didn't, she thought. *Yes, but that was before Danny went back there. He might be there right now telling Charlie I'm a lunatic who wants to kill him.*

She needed something more.

She switched on her laptop and waited for it to boot up. She googled Oswald Moseley's mass meeting at Bingley Hall in Birmingham and verified the date as Sunday 21 January, 1934. From there she found a newspaper front page for the next day and scanned the blocks of clustered print for stories that might be reported as breaking radio news the previous afternoon. There was only one story that looked suitable. Everything else seemed to be general news from the whole weekend that anyone might know about that Sunday afternoon in 1934.

She wrote down a few details of the story and then looked up a list of football results for January 1934. She'd printed them off and folded it in her pocket when the doorbell rang.

She froze.

No one ever called her here. No one knew her here. She peeped out of the window but couldn't see anyone down on the pavement. Whoever it was, they were standing close to the door.

She crept down the stairs and listened. The doorbell rang again. There was nothing to do but answer it.

She opened the door to find the redhead from the library, Kath Bright, smiling at her.

'You're back then, Rachel?' she said.

'I was just leaving, actually.'

Rachel stepped out and closed the door behind her.

'Oh really? Going anywhere special?'

Rachel looked down at her 1959 suit, which did not look too much out of place in 1934, and clutched her canvas bag closer.

'Or should I say any*when*?' Kath smiled at her own joke and seemed friendly.

Rachel felt a pang of guilt. Kath had picked her up off the floor, at the absolute darkest point of her nightmare; picked her up and given her the strength to escape it.

'Thank you,' said Rachel. 'You rescued me. I don't think I'd have done it without you.'

Kath shrugged. 'I bet you would. Like I said, you're more talented than any of us.'

Rachel shook her head. She didn't feel talented at all. She didn't feel like she understood any of this.

'You should come with us,' said Kath. 'We could do with your help.'

Rachel shook her head. 'I haven't got time.'

Kath frowned and Rachel realised what she'd said. She clutched the bag tighter.

'What have you got there?'

'It's nothing. It's something I have to give to Charlie.'

Kath grabbed at the bag and opened it, seeing the book before Rachel snatched it back.

'I have to give it to him,' said Rachel. 'Actually, I already *have*.'

Kath bit her lip, nodded and seemed to understand. If she knew she'd already done it, then she had to do it.

'When are you going?' she asked.

'Now.'

'I mean *to* when?'

'Oh,' said Rachel, feeling stupid. 'January, 1934.'

Kath's face fell. 'Oh God.'

'What?'

Kath took Rachel's hand, squeezed it gently. Rachel couldn't help remembering how much that same touch had saved her from dying in a padded cell.

'Look, Rachel. I understand you have to go back. I really do. And I'm not going to stop you. But… well, it's too much of a coincidence. There's something you need to know before you go back there. You *have* to come with me. Now.'

— 9 —

Kath took Rachel to the car park behind the shops where her Mini was parked.

'Get in,' she said.

Rachel paused. 'Where are we going?'

'Newport Road,' said Kath, matter of factly, as if it were obvious.

Rachel got in beside her and Kath pulled out down the car park slope to the exit. Rachel giggled to herself as they waited for a break in the traffic.

'What?' said Kath.

'I'm sorry,' said Rachel. 'It's just the thought of you travelling in a car. Instead of, you know, just thinking yourself somewhere.'

'Oh.' Kath laughed.

She inched into the traffic on Alcester Road, turning right, through the traffic lights at the Moseley village crossroads.

They sailed up the gentle rise and past the Prince of Wales pub. Rachel wondered idly about her bar job there. She'd probably been replaced already, disappearing with no notice given. She felt bad about letting them down. There was no way she could explain why she hadn't given them a phone call or an email. Whatever the emergency you could always do that. Unless you'd disappeared into a nightmarish Untime that looked like Kings Heath train station. There was no point explaining that one.

'Do you still use the gravestone in St Marys?' asked Kath.

It felt strange discussing this with someone, out in the open, as if it were normal. Other than at first, with Danny, before he changed sides, this thing had always been a secret she carried alone. She wondered if Kath Bright might become her friend.

'Yes. I do. I mean, I did just now. I know I'm supposed to be able to do it by myself, but... It's just easier.'

Kath nodded. 'I still use the Dovecote. That's where it all began for me. I've done it without a few times but it's difficult.'

'It seems to have a life of its own. I mean, I fall asleep or faint or something and I'm in a different time.'

Kath drove on down the hill towards Balsall Heath, past the derelict tram depot and the near-derelict Moseley Dance Centre next to it. Rachel noticed that Kath kept her eyes on it as she passed, as if looking for signs of life beyond the grime-coated windows. A bright new banner flapped in the breeze and promised a vintage dance night called *Hot Ginger*.

'That's your innate talent trying to tell you how easy it is,' said Kath. 'It's your logical mind that's refusing to believe it.'

They took a sharp right down Brighton Road, under the railway bridge.

'Yes, maybe,' said Rachel. It truly was much easier to believe it was a spooky gravestone causing this rather than any ability she had.

Kath turned right again up Kingswood Road and then took a sharp left into Newport Road.

'Mitch can do it better than me,' she said. 'But even he has trouble. He's more of an empath. He *feels* it.'

Half way down the quiet back street, she parked up. Mrs Hudson and Mitch were standing before a derelict house, deep in conversation.

The row of terraces all looked recently renovated, except for this one ruin that stuck out like the rotting tooth in a newly-capped row. The roof was dark and sunken like the bruise on a peach, the few square yards of garden were overgrown, and the door and window frames a tired blue that was a mass of flakes, the glass panes all grey and cracked.

It was a total dump.

Mrs Hudson and Mitch turned and looked surprised to see them.

'I know I shouldn't have,' said Kath. 'But wait till you hear where she's just visited.'

Mrs Hudson forced a kindly smile that hid her alarm. 'Let me guess,' said the old woman. 'January, 1934?'

Rachel frowned. 'How do you know?'

'Why then?' said Mrs Hudson, suddenly stern. 'What are you up to?'

Rachel stepped back, stammering. 'Nothing. That's where I arrived. After I escaped the station. *You* helped me get out of there and that's where I woke up, so I don't know why you're implying that I'm up to something.'

'No one's implying…' said Mitch.

'I didn't want any of this! I just want my life back!'

Kath took her arm and whispered soothingly, 'We know, Rachel. And we're going to try and help you.' She shot a warning glare at Mrs Hudson, who turned and faced the house again. 'But it's quite a coincidence to us that you've just returned from 1934, because that's where we've only just detected something very strange happening.'

Rachel tried to read their faces. Mitch urged her forward, pointing at the house.

'January 1934,' he said. 'Here. Something happens.'

'Saturday the 27th of January,' said Mrs Hudson bitterly.

'What happens?' Rachel asked. 'How do you know?'

'I told you Mitch can sort of feel things,' said Kath. 'He gets a sense for things: disruptions, ruptures in time. He feels them. And he's felt one happening here, on that date.'

'Well,' said Mitch. 'This is where the anomaly is at its most powerful. And it's off the charts. As if there's a great deal of activity around this house.'

'But at the Institute too,' said Mrs Hudson.

'She means Moseley Dance Centre,' whispered Kath.

'Yes,' said Mitch, impatiently.

Rachel could tell they'd argued about this a lot.

'But here it's *really* powerful,' said Mitch. 'Multiple visits. *This* is where the problem's located.'

Rachel looked from one face to the other. 'Is it someone's touchstone?'

Mitch shrugged. 'The level of activity matches that. But there's something else too. A very bad energy. Something very wrong happens here.'

Kath pulled a piece of paper from her jacket pocket and unfolded it to reveal a photocopied page from Kelly's Directory 1934.

'Here. It lists a Mrs Alice Ogborne living here. A widow. The 1931 census says it's her; a son, Harold, aged 18, and daughter Judy, 15. Do you think that's who it is?'

Mitch shrugged. 'I can't tell.'

'Sometimes,' Kath whispered to Rachel, 'we get a lot of disturbance around girls in their late teens. We don't know why.'

Rachel thought about herself and how this ability had manifested itself as she started University.

'But this is stronger than that,' said Mitch. 'There's a lot of bad energy around this house. It goes on for years. I can feel it. But something really unspeakable happens here on the night of 27th January, 1934.'

Mrs Hudson let out an exasperated sigh. 'Which just happens to be the exact same night of a certain crooner's concert just around the corner. The very night my parents met and fell in love.'

Rachel felt that feeling again: something crawling all the way up her back and her neck, with its scaly hand settling on her skull. It was the feeling she got when she sensed something very bad was about to happen. More and more it was a feeling that was becoming exclusively connected to Danny.

'A crooner?'

'Yes,' said Mrs Hudson. 'A very special crooner who made a very special visit here and no doubt caused the births of a great many children nine months later. One of them being me.'

'I think my friend Charlie is arranging that event,' said Rachel. 'Is his name… Benny Orphan?'

They all looked at her with shock now.

'What do you know about it?' said Mrs Hudson.

'What I said. Charlie's my friend in the past. He's helped me every time. I've just met him again in 1934 and he's organising that concert. He's very keen that it's going to happen,' she added.

'You'd better be right,' snapped Mrs Hudson. 'That concert *has* to happen.'

'Why would I try to stop it?'

'Someone wants to.'

'It's obviously Fenwick,' said Kath. 'You said so yourself.'

The slimy hand that had tickled its way up her back and neck now dug its nails into Rachel's skull.

'Oh God.'

They all looked at her.

'What is it, girl?' snapped Mrs Hudson.

'Just before I came back. I saw Danny arrive. He's gone to 1934.'

Mrs Hudson buried her face in her hands and slumped down onto the garden wall.

'I'm sure he has no intention of preventing your parents meeting,' said Kath.

'Are you?' said Mrs Hudson. 'And what gives you such faith in his inherent goodness, Katherine?'

Kath reddened and looked at the pavement. 'I just don't think he's evil.'

'I do,' said Rachel.

'No one's evil,' sighed Mrs Hudson. 'But some people do evil things because they're selfish. They only see their own needs. Fenwick was the same: he got drunk on his own sense of power and pursued it regardless of the damage it's done to anyone around him. Danny is no doubt the same.'

'It's Amy Parker,' said Rachel. 'He saved her life in 1912 and that's what wiped out my life. He's been preventing me from correcting that ever since.'

'Who is she?' asked Kath.

'He's obsessed with her,' said Rachel. 'If he's gone back to 1934 you can bet your last farthing it's to see her.'

'Well, that's something,' said Mrs Hudson. 'But I still don't like it. I don't want him anywhere near the moment my parents first get together. I'm sure Fenwick is leading him there.'

'I'll go there and stop him,' said Rachel.

'I don't want you going there and changing anything,' said Mrs Hudson.

Rachel unconsciously gripped her canvas bag a little closer to her side. Kath looked the other way.

'You've got to let me go there,' said Rachel. 'My friend is arranging that concert and I can help him. It makes sense.'

Mrs Hudson rubbed her eyes and sighed and pushed herself back to her feet. She stared at Rachel for a while, as if she were trying to burrow her way into her soul.

Was she reading her mind? Would she find out about the almanac?

'I thought you were only interested in getting your life back?' said Mrs Hudson.

She was right, Rachel realised. It was stupid to want to go to Charlie. There was no way Charlie could help her get her back to her old life with her dad. He'd already done everything he could.

'1980,' she mumbled. 'That's where it happens. I think. This Amy Parker who should have died: she has a granddaughter who meets my dad in 1980, instead of my real mum. But I don't know how to get there. If I could do it, I would. But I just go to 1934 instead.'

Something in Mrs Hudson's face thawed. She saw the lost girl in Rachel. She nodded and hugged her.

'Oh, you poor girl. Don't worry. We'll help you. Of course we will. Please forgive me for being so wrapped up in my own troubles.'

Rachel felt tears spring to her eyes and blinked them back.

'But as you can only get to 1934, and as it seems you could be very useful there, why don't you help us? And then we'll help you in 1980?'

Rachel nodded and smiled. 'Thank you.'

Kath and Mitch were grinning. They both patted her on the back.

'Welcome to the team,' said Mitch.

She felt a wave of pride swell inside her. It looked like all she had to do was make sure this concert happened, for Mrs Hudson's sake, and then they would help her with her own problem. In some other time. Some other time that didn't involve Charlie.

Perhaps this had been Charlie's sole purpose all along: the man who was arranging the concert where Mrs Hudson's parents would fall in love. If that happened, Mrs Hudson could then help Rachel get her own life back.

It seemed such a small part to play for a man who'd become so important to her.

'You go to this friend of yours, Charlie,' said Mrs Hudson. 'Make sure *nothing* changes. Use whatever influence you have with him to make sure this concert happens. We'll take care of this anomaly here. And we'll join you on the night in question.'

Mrs Hudson turned and gazed up at the dirty windows and the flaking blue paint. The meeting was over.

— 10 —

'I think she's a little bit tense,' said Kath as they walked back to her Mini. 'She's usually much nicer.'

Mitch trotted over to them and murmured, 'Go to my shop. You'll need some money.'

They both nodded and looked at Mrs Hudson, still gazing at the derelict house.

Kath drove back to Moseley and stopped at Mitch's junk shop, Buygones. She said nothing about Rachel's almanac and her intention to hand it to Charlie, which was most definitely an attempt to change the past. It was an unspoken secret between them.

Mitch came by a little later, after driving Mrs Hudson home, rattling his keys and opening up for them.

He opened a drawer below the counter and Rachel caught a glimpse of a series of envelopes with random years written on them. He pulled out one marked 1933, heavy with coins, and emptied it out on the counter.

Various dirty copper and silver coins poured out, all bearing the King's head. There were some large white banknotes too.

'Okay,' said Mitch. 'This is a farthing. You get four of these to a penny. Here's your shilling — that's twelve pence. People also called these a bob. There's also these thrupenny bits. They call that a *joey*. Worthless even during a Depression. You get four joeys to the shilling, or two of these sixpences. They're also called tanners. Now, it's not like decimalisation. You don't get a hundred pennies to the pound, it's 240. That's twenty shillings. This is a pound note. Or a twenty bob note in the vernacular. This is a ten bob note — that's 120 pence, or ten shillings, so half a pound. That's the simple stuff. These two here make it a bit more complicated. This is the florin, which is a two shilling piece, worth 24 pennies, and this is the half crown, which is worth 30 pence, or two and six. Have you got that?'

Rachel looked him in the eye. 'Oh yes, totally.'

Mitch smiled and dug around in a box full of purses, pulling out a fetching lime green one with a metal clasp. He poured most of the coins into it and a few notes.

'You probably won't need the notes as almost everything costs a few bob. If you get rumbled, just pretend to be American. Always works for me.'

Rachel took the purse and slipped it into her handbag.

'Thank you, Mitch. That's really kind of you.'

'Good luck,' he said. 'I have to say, I'm really excited to have you on board.'

He shook her hand and she felt suddenly nervous, as if she'd been mistaken for a famous person.

'Do you want me to walk you to…' Kath let it trail off, feeling stupid.

'I'm fine,' said Rachel. 'I've got some clothes at my flat I can take with me. I'll collect those on the way.'

She went to the door and turned to see them watching her.

'I'll see you in 1934 then?'

'We'll be there,' said Mitch. 'Good luck.'

She waved and walked out, rushing to her flat. Being in Mitch's shop had reminded her of the suitcase. She had a case full of old clothes, given to her by Maddy Parker after her mother died in '66. There was a particularly lovely ball gown. Maddy had wanted it all thrown out before the funeral. Rachel had offered to take it off her hands.

When she'd woken up back in her apartment, the case had been there, and she'd never known if it had somehow materialised with her or if Charlie had just kept it there for her all those years.

It was at the bottom of the wardrobe. She pulled out a few things that were obviously too old for her, threw the almanac in there and snapped it shut.

No one noticed the girl in the late-fifties suit with the old suitcase as she walked into St Mary's churchyard. She simply looked like one of any number of girls wearing vintage fashions in 2013.

An hour ago, she thought, she'd only intended to go back and throw the book at Charlie and then have nothing more to do with him. Now she smiled as she walked towards the touchstone. She smiled because she had a mission, and the mission involved getting to know Charlie all over again.

— 11 —

Amy Parker smoothed out her dress and checked her face in the kitchen mirror. The light was useless here, by the back door where the tin bath hung next to the privy. She ought to check her face in the dressing table mirror in her bedroom.

She dug lipstick from her handbag and put it to her lips, then changed her mind.

It was the Ogbornes' tea party next door, not a ball. And besides, today wasn't about her; it was about Little Amy.

She half laughed bitterly to herself.

Little Amy, the teenage girl who was about to call with her mother, Mrs Dowd. How everyone chuckled at the confusion over their names. Then the devastation as they'd called the girl 'Young Amy' then realised with embarrassment that that meant she'd have to be 'Old Amy'.

Old. At the grand old decrepit age of thirty-four.

She didn't feel old. A lot of women married at about her age. But she sensed her options were thinning out rapidly. There weren't many men in Moseley who showed any interest in her, due to the whiff of scandal regarding her father.

She heard their whispers. The women more than the men. The women were cruel, malicious, full of spite. The men tried to ignore it, but privately made a mental note to avoid her.

Constable Davies was about the only man around who smiled at her, even touched the peak of his hat when he passed her desk at work.

She wondered if he would be at the dance this weekend. She let herself imagine him asking her to dance, taking her in his arms, swirling to the music, his body against hers, her hand resting on his broad shoulder.

No.

He wouldn't ask her to dance. No one ever did. She was damaged goods. She was the girl whose father had died in the loony bin.

She was Old Amy, Big Amy, On the Shelf Amy.

But there had been the boy, Danny Pearce, who'd appeared suddenly, mysteriously, and rescued her from her insane father, and just as suddenly disappeared again, never to return. There had been many times when she thought she'd seen him. But it was always mistaken identity. And even a man who looked like him suddenly seemed less handsome when she discovered it wasn't him.

The doorbell chimed.

She focussed on her own face and realised she'd been staring at her reflection in the misty mirror for ages. She scowled and dashed to the front door.

Mrs Dowd stood there in a floral summer dress that looked like it had been made from a pair of curtains ripped down from a ballroom window. Her mole eyes squinted through pint glass spectacles.

Now here's someone who really deserved to be called Big and Old, thought Amy. And then felt guilty for her bitterness.

Little Amy stepped from behind her mother's giant frame and Amy took in a startled breath.

Little Amy Dowd looked beautiful in a white flapper's dress and matching cloche hat. Her pretty eyes sparkled with genuine warmth as she rushed to hug her.

Was this the only person in Moseley who actually liked her?

'Hello, Auntie Amy!'

Amy gave her a peck on the cheek and held her out, looking her up and down.

'My! You look absolutely lovely.'

She was not Little Amy's aunt. There was no family relation at all with the Dowds. But this was how it was. A youngster could not call her parents' friends by their first names, so you became their aunts and uncles.

Mrs Dowd blinked up at the sky. 'Nice day, considering.'

'Surprisingly warm for January.'

She ushered them through to the parlour where a pot of tea was waiting under a cosy. Mrs Dowd slumped into the sofa as if she'd walked a hundred miles to be here, instead of a hundred yards. Little Amy slid into a spot beside her.

'I thought we were going next door for tea,' said Mrs Dowd.

'Well, I suppose we are,' said Amy. 'This is sort of the pre-tea.'

Little Amy giggled. Mrs Dowd grunted and took a teacup and saucer, slurping at it.

'Are they in?'

Amy nodded. 'I saw Mrs Ogborne in the garden this morning.'

An embarrassed silence fell between them. Little Amy looked from one to the other and for the first time, Amy could see she was only a girl, not a young woman. The whole thing felt ridiculous.

'Auntie Amy?'

'Yes?'

'Can I turn on your radio?'

'May I!' barked Mrs Dowd. 'How many times?'

'May I?' said Little Amy.

'Of course,' said Amy. 'It's in the next room. You know where it is.'

Little Amy dashed out and the sound of a dance band cooing their way through *Why Should I Beg for Love?* wafted through to the parlour.

'That girl,' complained Mrs Dowd. 'Always with the songs. Can't go anywhere without the radio on. She's more excited about this bloomin' Orphan fellah pitching up than she is about today.'

'I suppose she knows Benny Orphan better than she knows Harold next door,' said Amy.

'How could she? That's bloody daft.'

'I mean. Well, Benny Orphan makes you feel like he's singing just for you. Every night he's on the radio, whispering sweet nothings in your ear. Young girls like that.'

Amy gave up explaining. It wasn't only young girls who liked that. Mrs Dowd looked at her like she was crazy.

'She's never *seen* Benny Orphan. She's seen Harold Ogborne.'

'Yes. I suppose so.'

Amy pictured young Harold next door, a spotty teenager with a scrawny neck, fidgeting, waiting for Little Amy to arrive. It was going to be awful.

They were going to marry her off to the boy and kill her dreams, and Amy was going to be one of the co-conspirators. And all because she lived next door to them and it seemed more appropriate that she should be the go-between.

'Harold's a good lad too,' said Mrs Dowd. 'Not like most young men his age. Left school early. Walked straight to Braddock's factory round the corner and asked for a job. On the machines in no time. Four years he's been there now. Eighteen this year and already the man of the house. A wage earner. Good thing to have.'

'Yes,' said Amy. 'Quite right.'

How could Benny Orphan, handsome, rich, debonair crooner, possibly compare to all that?

'Between you and me,' said Mrs Dowd, lowering her voice to a whisper. 'I think he's going to pop the question on Saturday. At the dance.'

'That's romantic,' said Amy.

She felt happy for the girl. Then realised that Little Amy would be married before her. She really would be On The Shelf Amy then.

'I suppose we'd better get round there,' said Mrs Dowd.

'I'll go and get her,' said Amy, putting her teacup aside and smoothing her dress down.

Little Amy was sitting with her head right next to the radio, humming along.

'Can I just hear the end of this song?'

Amy sat beside her and nodded, wondering if the girl wanted to delay the meeting with Harold.

They listened together for a while as some unknown crooner whispered their dreams.

'This is like the man in my dreams,' said Little Amy.

'The what?'

'There's a man that I've dreamed about. I can see his face and everything. I've seen him a few times in my dreams. It's almost as if no real man can match up to him. I think I'll see him for real one day.'

Amy reached out and stroked the girl's forearm.

She knew exactly what she meant.

— 12 —

Rachel climbed the iron steps to Charlie's door and slipped the note through the letterbox. She rang the bell and had scooted down the steps and out of the yard before Charlie had read the note and opened the door.

The note said:

Mohan Singh, Indian aviator, flying from Croydon to Cape Town trying to set the world record, will crash his plane near Paris this afternoon. He will escape with nothing but a broken leg. If you want to know more, I am sitting in Drucker's across the road. Please come. — Rachel.

Drucker's looked almost exactly the same as it had — or would do — when she'd sat there in 1966. She could have sworn some of the same old ladies were sitting in there, wearing the same outfits.

She waited a long time and had almost finished her entire pot of tea before Charlie walked in.

She looked up expectantly. His face was frozen, like someone who'd just heard of the death of a friend. He placed his hat on the hat stand and sat opposite her. His world had changed.

'How did you know that?' he said, finally.

'I've already told you.'

He wrung his hands. She'd never seen anyone actually *wring* their hands before.

'It can't be right.'

She put a hand on his.

'I know, Charlie. It's too weird. But listen. How did I know about the Billie Holiday record? How did I know your name?'

He shrugged and wouldn't look at her. She took a slip of paper from her handbag and slid it under his fists.

'And how do I know that these are the exact football scores for the next week?'

He opened the sheet and read the print-out. He seemed to read it for a long time, as if he couldn't take in the words, then he stifled a laugh.

'So both games on Wednesday night will finish 4-1. That's ridiculous.'

'Looks like it. But you might want to put some money on it and test it out.'

'Betting is illegal,' he said.

'I know, Charlie. But you know a man who can take your money.'

He looked in her eyes now. 'How do you know that?'

She smiled and said nothing. He nodded. Yes, she knew everything. He took in a deep breath, as if he'd been too scared to breathe since he walked in.

'What do you want?' he said.

'I want to stick around for a week.'

'Stick around?'

'Stay here,' she said. 'I'll help you make sure this concert of yours happens on Saturday.'

'Why wouldn't it happen?'

What to say? Should she tell him there was a former friend of hers who might have come to sabotage Charlie's concert so he could wipe out the existence of an old woman who hadn't been born yet?

'Let's just say there might be some people who don't want it to happen.'

Whatever that meant to Charlie he seemed to understand it. He even seemed grateful.

'I'll help you,' said Rachel.

'And what do you want in return?'

'Your spare bed,' she said. 'In return, I'll make you rich.'

Charlie looked down at the print-out and the Wednesday night scores that said:

Third Division (North)
Accrington Stanley 4-1 York City
Darlington 4-1 Rotherham United

'This is utterly bonkers,' he said.

She patted his hand again.

'I know, but don't worry. The next time it'll be you explaining it all to me.'

— 13 —

Amy Parker stared at the Ogbornes' carpet and willed it to open up and swallow her whole.

The tea party amounted to the two mothers chatting conspiratorially while Judy, Mrs Ogborne's 17-year-old daughter grinned for no reason. Little Amy sat on a creaking wooden chair, examining her white shoes. Harold was across the room from her, staring at her and not saying anything.

Harold didn't look like someone who wanted to see Little Amy. He certainly didn't look like someone who wanted to ask her to marry him. In fact, he looked vaguely annoyed about something.

The atmosphere felt as thick and inedible as Mrs Ogborne's seed cake, which had a distinct taste of birdseed and cardboard.

Amy gazed at the clock on the mantelpiece, watching its slow hand tick round and round, each second feeling like a day. She gazed out of the small window that looked down the narrow side yard, a tantalising glimpse of green lawn beyond it. An even more tantalising glimpse of the apple tree in her own back garden. How she longed to be there now. Alone.

Her eyes scanned the room for something, anything with which to strike up a conversation.

The gramophone, with a giant horn and a stack of records wedged behind it.

'That's a nice gramophone,' she lied.

Little Amy's eyes lit up.

'We never use it,' said Harold.

Amy wanted to slap him. He was nothing but a boy with skinny wrists trying to be the man of the house, talking to her like she was his skivvy.

'Do you have any good records?' asked Little Amy.

Judy sprang out of her chair and dug them out. Little Amy went to her side and examined them as Judy flipped through them.

'Oh! Benny Orphan!' cried Little Amy.

Judy was winding up the gramophone and putting it on before anyone could tell her no. The crackly strains of *I'll String Along With You* filled the corner of the room, Judy and Little Amy swaying side to side, waiting for Benny Orphan's voice to join in.

When he did, with his mellow tone and a smile in his voice, Little Amy gasped out loud.

'Oh! He's so handsome!'

Harold gazed at her and Amy could see the naked attraction in his eyes, but something else too: a spark of contempt.

'He's one of them Jews, ain't he? Bit oily if you ask me.'

'Now now, Harold,' said Mrs Ogborne. 'That's not very polite. Little Amy likes him, as you well know.'

There was a strong hint in the last four words that were almost delivered with a rolling pin.

Harold put on a fake smile. 'I prefer that Al Bowlly fellah. And he's *English* and all.'

'I don't think he is,' said Amy.

Harold looked like she'd slapped him. He didn't like women who disagreed with him, she thought.

'Al Bowlly's as English as Saint George,' he said, sniggering, as if she was wrong in the head.

'He was born in Mozambique,' said Amy, simply. 'His dad's Greek, mother's Lebanese. Or the other way round. I read it in Women's Illustrated.'

Little Amy and Judy looked amazed. Harold shuffled uncomfortably, as if his armchair had grown spikes.

'He wanted to go and see that Oswald Moseley today,' said Mrs Ogborne. 'I wouldn't have it.'

'He's a sensible politician, Mam,' said Harold. That absurd voice again: a boy pretending to be a man. 'The Daily Mail says so. That's Lord Rothermere, that is. They say he's the man to fix broken Britain.'

'He's more like a broken bloomin' record,' said Mrs Ogborne.

Little Amy giggled. Judy laughed.

Harold's face went red and Amy noticed his fists go white on his lap. She decided to change the subject.

'Well, we'll all be seeing him next week. Benny Orphan. Who'd have thought it; him coming to sing here. Right at the top of our road almost.'

'I can't wait,' said Little Amy. 'To think, we're actually going to see him. In the flesh. And he has a raffle every time he performs. One lucky lady gets to stand on stage with him and be serenaded.'

'You're looking forward to it, aren't you Harold?' said his mother, pointedly.

'Arr. I suppose so.' He relented a little and seemed to remember that this was going to be his big romantic occasion. 'He sings a good tune, I'll give him that. The posters say that he's coming with that Lew Stone's orchestra. Now they are a top quality band.'

Amy tried not to laugh. Harold Ogborne talking as if he was Britain's authority on popular music. What was it about being a potential husband that made men puff out their chests and say ridiculous things?

She gazed out at the garden again, longing for fresh air.

'It really is a lovely day out.'

Mrs Ogborne seemed to take the hint. She patted Mrs Dowd's hand and said, 'Why don't you come and see the garden?'

They all trooped out through the dank kitchen. Harold made a show of wanting to stay put in his chair but his mother gave him a warning glare and he sauntered out after them with his hands in his pockets.

Amy breathed in deeply, like a prisoner in the exercise yard. She wanted dearly to climb over the fence to her own back garden and slam the door shut.

They trooped to the bottom of the garden to see the dirt bed where the daffodils would grow. Mrs Ogborne talked at length about the various flowers and where they might all reappear in three months' time.

Little Amy left them suddenly, walking up the lawn towards the house. Was she going to use the privy?

She stopped dead suddenly and yelped.

They all looked with alarm. Had she trodden on something sharp? Amy rushed to her side.

'What is it?'

Little Amy pointed at the house.

'There. Did you see him?'

Amy followed her shaking finger to the dining room window that looked out down the side yard.

'Who?'

'There was a man, standing there, watching us.'

The others had gathered around.

'What is it, girl?' said her mother, a note of irritation in her voice.

Amy could tell that this meeting had not gone according to the script both mothers had in mind and she wondered if they were going to blame her for it.

'She says she saw a man, in the house,' said Amy.

'A man?' said Mrs Ogborne. "There's no man in our house.'

'At the window,' said Little Amy. 'Right next to the gramophone. I saw him. He was watching me.'

'You're just imagining it,' said her mother, taking Little Amy's arm and marching her back to the house.

The others followed and could hear Mrs Dowd whispering threats in her daughter's ear, telling her not to make a spectacle of herself.

It was all falling apart.

Amy followed them all back into the house. There was some more small talk before Mrs Dowd made the excuse to leave and they all looked forward to meeting again next Saturday night at the dance.

Amy stepped out of the front door and joined Little Amy at the end of the path. The two mothers murmured some more to each other.

'The man I saw,' said Little Amy. 'It was *him*.'

Amy took the girl's hand. 'Who?'

'The man I told you about. The one in my dreams. I think he's a ghost.'

— 14 —

Rachel woke with a start and shouted 'Dad!' She looked around wildly. Unfamiliar surroundings. Art Deco ornaments.

Charlie's flat.

A taste of déjà vu. She had woken up exactly like this, dreaming about her lost father, when she had woken up in Charlie's other flat. A morning in 1940.

She would wake up there in six years.

It was a two-storey flat above the shops. The lounge and kitchen downstairs. One large room with a bathroom off it. And a steep set of stairs leading to a square landing with two attic bedrooms, one facing the front, one facing the back of the shops. She had to be careful not to bang her head on the sloping ceiling when she got out of bed.

She could hear Charlie downstairs. Music wafting up to her.

She scooted downstairs and found the bathroom. It was bare and functional and cold. Floorboards, exposed pipes. Not a single thing to decorate it, as if it were the flat's afterthought. She wondered if it was a 1930s thing or just a single man thing.

She strip washed against the sink, with cold water, and ran upstairs again to dress hurriedly. Every time she visited Charlie in the future he would have a set of era-appropriate clothes waiting for her, but this time she'd had to sort it out herself.

This was the time she would have to leave him instructions: a list of dates she would arrive over the next thirty years.

She could only tell him of the 1940, 1959 and 1966 dates. It didn't seem that there were any others after that. She didn't know of any. She would meet him those three times and then, some time much later, he would leave instructions with a solicitor to gift her his apartment and a trust fund.

It was an older Charlie who'd done that. Older than the 50-year-old man she'd left in 1966. She wondered again how long he'd lived. Was he still alive in 2013 but loath to see her? He would be 97.

How sad, she thought. For me it's the last time, but for Charlie it's all to come.

She put on her lipstick and walked downstairs to greet him.

He looked up with surprise. He was sitting doing the crossword at the window table, tapping his fountain pen to the music.

'Good morning,' he said.

The words were *good morning*, but they sounded like *Oh, you're actually really quite pretty*.

He stood up and almost offered his hand to shake, then flapped his arms out as if to say *well, here's my humble abode.*

'Good morning, Charlie,' she said, and she realised for the first time that they were the same age. Charlie was twenty years old, just like her. He'd always been older than her every other time they'd met.

He made tea in the teapot, using the same tea leaves as yesterday, and rustled up some toasted crumpets. There was a poor sliver of butter and a few dregs of strawberry jam from a jar with a gollywog on it.

'I didn't have much in, I'm afraid,' he said. 'I don't tend to eat much, as a rule.'

He looked a bit thin. She'd put it down to youth, but now she realised he might just be poor. This was Charlie the penniless youth, not the dashing lieutenant or the businessman.

'I tend to spend my wages on expensive American imports,' he said, nodding to the gramophone record where Teddy Wilson played piano behind Billie Holiday singing *If You Were Mine.*

'Where do you work?'

'I'm bar manager at the Prince of Wales,' he said. 'I rather like it. I can start late in the day and the money's not too bad.'

'I can't believe it,' she said. 'I worked there in 2012!'

Charlie's eyes bugged out and he almost choked on his crumpet. He coughed and gathered himself.

'Are you okay?'

He nodded and took a sip of his tea to clear his throat.

'Excuse me,' he said. But when you say things like that it sounds like something from Buck Rogers. I can't believe we'll still be drinking in pubs in 2012. Won't we have flying cars and food pills and such?'

'I'm afraid there are never flying cars and food pills,' she laughed. 'Even in 2013, we're still waiting for them.'

He stared at her with awe and she knew he wanted to ask her more about the future and everything life had to offer in the twenty first century.

The doorbell rattled.

'I bet that's Henry,' he said.

He went to answer the door and Henry bustled through saying 'I come bearing glad tidings…'

He broke off when he saw Rachel sitting at the table and stared with amazement for a second, then his face broke into one giant grin.

Charlie came in behind him, shoulders hunched with embarrassment.

Henry took his hat off. 'Well, good morning, Miss Hines. What a pleasure it is to see you back here.'

'Rachel's staying for a while,' said Charlie. 'She wants to help us with the concert.'

Henry took a seat at the table and kissed her hand.

'How marvellous! Welcome aboard,' he said. 'May I?'

He indicated the last lone crumpet. Charlie nodded and Henry attacked it.

'You were saying?' said Charlie. 'Something about glad tidings?'

"Oh yes,' said Henry through a mouthful of crumpet and jam. He pulled a slip of thin paper from his coat pocket and laid it on the table.

It was printed *Post Office Telegraphs* and there were white strips of text that seemed to have been typewritten in capitals.

ALL GOOD FOR SAT 27 JAN PLEASE BILL AS LESTER JOHNSON & HIS COLOURED JAZZ ORCHESTRA IF YOU CAN PAY, FEED & HOUSE THEM

'And you call this good news?' said Charlie.

'We've got the band,' said Henry.

'We have to pay for new posters, and pay the band. And organise food and housing for them.'

'Charlie,' said Henry, pouring himself tea. 'We were going to pay Lew Stone's band anyway. These guys will be cheaper.'

'Do you think the hotel will have these men? You know, being… coloured?'

Henry shrugged. 'It's a theory we'll have to put to the test.'

'Why wouldn't they?' asked Rachel.

The two men seemed surprised she'd asked.

'Because people here are bloody ignorant,' said Charlie.

'And why do you call them *coloured?*'

Again they looked at her as if she was mad.

'Why wouldn't you?' asked Charlie.

'Where I come from,' she said. 'It's a bit rude to say *coloured.*'

'Really? What do you say?'

'Well, *black.*'

Charlie choked on his tea. Henry looked at her curiously.

'We really don't use that word,' said Charlie. 'It's very impolite.'

'Oh,' she said. 'Where I come from, it's the opposite.'

Henry looked suspicious. 'Where exactly are you *from*, Rachel?'

She looked at Charlie. What lie to tell? In 1940, Charlie had told everyone she was his niece from the country, but that wouldn't work now. Henry knew he had no niece. She remembered Mitch's advice.

'I'm actually from America,' she said.

'America!' cried Henry, delighted. 'Which city?'

'Er, New York.'

'You don't sound like an American. But you don't sound English either.'

'Upstate New York. There are actually more American accents than you hear in the movies.'

Charlie prodded the telegram.

'Can we tell him to wait until we've got money from the takings?'

'The band we can pay at the end of the night,' said Henry. 'The posters, I'm not so sure. He'll want the money up front. I've got a couple of joeys, if it helps.'

'Well, we're buggered then,' said Charlie. He looked at Rachel and blushed. 'I'm sorry. Excuse my language.'

She smiled and shrugged it off and reached for her handbag.

'I could give you the money.'

They looked at her like she'd said *I'm from the year 2013*.

She pulled a handful of banknotes from her purse. Henry and Charlie stared open mouthed.

'Dear God,' said Henry. 'Where did you get so much money?'

Rachel laughed shyly. 'Is this a lot?'

She put the crisp banknotes on the table and they both stared at them.

'Will this be enough for the posters?'

'With bells on,' said Henry. 'That would actually fill the dance hall with jazz bands for a week.'

'Oh,' she said. 'Well, you can have it.'

Charlie pushed the money back across the table to her. 'We couldn't possibly take your money, Rachel.'

'But I have it. And you need it. And I want to put the concert on as much as you.'

They both stared at the notes. They seemed to have a hypnotic effect on them.

'I think, as an American,' said Henry. 'You don't quite realise how much money you might be flashing around.' He picked up the newspaper and rapped the front page for emphasis. 'Look at it. Hunger, poverty, financial collapse and three million unemployed. War heroes singing for their supper.'

Rachel cleared her throat. 'We have a Depression in America too, Henry,' she said. 'I don't have enough money to solve all of Britain's problems. But I do have enough to solve yours. Yours and Charlie's.'

Henry grinned. Charlie stifled a laugh. Rachel realised she had blown away a great cloud of doom that had been hanging over these men for a long time.

'Rachel,' said Charlie. 'We'd be very happy to accept you as a partner in our enterprise. And we'd be more than happy to take your money.'

He picked it up and handed it back to her.

'But for the moment, I suggest you keep it safely hidden away in your purse, and we'll use it when we need it.'

'Which will be later today, at a certain printers',' said Henry.

Charlie lifted his teacup. 'Let's drink to our new partnership.'

'And the possibility of fresh tea leaves,' said Henry.

They toasted each other and slurped the weak tea and Rachel stuffed the banknotes back in her purse.

'Do you think we'll get any trouble?' said Charlie suddenly.

'What for?' asked Henry.

'You know. Putting on a coloured band? It's never been seen here. They don't like anything new. You got attacked yesterday for being a Jew…'

'I didn't get attacked, Charlie.'

'Ten thousand people at the British Union of Fascists' rally last night,' said Charlie, jabbing the newspaper. 'In Birmingham.'

'Pah!' said Henry. 'Who cares about them?'

Charlie shrugged and drank his tea. 'Just saying. We might need to hire some muscle is all.'

— 15 —

Amy Parker looked up at the prisoner being led out of the cells as she unrolled the arrest report from her typewriter, separating the flimsy sheet of black carbon paper and the pale purple-printed copy sheet. She filed them in the different manila card folders without looking.

Sid Haye didn't have the cowed demeanour of most people being released after a night in the cells. They usually came out looking sheepish, glad to be almost free and on their way, hoping the officers wouldn't change their mind and keep them another day.

But Sid Haye marched up to Sergeant Webster's desk whistling the *Internationale*. She could see that Constable Davies behind him was itching to give him a slap. He shoved him towards the desk.

'Morning, comrade,' said Sid with a cheeky grin.

'You watch that mouth of yours, Lowe,' said Sergeant Webster. 'It's got you in enough trouble as it is.'

'And a great deal more, I'll wager,' said Sid. 'Or I wouldn't be doing my job as a member of the Communist Party of Great Britain.'

Davies pushed him in the back.

'You be careful I don't do my job as a member of Her Majesty's police force.'

'As a hired hand of the capitalist state machine,' said Sid.

'I've heard enough,' said Webster. He wrote the release time in his ledger. 'Out you go, sunshine.'

Sid backed out of the station, jacket clutched in one hand, insolent grin all over his face.

'Funny, ain't it, how you arrest the likes of me, but not one of the fascists who were running round kicking people's heads in last night? It's almost like you're protecting them.'

Davies blushed with fury. 'You better watch you don't get *your* head kicked in!'

'Constable Davies,' said Webster in a warning growl.

They watched Sid Haye saunter out, whistling the *Internationale*.

'Aw, what I'd give for ten minutes alone in a cell with that commie b—'

He stuttered and remembered Amy was present, nodding towards her.

'Bleeder.'

'Language, Davies.'

Amy looked at the clock.

'That's me done for the day, Sergeant Webster,' she said, rising and reaching for her handbag.

'Righto, Amy. See you tomorrow.'

She walked through the reception area. Davies nodded and mumbled a goodbye to her, looking at his boots.

She walked out and breathed fresh air. It was a beautifully sunny and mild morning for January. They said it was going to be sunny and mild all week.

She wasn't sure how much longer she could take working part-time at the police station. It wasn't the lack of glamour or promotion opportunities, so much as the constant presence of a man who was only ever interested in her when no one else was around.

She dashed the last few yards to catch a tram heading to Moseley village. It sailed past Sid Haye sauntering up the long street.

She closed her eyes as the tram passed 12, Alcester Road, trying to shut out the memory of her father.

Amy stood frozen in the street, staring in panic at her father, a monster spat from the house's mouth. She heard the tram's whistle too late, twisted to see it almost upon her.

The brakes screeched, the bell rang, someone screamed.

Danny lunged and tackled her out of its path.

The tram clattered by and hissed to a stop as Danny held her tight on the floor. She had a moment to realise they were alive, her soft body under his, her breasts rising against him, panting, alive. The tram passed by and Mr Parker came screaming at them brandishing a cane.

'You whore! You vile whore! Abomination!'

Danny jumped to his feet between them and thwock! took the cane right across his face, stumbling to one side, blood spurting from his cheek. Parker raised the cane again to strike Amy, then stuttered, confused, as the cane was snatched from his grasp and a crowd of passersby jumped on him and pinned him down. A woman pulled Amy to the far kerb, wrapping her arms around her.

Someone pulled Danny to his feet and dragged him away. He stared after Amy, dizzy, groggy, face bleeding, but triumphant, seeing Amy safe and her father still screaming biblical abuse at her from under a scrum of burly men.

'I did it,' he said. 'I stopped it.'

Amy stared back as he was dragged away from her. She understood it now. She caught his eyes for the last time as someone — a girl, was it? — pulled him away.

The tram was passing the Prince of Wales when she opened her eyes again. Another good reason to quit the job at the police station — having to pass that spot every day. If she got a job in Moseley or Kings Heath she could avoid it.

She hopped off at Moseley village and viewed the situations vacant cards in the newsagents' window. She could buy some potatoes at Shufflebotham's on the corner of Woodbridge Road and some rye bread from Luker's and walk home down Church road. It was pretty much coming back the way she'd come but she preferred the quality of the shops in Moseley village and the walk did her good.

There was an insurance firm and a solicitor in Kings Heath both wanting clerks, but they didn't say if they were part-time positions. She noted down the telephone numbers.

A man was watching her.

She focussed out of the index cards and onto the surface of the glass where the reflection showed the street behind her: cars and vans flashing past, and a man outside a barber's shop, standing staring at her.

It was him.

Her heart caught, missing a beat.

A familiar rush of nausea. This had happened so often and it never had been him. She was over the feeling already and resigning herself to turning round and seeing that it was just another man. Just another man, who meant nothing to her.

She turned and looked.

His startled eyes stared back.

It was Danny Pearce.

She felt her face go cold. Her belly flipped over like that time she'd taken the ferry across to France. The world was swimming. She was underwater.

He stared back at her from the other side of the street. Each time a van flitted between them she expected that he would have disappeared. But he remained. Danny Pearce. Looking exactly as he had that day in 1912. The same boy. As if 22 years hadn't passed since then.

He was going to disappear. He had to disappear. Like a mirage, an hallucination, a dream. He had to disappear because it didn't make sense. He was here again and he didn't look a day older.

He smiled. Then he looked both ways. He was coming to her. He crossed the road, walking towards her, closer and closer. A gust of wind flashed between them.

'Amy,' he said.

Someone answered for her. It couldn't have been her because she couldn't speak, but the voice sounded like hers.

'Danny? Danny Pearce?'

'I've come back to you, Amy,' he said.

The ground shifted beneath her. Do not faint, she told herself. This is not real. This is not happening. You might be mad but do not let it show. Do not let anyone in Moseley see that you are mad.

Just like your father.

She pushed him away and ran into the road.

The shriek of brakes. A horn blared.

She ran and found herself on the other side of the road. Voices shouting after her.

She ran up the street, past the Fighting Cocks, the shops a blur. She turned the corner at Shufflebotham's and ran up Woodbridge Road, scared to look back.

She didn't stop running until she was half way down Church Road. She caught her breath as she turned into Newport Road and looked back to make sure he wasn't following her.

No one.

I am mad. Just like my father. They will come and take me to Winson Green Insane Asylum.

Mrs Ogborne called out to her as she bustled her way into her house. *Answer her. Do not let them think you are crazy like your father.*

She called a hello and slammed the door.

Hide. Hide away. Don't let them come for you.

She locked the door and slumped to the floor in the hallway, sobbing.

And she remembered Little Amy from yesterday. The stupid girl in love with a man from her dreams who was nothing but a ghost that would one day drive her mad.

She knew now that they had much more in common than their name.

— 16 —

Whenever Rachel walked into Silver Street, she always thought of Shakespeare, but this time she was overwhelmed by the changes. In 2013, everything had been replaced by soulless shoebox blocks, but for the little huddle of shops on the right as you entered. In 1934, those cottages ran both sides of the street as far as the eye could see. It was a vibrant and bustling side shoot of the high street.

The Kings Heath Press was at number 32, where she was more used to seeing the Lidl store. She followed Charlie and Henry inside and watched as they chatted with the overalled gentleman across the green counter. It looked more like a factory reception than a print shop, and she realised that was because in this time printing was an industrial process. Over the years it had become cleaner, whiter, more pristine. She wrinkled her nose. The place had a ripe smell that caught you right at the back of your throat. But she was too fascinated by the process to go outside and leave Charlie and Henry to it.

There were leaflets, posters, pamphlets of all types running off the presses, and it occurred to her for perhaps the first time in her life what a revolution the desktop printer must have been.

She'd been too young to appreciate its impact on everyday life in the late twentieth century. She had been born with them everywhere. As a History student she, of course, possessed an abstract knowledge that they hadn't always been around and that people had relied on an actual print shop to print off whatever they needed, but only here — standing in a busy workshop, seeing the dozen or so men dealing with the huge output of material, the sweat and grime of it, contrasted with the pristine quality of the printed paper output — only now could she appreciate how amazing it was.

A few other customers had called in from businesses all around Kings Heath with jobs, all handwritten on foolscap sheets, and had discussed their requirements with the men who ran the shop.

She wondered how she might explain to Charlie that all of this was gone in 2013; that if you wanted something printing, you pressed a button on your computer and watched it roll out of your own little print machine, and in full colour.

Charlie and Henry were debating font sizes and whether they could afford a second colour, when Sid Haye walked in.

Rachel watched him, his cocky saunter, his grin of recognition when he saw them. It was not a nice smile, she knew instantly.

'Good afternoon, comrades.'

Charlie and Henry turned and looked at him for a silent moment. They didn't make a sound, but Rachel sensed it as an inward groan they shared.

'Hello, Sid,' said Charlie disconsolately.

Sid pulled out a folded scrap of paper and presented it to them.

In crude pencil Rachel could make out *Why the real enemy is the National Government, not Mosley's Fascists'* as a headline. There was other, smaller writing below it but she couldn't read it.

'You're the first to know about our next public meeting, Saturday night,' he said. 'I know you'll be there.'

'We're busy Saturday night, Sid,' said Henry.

'Too busy to defend the oppressed workers against the brutal oppression of the British government? What could be more important than that, eh?'

'We've got a concert that night,' snapped Charlie. 'You know full well.'

'Ah,' said Sid, as if remembering. 'Your bourgeois crooner singing love songs to stupefy the masses. I remember.'

Sid snatched the sheet of paper from Charlie's hand and scanned it. He gave a low whistle.

'A *coloured* band, eh? In Moseley?'

'Yes,' said Henry. 'Do you have an objection?'

'Not me. Of course not. I think it's very progressive.' Sid handed the sheet back to Charlie. 'Our friends in the British Union of Fascists might disagree, though.'

'Yes,' said Charlie. 'I thought that too. Perhaps you and your members might volunteer to provide us with some protection?'

Sid held up his own leaflet draft again.

'I'm afraid the Communist Party of Great Britain will be waging the *real* fight against social democracy, my friend.'

Henry laughed. 'Yes. In a meeting room with a handful of people who already agree with you, instead of on the street, where you might actually find some fascists.'

'Well, that's symptomatic of your bourgeois thinking on the issues that face us, comrade. We've got the Daily Mail supporting Oswald Mosley and telling us all how nice Herr Hitler is. Lord bloody Rothermere, himself; pillar of the British establishment. Meanwhile you can get ten months' hard labour for organising a march for the unemployed. But the tide is turning. Look at the King and Country motion in Oxford. It's our policies in the Communist Party that will defeat capitalism and win freedom for all oppressed workers. And that's the only way to defeat fascism.'

'Yes,' laughed Henry. 'Just like your policies led to the defeat of Hitler in Germany. Great work there.'

The smug smile disappeared from Sid's face and Rachel could see a glower of resentment. Henry had said the one thing that could strike this man in the heart.

She realised now the full force of something she'd only ever studied in dusty textbooks before. She'd read about the rise of Hitler and the disaster of Stalin instructing the Communist Party of Germany to oppose the social democratic centre instead of the rising Nazis. You read it in a book and couldn't understand how anyone could mistake Hitler as the real menace that must be stopped.

But here she was in 1934, where all of this was still playing out. Hitler had only just become Chancellor. The Daily Mail and a large portion of Britain's ruling class, including a certain Prince of Wales who was about to become King, thought Hitler was a sensible politician, a strong leader, the kind we needed. And the tragedy was that the Communist Parties around the world, under orders from Stalin in Moscow, were pursuing a ridiculous line of attacking democracy, flawed as it was, instead of the Nazis.

She saw for the first time how this was not about abstract ideas, but about real people like Charlie, Henry and Sid making real choices: real people in humdrum streets trying to change the world.

The print shop foreman returned to the front desk and took Charlie's rough draft, promising the posters would be ready in four hours.

Charlie pocketed his receipt. 'Good luck with your meeting, Sid.'

He headed for the door. Henry followed, grinning, raising his hat.

'You might find your bourgeois singer crooning to an empty dance hall,' said Sid. 'There's a lot of people listen to the party around here and we'll be advising them strongly against attending your event.'

'Good luck!' called Henry.

Rachel stared at Sid for a moment. She wondered if she should tell him about the disaster that was about to unfold: the rise of Hitler, the embarrassment of the Nazi-Soviet non-aggression pact, the outbreak of war, Hitler's eventual invasion of Russia, the discovery of Hitler's death camps.

How to tell him that every decision he was making was wrong? He reminded her suddenly of Danny. She'd warned him about pursuing Amy Parker and saving the girl's life, but he'd ignored her, with that same smug look of self-righteousness.

And disaster had unfolded.

She just shook her head and walked out. There were some people you couldn't tell anything to.

— 17 —

Time is a human illusion. All times co-exist in the stupendous whole of eternity.

Danny turned his Kindle off and hid it inside the secret pocket in his suitcase. There was enough power in the battery to last him his entire stay here so it wouldn't need recharging, which was lucky because the plug sockets were ones he'd never encountered before.

Hinton was right, he thought. Everything was simultaneous. It was the best theory for his experience he'd read so far.

He'd considered carrying the Kindle with him to keep it safe, but having it on his person meant it could be found if he was arrested. And he'd been arrested too many times in the past.

It was safer in a secret pocket of a locked suitcase.

He walked out of the Alcester Lodge Hotel and into the mild night air of Moseley. There was a different taste to it. Something he couldn't define. It might have been the lack of pollution.

The hotel was drab but comfortable. He had no intention of staying there much longer. Hopefully not another night, if everything went well with Amy tonight.

He walked down the rise towards the village, passing the Dovecote, and mulled over his options.

Her reaction this afternoon had shocked him, much as her reaction to him turning up at her door in 1966 had shocked him.

There had to be a way he could get through to her. It made him angry with her: that he could travel through decades to be with her, but could never get through to her enough for her to hear what he had to say.

He was going to call on her, knock her front door and explain everything to her. Surely honesty would work? She had seemed to understand back in 1912. The moment he'd rescued her. She had surely understood then that Danny Pearce had known something about the future; that he wasn't just a boy from 1912 who had taken a shine to her?

That feeling again. Every time he thought about Amy Parker. A strange foreboding sensation. Something awful that he couldn't quite recall. A premonition?

It wasn't the usual feeling he associated with Amy Parker: a yearning, empty void in his belly — a feeling that was probably love. Was that what love felt like? Feeling hungry and sick with hunger and unable to eat all at the same time? That was surely love.

This feeling was different.

This was a feeling that something terrible might happen, and that something terrible had already happened, and that both things were the same thing.

Could it be a symptom of being in 1934? A decade where almost everyone had felt the same. The whole of Europe sliding toward the abyss of war and holocaust and no one able to stop it. He had flicked through many books on the subject so that he had an acute awareness of this sense of doom that everyone seemed to possess in the thirties.

Everyone in the decade seemed to know that war was coming, and no one had swerved to avoid it.

He came to the village and couldn't help glancing over at the alley that led to the churchyard. A sudden gust of wind howled down it and almost blew his hat off.

Three figures were clustered at the alley's mouth, huddled in the darkness. They seemed to be painting something on the wall. A girl and two men.

He watched them from the other side.

One of them was Rachel.

He stepped back into the doorway of Boots, still there, as it seemingly always had been, on the corner. Hiding in a shop doorway and watching a woman on the other side of the road. The second time that day.

He peered through darkness. It was Rachel.

He realised now that they weren't painting. They were putting up a poster. One of the men had pasted the wall; the other unrolled the poster and the first man had pasted it in place.

Rachel was looking around to see if they were being watched. She looked right across at Danny. He pressed further back into the shadow of the doorway.

She hadn't seen him. Hadn't reacted if she had.

Satisfied with their work, they continued walking up the road.

Danny looked both ways, allowing a car to pass, and crossed the village green to view the poster. It was the same poster that Fenwick had given him. He took the poster from his pocket and unfolded it, the photograph of Amy almost falling out.

Benny Orphan in concert at the Moseley and Balsall Heath Institute, with the syncopated accompaniment of Lester Johnson's Coloured Jazz Orchestra.

He looked at the photo. Amy Parker was going to be there, at that concert. Amy Parker in her ball gown and looking just like she had this morning. A younger girl with her. Both staring at the crooner who must be Benny Orphan.

So Rachel was behind the concert.

He wondered at their paths crossing again. Every time he tried to make a connection with Amy Parker — whatever moment in time it happened to be — there was Rachel.

She had opposed him from the start. Had wanted Amy to die at her father's hand. Had raged that it was altering something that had already happened. Had tried to stop him from pushing Amy out from in front of the tram.

And then she'd claimed that that act had somehow wiped out her existence. She'd been there at the end: her and this friend of hers, Charlie: policing him at Amy's funeral in 1966 and forcing him back to the present.

He followed them at a distance. They'd stopped to paste up another poster to a lamp post outside the Fighting Cocks pub.

A small crowd had gathered around them so he felt comfortable in walking closer. The crowd seemed to be drinkers from the pub, and as he inched closer to the fringe of the crowd he heard someone shout 'Go and tell Harold about this!' at which one of the men ran inside.

There seemed to be a lively debate taking place, drinkers shouting questions at the two men who were with Rachel.

The one man had a fixed smile on his face and seemed unperturbed, but the other looked nervous and was glancing up and down the street. He whispered something to Rachel. She shook her head.

Danny recognised him now. It was the man called Charlie. He had looked older and wiser in 1966 but was nothing but a teenage boy here.

Danny felt anger rising inside him. Here was Rachel, who had her own man she'd fallen for in the past. It was all right for her to do that, but not for Danny. She was always there in whatever past he visited, trying to prevent him from being with Amy. But not this time.

A mob of drinkers belched out of the pub and crowded round. One of them must have been the man called Harold — a young, wiry looking ferret-faced teenager with a sneer on his face. He pushed his way to the front and read the poster.

'Arr, it's like that is it?' he shouted, putting it on for the crowd. 'Bringing a band of darkies here now, are ya?'

There was a swell of outrage from half the crowd, jeering Harold on. Others in the crowd told him to shut his trap. Everyone was arguing with everyone else.

Danny noticed a handful of the men behind Harold were wearing black shirts, some of them polo necks, others wearing a black shirt and black tie combination, including one woman. They were wagging fingers at various members of the crowd who were shouting in their faces.

'We don't want their sort here!' shouted Harold.

A roar went up. The crowd surged like a rugby scrum and Danny was knocked back.

'Shut up, you horrible racist!'

It was Rachel's voice. He heard others in the crowd express surprise and confusion. 'What did she say?' 'Huh?' 'What was that?' He realised no one had ever heard the term 'racist' before.

The confusion lasted only a few seconds before the mêlée erupted with renewed vigour.

One of the Blackshirts tried to snatch the bucket from Charlie's hand. Charlie pulled away. Everyone was shouting.

'It's Jew Henry!' shouted the Blackshirt woman.

The bucket catapulted into the air suddenly and thick-gooey paste hit her face.

The crowd became one great angry mass of fists and shouts.

Danny saw Charlie turn and rush Rachel away. He said something that made her cross the street alone, head down. Danny followed Charlie's quick glance and saw a policeman running towards them.

Rachel had stopped on the other side of the road and looked back. She was frozen in surprise, looking right at Danny.

He had to get out of there.

Rachel turned and ran into the black entrance in the middle of Victoria Parade.

The policeman ran for Danny, hand out. Danny recognised him. One of the cops who was going to arrest him in 1940.

Please, not again.

But the policeman didn't notice Danny.

Of course. He's never seen me before.

Constable Davies barged Danny to the side and waded into the thick of the scrum.

Do not get arrested again. Get out of here.

Danny about-turned and walked swiftly away from the crowd. More policemen were running towards the disturbance. He looked back and could see that Charlie and the man called Henry were being arrested.

Danny walked swiftly back up the hill to his hotel, an angry wind chasing him, and didn't breathe easily until he'd closed his hotel room door behind him.

— 18 —

'You're sure it's here?' asked Kath, parking her Mini as close to the side of the access road as she could.

She was technically parking in the entrance to the hospital but they would probably get away with it for a while before anyone moved them on, particularly as they were parked outside the gate house.

She checked Mrs Hudson in the rear-view mirror. The old lady smiled slightly. She never questioned Mitch's intuitions.

Kath could see the top of the Dovecote above the hedge.

'Do you think it's connected to why I use the Dovecote?'

'No,' said Mitch.

He was slumped in the passenger seat beside her, wrapped up for winter, even though it was hot, still looking tired. Time Flu made him irritable, she remembered. It made him blunt.

'It's just, you know, a bit of a coincidence. He works here in the grounds of the hospital. And the dovecote's in the same grounds.'

Mrs Hudson spoke up from the back seat. 'Perhaps he's feeding off its energy, the same as you, dear.'

Mitch snorted.

She knew he was a hardliner on the whole touchstone question. Random bits of stone in graves and dovecotes didn't have any kind of power to send people back in time; it was all an innate skill of the person. She knew he was right, and he was the person most qualified to know, but she could never quite shake it off.

'He's coming,' said Mitch.

They watched the access road that dipped down the hill to the building that had once been a stately home but was now a hospital.

A figure came walking up, looking at his feet. A man in his twenties with the kind of silly haircut that all men in their twenties seemed to favour these days. He had a canvas bag slung over one shoulder. He wasn't fat, thought Kath, but he looked heavy. It was like he was carrying a great weight that you couldn't see.

'It must be Jez,' said Mitch suddenly, with the force of revelation. 'I've been hearing *Jess* in my head. He's *Jez*.'

Jez passed their car without seeing them and walked out of the hospital grounds, turning left, walking down the rise towards the village.

'Are you sure about this?' asked Mrs Hudson.

Kath got out and let Mitch slide over into the driver's seat.

'I'm not having either of you walking all over Moseley,' Kath said. 'Look after her.'

She patted the roof of the Mini and walked out of the entrance, turning left and following Jez down towards the village.

He crossed over to the village green and took the east side of the street, turning at *Cafephilia*, the new coffee shop on the corner of Woodbridge Road. Kath gave it a quick glance. She loved the giant photo they'd put on the wall of the same street corner, back when it was Shufflebotham's Grocers in the thirties.

Jez tramped on up past the now boarded up Luker's bakery and on past Patrick Kavanagh's. She called Mitch on her cell phone.

'He's turned down Church Road. I think you're right.'

She followed him at a distance of twenty yards down the steep slope. He didn't look back once.

And then he turned into Newport Road.

She called Mitch again to tell him.

'We're coming,' he said.

She hung back by the phone box, not wanting to tail him up a quiet, residential street where it was impossible to hang around without looking suspicious. She craned her neck to see.

He turned into the same house, the near derelict one with the faded blue paint.

Once he was inside she strolled slowly up the street. Mitch drove in from the other end and parked across from the house. She quickened her step and got in, feeling awkward that she was sitting in the passenger seat.

Mitch was rubbing his eyes and wheezing to himself.

'He's in there... there's a... oh, he's in 1959.'

'What do you mean?' asked Mrs Hudson.

'He's in the house... he's in there right now, in 2013... but he's also in 1959. A couple... there's a couple, arguing. He's watching them. They can't see him.'

Kath wanted to ask him how he could be visiting 1959 but apparently invisibly. And who were the couple? But she didn't want to break his concentration.

'They're coming out... Anger... so much of it...'

The front door opened suddenly, rickety, unsticking uncertainly, and Jez came out. He walked to the little gate and carried it open, the bottom hinge broken.

'He's watching them... the couple...'

'What couple?' said Kath.

Mrs Hudson shushed her.

'Can you not see the couple?' murmured Mitch. 'He's watching them.'

Jez crept along the pavement cautiously, as if he were watching a couple of microscopic bugs dancing in the air, then he reached out for something.

'He's trying to touch her... Oh God, she felt it!'

Jez disappeared. Kath thought she'd blinked, missed him run back in, but no: he had been there, and then he was no longer there, so you thought you'd only imagined him being there.

'Where did he go?'

'He's back inside,' said Mitch, slumped now, trying to breathe deeply.

'He just flitted back inside?' said Kath. 'In the same time zone?'

'He *was* in 1959,' said Mitch, as if it was obvious. 'Now he's back here in 2013.'

Kath stared back out at the pavement where he'd been; where she'd *seen* him.

'So we know he's visiting this old man, Harold Ogborne, now,' said Mrs Hudson. 'And he's somehow flitting back to the past, to see the wife?'

'She's dead,' said Mitch. 'She died in 1979.'

'What's he up to, this Jez?' asked Mrs Hudson. Behind everything she said, Kath could still hear the same question: *what does this have to do with the night my parents fall in love?*

'I don't think he knows,' said Mitch. 'He's just attracted to her. She's drawing him towards her.'

'And who *is* she?'

'Her name's Amy,' said Mitch.

'Not this Amy Parker?' asked Mrs Hudson. 'The one Danny Pearce is so attracted to?'

'No,' said Mitch. 'It's not her. This Amy is younger.'

Kath heard herself almost sigh with relief. Danny's obsession with Amy Parker disturbed her.

Mitch closed his eyes, exhausted. 'Take me home now. I need to sleep.'

Kath opened her door and stepped out. 'You'll have to slide over. Unless you want to drive?'

Mitch realised he was sitting in the driver's seat. He nodded and started to hutch across, like a man who was a good thirty years older than he was. Kath walked round and took the driver's seat, casting one more glance back at the ruined house.

She got in and drove off.

'This Jez chap can't be that innocent,' said Mrs Hudson. 'We're detecting a huge disturbance here;

something enormous. He's not just staring at a girl from the past.'

Kath wasn't sure if the old woman was only talking to herself.

— 19 —

She needed Mrs Hudson.

Rachel paced Charlie's room, coming back to stare at Moseley village through the net curtains again and again. The morning traffic was still busy. Rush hour had come and gone.

Or Mitch or Kath Bright.

She needed them here right now, because she had no idea what to do. Charlie and Henry were probably still in a police cell and she didn't know if they were coming back. She realised she would have to arrange the entire concert herself now and had no idea what to do about it.

If Mrs Hudson, or Mitch, or Kath would only come and help her, everything would be fine. But this was what they'd left her to do while they got on with more important business. It seemed such a little thing. Go and make sure this concert happens, Rachel. What could be easier?

Except since she'd got involved, the concert was now even further away from happening. They'd attracted the attentions of Blackshirts and the police and the two men who knew how to put the concert on were both in a cell.

She could go and ask to see them. A few words with them. Perhaps Henry or Charlie could hand her their notes. There would be people she might call: the agent they'd mentioned in London, whoever it was that ran the dance hall. There would be security to man the door. Did the venue supply those? Would she have to arrange a hotel for Benny Orphan? What about for the band?

The more she thought about it, the more there was to do, till it swamped her and she felt herself sinking, drowning.

And she knew she couldn't go to the police station in case Davies saw her. Davies had never recognised her in 1940 so it followed that she had never been to the station in 1934. So not going to the station was the best decision to make and it would all, somehow, work out for the best.

Unless the concert didn't happen and Mrs Hudson's existence was somehow wiped out.

She gazed longingly across the village green at the entrance to the alley. She could walk right over there and go to the touchstone and be back in 2013. Easily. She could even try to come back here earlier. Make everything better this time. Warn Charlie about the Blackshirts and the possibility of arrest.

She had watched the disaster unfold from the darkness of the Victoria parade alley. Danny had watched the trouble start and then walked away as soon as the police had appeared, obviously scared of being arrested again.

What was he up to? Was he involved with the Blackshirts? Was this how he would sabotage the concert as Mrs Hudson suspected?

She had followed him, skirting the shadows on the other side of the street. He had crossed over and walked up the rise ahead of her, not looking back once, and almost run into the Alcester Lodge Hotel.

By the time she'd walked back to the village, the paddy wagon had arrived and Charlie and Henry were being led away. When the police were gone, the laughing Blackshirts tore the posters down and stamped on them.

In the end, there was nothing to do but retreat to the flat; thankful that Charlie had given her a spare key.

There was nothing out there now to suggest any of the trouble that had happened last night. It was a respectable suburban village green straight out of a Ladybird book.

Peter and Jane Pretend the War's not Coming.

A key scraped into the lock. The front door opened in the narrow strip of hall. Footsteps stomping in.

Would it be the police, come to search his flat?

The door creaked open and Charlie's tense face melted with relief.

'You're here,' he said. 'Thank God.'

She ran to him and almost knocked him back against Henry.

'Oh Charlie! You're back! I was so scared for you!'

He unpeeled her from him, blushing, grinning, smoothing his hair down. It was wild and unruly without the Brylcreem.

'Don't I get a welcome hug, too?' said Henry.

She laughed and kissed him on his rough cheek and he blushed too.

'We were worried about you, Rachel,' said Charlie. 'Anything might have happened.'

'I was worried about *you!* You were arrested!'

Henry slumped into the sofa, his bones creaking. 'Ah! I ache everywhere.'

Rachel filled the kettle with water and lit the stove.

'Oh yes. Tea. Much needed.'

Charlie fell into the armchair and yawned. They both looked like they'd not slept all night.

'Well, that's a hotel I'm definitely not patronising again,' said Henry.

'Room service was awful,' said Charlie.

'That man Davies, the concierge. He didn't like us very much, Charlie. Did you notice?'

'I think we can safely say he's not a jazz fan.'

'Perhaps we should have tipped him.'

Rachel laughed to herself and thought of the irony. In six years' time, Charlie would be a Lieutenant and get to order Davies, still a lowly Constable, around. She saw now the simmering envy that had always existed between them, the envy that would erupt in 1966 and lead to Davies trying to kill them both.

Charlie looked suddenly sullen. 'Do you think we were wrong to put the posters up all around Moseley?'

'We should put up more!'

'The Blackshirts will only rip them down again.'

Rachel turned from the hob. 'Who was that horrible woman shouting at you?'

Henry waved a dismissive hand. 'Oh, that was an old school chum of mine. Julie Hickman.'

'You *know* her?' said Charlie, aghast.

'I don't think she's ever recovered from my rejecting her advances in the third year. Unrequited love is one of the prime causes of anti-Semitism. It's a fact. I guarantee you there's a beautiful Jewish girl somewhere in Germany who turned Adolf Hitler down, and look what it's caused.'

Charlie chewed his thumb and looked out across the village to where they'd been arrested last night. None of the posters were there.

'So we just put some more posters up?'

'Yes!'

'And get arrested again?'

Henry shrugged and the life seemed to go out of him. The kettle whistled. Rachel made the tea and set it on the table by the window.

'Why don't we print some flyers?' she said.

They both looked at her. It was that look people gave you in the past when they didn't know what you were talking about.

'Little versions of the poster? To hand to people?'

'Handbills!'

'Yes, handbills. We could order thousands of them. Hand them out to everyone in Moseley.'

Henry's eyes lit up. 'I could put some in Manny's fish and chip shop. Give them out to every customer.'

'We could hire some people to give them out,' said Charlie.

'Could we get some people?'

'There's no shortage of people looking for work, Rachel.'

'Then let's do it,' she said. 'Let's flood Moseley with handbills. And town too. Why not?'

Henry clapped his hands. 'She's right. It's Benny Orphan. People will come from miles around.'

'I don't know,' said Charlie. 'Thousands of handbills, people to distribute them. It's a lot of money.'

Rachel pulled out her purse again and held up the crispy notes. They didn't even seem real. Toy banknotes from a children's game. But she could see the almost dizzying effect they had on Charlie and Henry.

'Is this enough?'

'Rachel. That's enough to pay everyone in Moseley to attend,' said Charlie.

'And Kings Heath.'

'Well how much do you need?'

Charlie stepped up and took a single note from her.

'That should do it. There'll be change.'

She shut her purse. There were a few more notes. There was a certain bet to place tomorrow and Charlie would need a stake for it. She would hand it to him later, when Henry wasn't there.

And that bet would mean even more money.

She felt a sudden wave of euphoria. This was all going to happen. She was going to make it happen.

She poured tea into two china cups and turned with them. Henry was snoring. Charlie's eyes were at half mast.

It could wait.

She reached for her purse and took a basket that Charlie had on a hook. There was no food in the place and they would need breakfast when they woke up. She could go and see what the shops looked like in 1934.

— 20 —

Danny took a deep breath, opened his hotel room door and crept down the carpeted stairs to the chintz adorned reception.

'Good morning, Mr Pearce,' sang the girl on reception.

Every time he passed through she looked him over with moo-cow eyes. A teenager who looked middle-aged thanks to the dowdy clothes she wore.

He tipped his hat and nodded to her, and it was only then that he remembered walking in here looking for a room in 1966. They were booked up. A woman in reception with horn-rimmed glasses, who looked sixty but was probably thirty. It must be her.

He stepped out into the morning sun, a chill blast hitting the film of sweat on his face, and took the same route as last night.

Take two. It felt safer now. He should stop walking out at night altogether. He'd thought it would make it easier to avoid being seen but it was worse. The daylight definitely felt safer.

He held onto the brim of his trilby as he walked, wind whipping around him. Felt the envelope in his pocket. Insurance.

The arrests had spooked him.

It seemed that every time he went back in time, he ended up in a police cell. First in 1912, dragged away by an Edwardian brute of a copper. Again in 1940, knowing the police station was going to be bombed that night. And the policeman who'd bumped into him last night had only been the same one who'd taken him in that time, and again in 1966. And after he'd escaped his cell that time, the same policeman had handed him over to a gangster to dispose of.

The same face, only younger. Running at him. Hand reaching out. The jolt as his body hit him.

The relief when he'd shoved him aside to arrest someone else.

Walk slowly now, head down, do not draw attention to yourself.

He felt more and more like a man on the run.

Every time he travelled back in time, something bad always happened. And in 1959? What had happened there? He wasn't sure. It was beyond his memory, like a dream just out of reach.

Why did he bother going back in time?

Amy Parker. That's why. It was always because of Amy.

He crossed over to the village green and didn't even glance sideways up the alley to see the churchyard gate and the gravestones beyond it.

Past the Fighting Cocks, where it had all happened. Just the human traffic of respectable shoppers. No police. No fighters.

He was scared. He didn't care who knew it.

It felt safer to walk out in the day time. He would be fine as long as he avoided doing anything suspicious; as long as he avoided crowds or potential violent situations.

He would surely be safe?

He turned into Woodbridge Road and the impressive corner display of Shufflebotham's Grocers caught his eye. He crossed over to peer at a window display of ham hocks.

Overcoated women with hats like the Queen wore, wicker baskets hanging from the crooks of their arms, chatting in the store, pointing out this and that.

He almost jumped when he recognised Rachel inside.

She was chatting to a green-overalled gentleman and appeared quite at home. How come *she* never got arrested?

He ducked away quickly before she could turn and see him staring at her. Up the street, past Lukers. The lovely fresh smell of bread. Onwards. The Trafalgar Inn. The entrance to Moseley station. He stopped and looked down the slope to the quaint huts either side of the train track.

A feeling of déjà vu. Dread. Fear. Something that had happened in 1959. Something he couldn't remember. Something very, very bad.

He shuddered and walked on, head down.

Do not be distracted. Do not stand and stare at anything. Suspicious people do that. People who get noticed.

He turned down the steep slope of Church Road and followed it all the way down to the bottom, where it seemed strange not to smell spices from the Indian grocers, and the mouth watering scent of a score of Balti restaurants. It was still a quiet suburb where genteel Moseley frayed at the edges and became shabby Balsall Heath.

'Lower Moseley' he'd once heard someone jokingly call it.

He turned into Newport Street. The familiar sense of it. He'd walked here in 1966. Midnight. Knocking her door. She'd answered the door looking just as he'd remembered her. And then it hadn't been her. It had been her daughter, Maddy. Amy had been the old woman behind her, shouting venom at him.

This time it would be different, he told himself.

It was 32 years before that. She had no reason to be bitter. She only knew him as the man who'd rescued her from her insane father.

She had been scared yesterday morning when she'd seen him in the street, but that was only natural.

He was a ghost from a bad moment. The worst moment of her life.

But if he had time to talk to her, he might explain it all to her.

How was he going to do that?

He thought of the words. How to break it to her gently? *The thing is, Amy. I'm a time traveller.* Would she faint? Would she drop down and actually die?

He thumbed the envelope in his jacket pocket.

Here it was. The yellow gate, next to the blue one. He pushed it open and let it click after him gently, quietly.

There was a doorbell. He pressed it and heard it rattle faintly inside. Footsteps plodding down the hall, the latch clicking.

Amy Parker staring at him.

Just like in 1966, he thought, *when it was her daughter, Maddy, not her.*

Recognition in her eyes, then alarm. She looked pale and her eyes were swollen. Had she been crying?

'Amy,' he said. 'It's me.'

'No,' she cried.

She slammed the door shut.

'Amy! Please!' he called.

Do not shout. Do not make a scene. Do not attract attention.

He knocked at the door and called through gritted teeth, knowing she was still on the other side.

'Please, Amy. It's all right. Let me in.'

He bent down and pushed the letterbox flap open. A coffee brown hall. Amy was sitting against a mahogany hatstand, hugging herself.

'Amy. It's me, Danny. Please don't be afraid.'

She was shaking her head.

'Go away! You're not real!'

What was wrong with her? Wasn't it obvious he was real? Why was she being so dramatic?

'Of course I'm real, Amy. I'm here. I've come such a long way to see you.'

She turned and looked fearfully at his eyes framed by the letterbox.

'Just let me in and I'll explain everything.'

She was crying now, shaking her head.

'I can't.'

She pushed herself up from the floor and stumbled down the hallway, bouncing off the walls. The door at the end of the hall slammed.

'What's your game, mister?'

A man was standing over him. Next door. A knee-high wooden fence between them.

Danny stood up and eyed him and was surprised to recognise the man from the fight last night. The ferret-faced teenager who'd kicked up the fuss with the Blackshirts. Harold, they'd called him.

Do not get noticed. Do not get arrested.

'Recorded delivery,' he stammered, pushing the envelope through the letterbox.

He backed down the path and marched down the street, feeling Harold's cold stare on his back and a cold wind on his face.

The concert, he thought. If she wouldn't respond to his letter he would have to talk to her at the concert.

— 21 —

When Charlie and Henry woke up, they were pleased to see the food she'd bought. They had quite a buffet and she got the feeling neither men ate much as a rule.

Charlie had to rush to the Prince to work the lunch time shift, and Rachel stayed with Henry and worked on the design for the flyers. It looked rather boring, just text, and she suggested it might look better with a photograph.

Henry looked at her like she was mad. How could he take a photograph of Benny Orphan when he was in London?

But she'd seen vintage posters for concerts in the 1930s, admittedly all American, and a cut-out of the band leader or singer's head seemed to be a common feature.

She asked if they had any magazines with Benny Orphan in them. They could cut out his photograph.

Henry thought about it, and then a light bulb lit his face.

'Sheet music!' he shouted.

They ran out to a music store that sold sheet music the way a modern store would sell CDs, and Henry triumphantly pulled out a few songs that bore photographs of Benny Orphan.

They paid for them, took them back to Charlie's flat and cut them out.

Charlie came back, saying Mr Hollis at the Prince had let him take the afternoon off, but he had to be back for the evening. He was impressed with Rachel's re-design and looked at her with a strange sense of awe, as if she'd told a particularly delightful joke.

They went to the printers and ordered a mighty consignment of handbills. The printer huffed and puffed and said he'd never be able to get so many ready for the next day, so Henry suggested he do it in batches each day.

Later on, it came time for Charlie to head back to work and the closer the time came, the more he fidgeted. Rachel wondered what was the matter with him. Henry was heading to Hurst Street in town to a Jewish social club to talk to Manny Singer about security.

'I can't leave you here alone, Rachel,' said Charlie.

'I got plenty of practice last night,' she joked.

'She can come with me,' said Henry. 'I'll take her to Little Israel. Show her a good time.'

Charlie could see that Rachel was excited by the prospect so he shrugged and gave in. She could tell he didn't want to leave her. He shuffled off to work like a reluctant boy to school.

Henry and Rachel caught the 112 tram into the city. Henry was chattering away, telling her all about the Jewish quarter that comprised a handful of streets down town — Holloway Head, Hurst Street, Sherlock Street, Ashley Street and Benacre Street — and had been a Jewish ghetto for 200 years.

'And they still say we're newcomers,' he laughed.

She was distracted, watching the city passing, a city she barely recognised but for a few buildings. The city centre loomed ahead, but not the skyline she recognised. It seemed absurd, to be riding into a Birmingham city centre that didn't have a Rotunda and a post office tower.

They hopped off at the top of Digbeth by St Martin's church, its soot-black façade imposing, railed off. She gazed around in wonder at the empty market square and the imposing old market hall and tried to equate it with what stood there now. How could she ever describe something as space age as the Selfridges building to Henry? He really would think she lived in a sci-fi future world and expect the cars to fly.

'You're from New York, you say?' laughed Henry.

'Yes. Why?'

'You look like you've never seen a city before.'

She laughed and shrugged. 'It's just so very quaint.'

They skirted through back streets she didn't recognise and eventually came to Hurst Street, where every third shop seemed to have a Jewish name above the door: grocery stores, delicatessens, tailoring workshops, ticket writers, tripe dressers.

She wondered what he'd say if she told him that in 80 years all of this would be Chinese supermarkets and gay bars.

He led her to a fish-and-chip shop that branded itself a *Fried Fish Dealer* and laughed 'There's nothing more British than fish and chips. You ever tried it?'

'Of course I have, Henry. Everyone tries fish and chips when they come to England.'

'A totally Jewish dish, of course,' he laughed.

He pointed to the rooms above the shop and rang the bell of a blue side door, which creaked open for them.

A man stood in the doorway who looked like two men rolled into one. He wasn't fat. He was about six and a half feet of muscle, and very handsome, she noticed. His stern face cracked into a smile.

'Henry! My word, send for a lamb to slaughter.'

They hugged in the doorway and the big man ushered them inside. A handful of other men were playing cards at a table behind the door.

'Manny, this is Rachel. Visiting us from America. Good friend of mine, helping us with our concert. Rachel: Manny Singer.'

Manny bowed and took her hand, planted a kiss on it. 'I'm honoured,' he said.

'Any chance you could take some time to talk?' said Henry. 'Upstairs?'

Manny expressed surprise and nodded. He told the card players he was heading upstairs for a while. They waved but didn't look up from their game.

Upstairs were a couple of rooms with a makeshift bar and kitchen. Tables were dotted all around and Jewish men of all ages talked, argued, played chess and drank. A gramophone in the corner was playing jazz. A couple of older men playing chess were complaining, teasing, and demanding some Schubert instead. At another table a huddle of young men were shouting, waving their arms, stabbing their fingers at each other, debating the merits of Trotsky versus Stalin.

'Stalin has betrayed the workers of the world!' shouted one young man. 'Germany has fallen to the fascists and the rest of Europe will follow. You will see. And the only man in the world who warned us this was coming, and told us how to stop it, is exiled on some island off the coast of Turkey!'

'Ach! Always harping on about Trotsky!'

They banged their fists on the table but no one else in the room seemed concerned that they might fight.

'It's not often we're honoured with Henry's presence,' said Manny. 'Now that he's one of the upper class Moseley Jews, not the genuine ghetto Jews from here.'

'Pah! I live in Kings Heath. And I was here on Sunday.'

They were kind of acting up for her, performing a comedy double act. Manny ordered a bottle of pálinka and three glasses and they sat at a table. Rachel was worried the chair would break under him.

'Great boxer,' said Henry, as if reading her thoughts. 'I keep asking him to make a return to the ring, with me as his able manager, of course. But he won't listen.'

'Easy for him to say. He's not the one getting punched in the head.' Manny tapped his temple. 'I have a brain to protect.'

'Listen to him,' Henry tutted.

An old woman brought what looked like a slim bottle of water to their table with three shot glasses. Manny poured.

'I have intellectual pursuits,' he said. 'I'm taking courses in management and accountancy. I want to be the guy counting the money at the end of the night, not the guy being bandaged up.'

He raised his shot glass. So did Henry. Rachel dutifully followed.

'Egészségedre,' said Henry.

'L'Chayim,' said Manny.

'Bottoms up,' said Rachel.

The two men knocked it back so Rachel did the same. There was a moment of nothing, and then it was as if someone had fired a flamethrower into her open mouth. She coughed, choked, eyes watering.

Henry and Manny chuckled. Many poured another round.

'Be that as it may,' said Henry, resuming the conversation. 'It's your muscle we're interested in regarding a certain event this Saturday.'

'You want me on your door for Benny Orphan? That's a disappointment. I was rather hoping to be on the dance floor with a handful of warm girl. No offence there.'

Rachel smiled through the pain. It was cute what men thought might be offensive here.

'Might be a little more than just you working the door,' said Henry.

'Oh really?'

'The event has come to the attention of our friends in the B.U.F.'

'Blackshirts?'

'We got into a disagreement with them last night while putting posters up.'

'And you think they might take that disagreement to the dance floor?'

'It's a possibility.'

Manny nodded and thought about it. 'You'll need five on the door, and another five or more inside just in case they get past the door and start trouble inside. That's ten men for the night. Including me.'

'We can afford ten,' said Henry confidently.

'And tuxedo hire. Make them look non-threatening for your more discerning clientele.'

Rachel looked to Henry.

'I'll have a word with Rosen. He'll do us a deal.'

Manny named a figure. Henry accepted it and the two men shook hands. They raised their glasses again. Rachel joined them, knocked it back and tried not to cough this time as the fire hit her throat. It was now warming her whole face and she was worried she looked like a traffic light, the red about to turn to yellow and then green.

'You know Jimmy Connor?' said Manny.

'Of course,' Henry smiled. 'Another suburbanite Jew who's deserted the *stetl*.'

Manny laughed. 'I was forgetting. Another Hunk like you.'

Henry translated for Rachel's benefit.

'Jimmy Connor would be known as János Konrád back home. Family from Debrecen, Hungary, like mine. But came over way earlier. Total Brit now.'

'He knows all about the Blackshirts out your way. He can give you names.'

'What's he doing? Spying on them?'

Manny chuckled again. 'Turns out there's one in the factory he works. Braddock's is it? Whatever. Anyway, there's some young kid, Harold something, works there and never stops blabbing about Oswald Mosley this, the Jews that. Course, he doesn't know Jimmy's a Jew. And Jimmy never lets on, just lets him talk away.'

'Why doesn't he punch him on the nose?'

'Keep your enemies closer.'

'I think this Harold was there last night,' said Rachel.

'Oh, the ferret-faced wretch,' said Henry, remembering. 'He was called Harold?'

'I heard someone say his name. Makes sense.'

'Well, there you go,' said Manny. 'If anyone knows their plans it'll be Jimmy. Harold the Ferret's probably told him everything already. He's practically our hotline to Blackshirt central office.'

The two men laughed again and Manny set up another round. Rachel went along with it again but almost cheered when Henry suggested they stop drinking pálinka and have a meal.

— 22 —

When they got back to Moseley and Charlie came home, he suggested they move their operation to the Prince of Wales. He'd asked Mr Hollis if it was fine and the old man had said yes. He didn't mind him turning the snug into an office during the quiet hours. A couple of free tickets to see Benny Orphan had lubricated the deal.

So the following mid-morning, Henry and Rachel sat in the snug and plotted the publicity campaign while Charlie saw to the running of the pub.

They had stacks of handbills and a variety of young men in suits called in to collect them, Henry paying them with coins. Rachel noticed they all looked rather smart until you checked their shoes and saw how much the heels were worn down. Some even had split soles. They were all grateful for the money and walked out with stacks of handbills and a spring in their step.

'We should make a press release for the Birmingham Post,' said Rachel.

Charlie and Henry looked at her puzzled.

'It's a news story. Benny Orphan's a famous crooner. Lester's band are a big novelty. They'll write a story about it, surely?'

Charlie and Henry looked at each other and grinned.

'I like the way this girl thinks!' cried Henry, jumping up and kissing her. 'You've found a real gem here, Charlie.'

She blushed and shoved him away.

'You'd better write it, Henry,' she said. 'I'd get it all wrong with my Americanisms.'

He took out a fountain pen and started jotting in a notebook. Charlie went back to the front bar. Rachel suggested a few phrases but left most of it to Henry, sensing that the tone of a press release in 1934 would be much less zippy than one in 2013.

Charlie popped his head in a little later and indicated Rachel should come through. She left Henry writing and joined Charlie in the back corridor at the bottom of the stairs.

'What is it?'

'The chap I told you about — the one who takes bets. He's here.'

He nodded his head towards the front bar. Rachel peered through to the sunlit bar and ducked away.

He hadn't seen her.

'What?' said Charlie, puzzled.

'That's Bernie Powell,' she said.

'How do you know that?'

'Let's just say we're going to meet one day.'

She gripped Charlie's arm and huddled in the shadows where he wouldn't see her.

'He's dangerous, Charlie,' she whispered.

'What? Bernie? He's harmless. He's just a bloke who takes bets.'

'He's going to be dangerous. One day.'

'Really?'

It sounded like Bernie Powell was the nicest man in Moseley. But she knew he would one day turn into the kind of man who'd threaten to slice up her face. She wondered how it would happen: how he would change from a harmless bloke in the pub with a sideline in dodgy bets, to the most powerful gangster in the city by 1966. She shivered all over. He quite literally made her flesh crawl.

'Go on, then. Ask him. I'll get the money. But don't let him see me.'

Charlie nodded and lifted the flap up to the front bar. Rachel scooted into the snug and collected her purse. Henry was still writing in his notebook, tongue sticking out. She went back out and stood against the wall, listening to the conversation in the bar.

'Only there's a little wager I'm interested in. Tonight's games.'

'Your money's good with me, Charlie.' Bernie's voice, only thinner, weedier. 'Who've you got to win?'

'Not wins,' said Charlie. 'Results.'

'Results?'

'Both games to finish 4-1 to the home teams.'

There was a pause and then a little laugh.

'No chance. Never happen.'

'So you'd give me good odds, then?'

She could hear Charlie's cheeky smile.

'Funny kind of bet. You ain't got some insider tip have you?'

She heard Charlie laugh it off and then say almost with embarrassment, 'I had a dream.'

Another laugh from Bernie: louder, rounder.

'A dream, eh? Go on then. I'll take your money.'

'Let me just get my wallet.'

Charlie came through the flap and was surprised to see her there. She shoved a note into his palm and pulled him close, whispering.

'Change your bet. Get one of them wrong.'

'Why?'

'You're going to sting some people who could one day turn very nasty. Don't sting them for too much. Always make them think you're just a regular loser who occasionally hits a big one.'

Charlie thought about it, looked at the crumpled note in his hand, nodded.

He lifted the flap and walked back in.

'Here you are,' he said.

'Blimey, Charlie. That's a big stake. You ever dreamed right before?'

Bernie was laughing, but it was a nervous laugh.

'That's what I'm worried about,' said Charlie. 'Tell you what. Give me Accrington and Rotherham. Both to win 4-1. Separate bets though.'

'You said both home wins.'

'I know, but I fancy Rotherham to beat Darlington.'

'Never happen, mate.'

'You'll give me good odds then, won't you?'

'Go on then. Fool and his money and all that.'

Rachel walked back into the snug. It was quite possible that Bernie Powell had seen her back but he would never remember her, not by the time he met her face to face in 1966.

She sat by Henry, looking pleased with himself, and she tried to smile encouragingly, but she felt sick inside.

She had just set in motion a massive con on the city's illegal bookies. They'd threatened to kill them all in 1966 when they were legal.

What would they do now?

— 23 —

Amy Parker felt scared walking out of her own front door and up the street.

It wasn't the fact that the ghost of Danny Pearce might materialise before her. It was much more mundane than that. She felt scared because she had taken two days off work and thought it would look bad if she was seen strolling about on her own two feet.

It wasn't right that your employers might not accept that you could be ill without being bedridden; that sometimes illness was inside of your head. But there were plenty of other women who could type and would gladly take her seat at the police station. That was the fact of the matter.

She shouldn't be out there. But she had to. She had to know.

She walked up Newport Road and turned into Kingswood. Only a short walk. No one would see her. It was almost dark already.

She reached the house and rang the bell. Little Amy answered and was surprised to see her.

'Hello Auntie Amy. My mum's out.'

'That's all right. It was you I wanted to talk to.'

'Me?'

It was the strangest thing in the world to call on a teenage girl. But not as strange as seeing ghosts.

'Can I come in, please?'

Little Amy remembered her manners and showed her through to the parlour, the spotless front room that was only ever used for guests. She sat awkwardly on the edge of the sofa as if she had no right to be in this room. Amy wondered if it was the first time someone had ever called just for her.

She looked her over: a teenage girl, much like she'd been herself when Danny Pearce, her own personal ghost, had appeared in her life.

'I wanted to talk to you about Sunday,' said Amy. 'About what happened.'

Little Amy squirmed and looked at the carpet.

'About this man you saw.'

'I don't want to go back to that house. There's something not right about it. A feeling I get.'

'Are you sure you're not imagining it?'

Little Amy looked up, looked her right in the eye. She seemed to sense that Amy was not just another adult who would dismiss it as her over-active imagination despite what she'd just said.

'I know what I saw.'

Amy nodded. 'Yes. I'm sure you do.'

A part of her had hoped the girl would deny it all. She felt as if she'd dived in to save Amy from drowning, and was now being pulled under with her.

'Still. I'm sure if you go again you'll be fine and you won't see any strange men.'

'Why?'

Amy shrugged. She had no answer.

'Let's go to the concert on Saturday night,' she said with sudden optimism. 'You can dance with Harold. Let's just see what happens there.'

Little Amy smiled and her eyes lit up, more at the thought of the concert than of Harold, it had to be said.

'Do you like Harold?' she asked.

Little Amy bit her lip. 'He's a nice chap, I suppose.'

Amy nodded. 'Yes. He is.'

Neither of them really believed it, but it seemed the right thing to say. Some unseen force was drawing them together till they collided in a church aisle and it seemed no one could stop it.

'The thing about Harold,' said Amy, 'is he's real.'

She stood up suddenly. She had to get back before anyone saw her.

'I'll let you go,' she said. 'If you want to come round and talk to me about what dress you want to wear, feel free.'

Little Amy smiled and led her to the door. Amy turned on the doorstep and squeezed Little Amy's arm.

'I believe you,' she said.

She marched off and was round the corner quickly, wondering if she was the best person to be offering Little Amy support at the moment. She was quite possibly the worst person, seeing as she was clearly insane herself.

She looked up and her heart skipped a beat. There was a policeman at her door. He turned and saw her.

Constable Davies.

She cursed herself. Caught out.

Harold was at his door too. He said something to Davies and retreated inside. Had he told him about Danny's calling? And if Harold had truly seen him, it meant that she wasn't mad after all. It meant that the Danny who had called at the door was real. Not a ghost.

Davies shuffled on the doorstep, took his helmet off and tucked it under his arm, seemed sheepish.

'Hello, Amy,' he said. 'Just called to see how you were.'

'I'll be back in work tomorrow.'

She opened the door. He was right next to her. Almost touching. The door flew open and she was down the hall, taking her coat off and hanging it on the mahogany stand.

'Come in.'

He looked at his boots as he crossed the threshold and she knew this was going to be agonising. Still she said, 'Would you like a cup of tea?'

'No, no, no. This is just a fleeting call. I really don't want to impose.'

She led him into the parlour. He took an armchair seat across from her. He was sweating.

'I didn't mean to impose,' he said. 'I thought I would call by and enquire after your health.'

He was talking like he was writing a police report for her to type. And he still hadn't looked at her.

'I've been… well, just a little under the weather. I'm on the mend now.'

'You do look awful. That is… I mean ill. You look like you've been ill.'

'It's fine,' she said, as gently as she could.

'Your neighbour. He said you'd had some... bother. A caller.'

She breathed out and a landslide of worry avalanched from her shoulders. Harold had seen Danny Pearce at the door. And if Harold had seen Danny that meant he wasn't a ghost. He was real. She wasn't insane.

'Are you all right?'

He half raised himself from the armchair, wondering if he should come to her aid. She waved him back and couldn't hide her smile.

'I'm absolutely fine. I'm so much better in fact. As you can see.'

He smiled himself, although he couldn't know why.

'It was just someone I knew a long time ago. I didn't want to see him again.'

'Is he giving you trouble?'

'Not at all. Everything's fine. I was ill and didn't really want to answer the door.'

'Oh. I see. Because if he was, I'd...'

He stared at his boots some more. This was the moment he should kiss her, confess his feelings for her.

'You don't need to do anything, Constable Davies.'

'You needn't call me that,' he said. 'Well, outside of the station.'

'And what should I call you?'

'Well, my name.'

'I don't know it. You've never told me.'

'Oh. No. I haven't.'

He seemed to want to say something, swallowed a thought, shrugged his shoulders. It was as if he was talking to himself. Talking to himself, instead of to her.

'Very well,' he said, as if in answer to something she'd said. He bristled and nodded and stood up suddenly. 'I'll be on my way.'

He walked out and she followed him down the hall, held the door open for him, watched him clumsily put his helmet back on.

'I shall see you tomorrow, Miss Parker.'

He saluted, then clenched his fist, and blushed and marched down the street.

She closed the door and held it shut for a long time, in case he might come back.

He was a coward.

She thought now of how Danny Pearce had pursued her. Climbed to her window, demanded to see her, begged her to run away with him somewhere safe. But her father had discovered them. Danny had fought him. Danny had protected her. Danny had thrown himself in front of a tram to save her.

And now he was back, calling at her door, begging to see her again.

And Constable Davies couldn't even tell her his first name.

She went straight out to the back yard and yanked the tin lid off the dustbin with a clank.

An envelope sat on top of loose potato peelings, crumpled newspapers and jagged tin cans.

An envelope with her name on it.

— 24 —

Charlie hurtled through the side door at the Prince of Wales exactly on the dot, give or take twenty seconds. With relief, he lifted the flap and was about to go through to the front bar when he saw Mr Hollis on the stairs.

'Charles. Could you come upstairs, please.'

He watched Mr Hollis walk back to his parlour and cursed himself under his breath.

Stupid. He'd pushed it too far. Spent too much time planning this concert and even using the snug as an office, and now he was going to get the sack for being a minute late.

He trudged up the dim stairs and walked into the parlour and was surprised to find a policeman sitting with Mr Hollis.

'Charles. This is Constable Davies, whom I hear you've met recently.'

The light through the window fell on Mr Hollis's spectacles so it was impossible to read his expression. But as there was no chair for him, and Mr Hollis had made no indication that he should sit with them, it was unlikely that his boss was in the best of moods.

Mr Hollis held up an envelope.

'We've received this today. I wondered if you might know anything about it.'

Charlie read the letter, scanning the words, a lump rising in his throat. It was written in a barely legible scrawl, full of spelling errors. A page of threats and vitriol.

'I see,' said Charlie.

He was aware that Rachel and Henry were about to call to start work in the snug, and was hoping that Constable Davies wouldn't bump into her. Rachel had seemed quite keen that he shouldn't see her because of some future meeting they would have.

'Do you know what it is, Charles?'

'I think I do, Mr Hollis. It looks like a threat to burn down the Prince of Wales if we proceed with the concert on Saturday.'

'Ah,' said Mr Hollis. 'I rather hoped it wouldn't be about that.'

He took the letter back and handed it to Constable Davies. The policeman was finding it rather difficult to hide the smug grin on his face.

'Quite serious, I'm sure you'll agree, officer.'

'Very serious, sir.'

'So what are we going to do about it, eh?'

Davies puffed his chest out and appeared to be about to make a stump speech out of it.

'Well, sir, if I might suggest that this concert, which I know is being organised by Mr Eckersley here, is immediately cancelled. I think the problem might go away.'

'I'm sure it would,' said Mr Hollis.

Charlie felt his blood boiling. Don't let them stamp you down. Fight them back. Put the concert on and to hell with them. If it had happened a day earlier he would have been scared. It had been difficult enough to get the job, and it had kept him from falling into the abyss of unemployment, but now he had winnings to collect and a guarantee of more to come.

'Now. Is it true you've been arrested for brawling in the street, Charles?'

'No, it's not true, Mr Hollis. We were putting up posters for the concert when we were attacked by a group of Blackshirts. The same men who sent this, I'll bet.'

'But you *were* arrested?'

'Constable Davies here did take myself and my colleague, Henry Curtis, into custody for the night.'

'Standard procedure with a street brawl,' said Davies. 'Especially outside a public house.'

'I don't like the sound of this at all, Charles.'

'We were not charged. I'm sure Constable Davies can confirm that?'

Davies shifted uncomfortably. 'Well, that *is* true, no charge as such, but—'

'As we hadn't done anything wrong,' Charlie continued, 'other than raise the ire of some unsavoury characters who, quite frankly, object to us staging a harmless musical concert because they don't like the races of the performers.'

Mr Hollis looked back at Davies, and Charlie sensed that the inquisition had swung in his favour.

'So he wasn't actually charged with any offence, Constable?'

'No, sir. Not as such.'

'Well, this won't do. This won't do at all.'

'No sir,' said Davies, brightening up. 'I'm sure it won't.'

'You're bloody well right it won't.'

Davies' mouth fell open. So did Charlie's. He'd never heard Mr Hollis swear before.

'I tell you what I'm going to do now, Constable Davies. I'm going to lodge a very firm complaint with your station sergeant.'

Davies' face turned a light shade of purple.

'I'm going to tell him that I take a very dim view of my staff and I being threatened by two bob bullies while going about our lawful business. And if I hear of any further occurrences where this happens and they walk away scot free, while my man here gets locked up for the night, I'll be writing a very strongly worded letter to my friend, the mayor.'

Mr Hollis stood up. Davies jumped from his chair as if he'd been electrocuted.

'I'll be along to the station later to make a statement,' said Mr Hollis, snatching the letter from Davies' hand. 'And I shall expect some serious effort to be expended in tracing the culprits responsible for this filth.'

'Yes sir. Of course, sir.'

'Now thank you for your time.'

Davies plonked his helmet back on and headed down the stairs.

Charlie cringed and rushed to follow. *Don't let Rachel be down there.*

'Just a moment, Charles.'

Mr Hollis waited for Davies' boots to clump down the stairs and the side door to slam shut before he turned to Charlie with anger in his eyes.

'Charles, I'd just like you to know that if you need anything from me, anything at all, in connection with this concert. You just ask. That's all.'

'Why, thank you, Mr Hollis. You've been very generous already, letting us use the snug.'

'If you need money to make sure it happens, anything.'

He was taken aback by the old man's ferocity.

'That's incredibly generous, sir.'

Mr Hollis nodded, dismissing him. 'I can't abide bullies, Charles. You can't ever give in to those vermin.'

'No sir.'

He hesitated at the door, not sure if he should leave or not.

'And those Blackshirts give me the creeps. I saw enough of their sort during the General Strike. Bloody bullies and vermin, the lot of them. They'll not win this time.'

Mr Hollis had almost screwed the letter up, his fists white with rage. He came to himself and smoothed it out, placing it on the sideboard.

'Thank you, Mr Hollis.'

Charlie left him and skipped down the stairs, looking for Rachel.

— 25 —

Rachel had her hand on the brass door handle, about to push and enter the pub, when it flew from her grasp and a policeman barged out, shoving her aside.

He snarled a 'Sorry' that was more growl than apology and stormed off.

She watched him duck out of sight and felt her heart thumping in her throat. Constable Davies. If he'd stopped to apologise he'd have seen her. Then he would surely have recognised her again when she met him in 1940.

Or perhaps he wouldn't. Just a random girl he'd bumped into six years ago. Would you remember that? No one would.

And perhaps it didn't matter what she did and whether he saw her or not. The fact was that in 1940 he'd not recognised her from any previous time, and that meant that he wouldn't have any meaningful interaction with her now in 1934.

But the past can change. It changed for you. It wiped out your whole life.

She walked into the pub. No one seemed to be around. She stood awkwardly in the T-junction of the back corridor. Voices upstairs.

Someone came skipping down the stairs. Charlie. He was grinning ear to ear.

He took her arm and led her into the snug.

'What's up?' she asked.

'Something wonderful just happened,' he said. 'Old Hollis gave Constable Davies a rollicking. He's backing us to the hilt over the concert and wants the police to investigate the Blackshirt threats.'

'Threats?'

'Oh, yes.'

The door opened and Henry walked in with a bulging briefcase under one arm and a wreath in the other. He plonked the wreath on the table.

'What's that?' asked Charlie.

'It was on my door this morning.'

Rachel looked at Charlie. He didn't seem to understand it either.

'It's a wreath,' said Henry, handing them a postcard. 'There was a card attached, addressed to "Jew Henry". Not quite the valentine I had in mind from dear old Julie Hickman but there you go.'

Charlie read the card and his smile melted. He passed it to Rachel.

We are the coming storm.

'I don't get it,' she said.

'Another threat,' said Charlie. 'They wrote to Mr Hollis here too. Threatened to burn the Prince down if the concert went ahead.'

'They're all hot air,' laughed Henry. 'All dressing up and marching and puffing out their chests. They won't see out any of their threats.'

Rachel shook her head. 'You don't understand what they're capable of, Henry.'

He wouldn't, of course. Even though he was Jewish. Everyone in Europe was trying to believe there *wasn't* a coming storm, and they would go right on believing it until it blew their houses down.

Charlie looked at her with wonder. He knew now that she was pretty much an expert on what the future would bring and he could clearly see the fear in her.

'We're not cancelling the concert,' said Henry.

'Good God, no,' said Charlie.

'Never,' said Rachel. 'But we do need to be prepared for them, because they will try to hit us hard, and they are very dangerous people.'

She gave the card to Charlie.

'You should give this to the police as well. And tell them we know who's behind it all.'

It was only when she said it that she thought of Danny, hiding away in that hotel. Was he the one behind it? *Go to him. Go to him now and confront him with it.*

'Ah, the police don't care,' said Henry, slumping into a chair and digging out a ledger from his briefcase. 'They'll line up alongside the Blackshirts every time.'

Rachel took stacks of handbills and sorted them into neat blocks ready for the distributors to collect. She decided she would slip away to confront Danny at the first opportunity.

'That may be so,' said Charlie. 'But Mr Hollis is right. You have to complain about their bullying and force the police to take action against them. Force them to apply the law.'

He checked his wristwatch and noticed a face appear at the glazed door.

'They're here.'

He waved the man inside.

Rachel smiled at him: a skinny teenager in a shabby suit, holes in his shoes, shoulders hunched trying to make himself as small as possible.

'Take a seat,' she said, smiling kindly. 'We'll be as quick as we can.'

'Thank you, ma'am,' he muttered.

It nearly cracked her heart in two. These men, so young, so broken. She knew there were millions of them. A generation on the skids. Poor, hungry, desperate.

Henry took a pen and ink bottle from his briefcase and wrote down in his ledger the names of them all and the amounts they were paying them.

Charlie went to prepare the bar for the day. More men arrived and sat awkwardly, waiting to be given handbills and a few coins that changed their entire world. Their clothes were damp and musty.

Mr Hollis walked in and stopped short, surprised at the crowd of people in there.

The men all stood up, as if he were a minor royal.

'Good day, Mr Hollis,' said Henry. 'We're just giving these men their handbills to distribute and then they'll be on their way.'

Mr Hollis stared at the sorry band of humanity cluttering his snug and seemed appalled.

'Charles!' he called.

Charlie came through. 'Mr Hollis?'

'This won't do at all,' he said.

'No sir. Of course not.'

'These men are in no fit state to go tramping the streets of Birmingham,' said Mr Hollis. 'Serve every man a pint of bitter. And get round to Luker's and buy a couple of loaves.'

'Yes sir,' said Charlie, beaming.

Mr Hollis turned and addressed the band of now smiling men. 'I don't have any food to give you today, gentlemen,' he said. 'But tomorrow — they will be working again tomorrow, Charles?'

'Yes sir. And Saturday morning, too.'

'Good. I'll make sure there's hot soup for you to send you on your way tomorrow and Saturday. And a beer. And the same when you return. In fact, are they returning today?'

'The men are paid in the morning and again when they return and tell us where they've distributed the handbills, Mr Hollis.'

'Then I'll make sure there's soup for you all when you come back today.'

The men chorused a hearty 'Thank you, sir!'

'And thank *you*,' said Mr Hollis. 'You just make sure you get lots of people to come to this concert.'

Rachel offered to get the shopping, and Mr Hollis told her to buy four loaves from Lukers, and root vegetables and a chicken from Shufflebothams.

'I've got some jam and butter upstairs they can have with the bread. But for now let's pour those beers.'

He walked out to the front bar with Charlie, leaving a room full of humanity.

Rachel put her coat on. Danny would have to wait until the men had gone and she could slip away.

— 26 —

Once she'd returned with the shopping and the men had drunk their beer, wolfed their bread and jam, and set out with their handbills, each man grinning, Rachel made her move.

She left Charlie running the bar and looking forward to the call of Bernie Powell with his winnings, Henry off to the printers to get more handbills and Mrs Hollis making a giant pot of chicken soup in the pub kitchen.

Everyone was too busy to ask where she was going and she didn't volunteer the information, just put her coat and hat on and announced she'd be back in a mo.

She walked through the village, wondering how Mrs Hudson, Mitch and Kath were getting on with their half of the mission. When they'd left her to make sure the concert happened come what may, she felt she'd been given the house to tidy while everyone went on an adventure, but now she was worried the whole thing might be beyond her and had several times wondered where the hell they were.

She walked up and found the Alcester Lodge Hotel, its white painted frontage promising and failing to deliver seaside air and candy floss.

She walked into the dull reception area and found no one there. She waited a while, taking in the shabby chintz pallor of it, before noticing the brass bell.

An old woman came through and seemed surprised to see her. Suspicious even.

No, not old. She was young. As young as Rachel even. She just dressed like a grandmother.

'Can I help you?'

'I'm here to see Mr Pearce.'

'Mr Pearce?'

Was he using a pseudonym? Perhaps she'd simply have to wait outside and hope he eventually showed his face.

'Yes. Mr Pearce. He is staying here, isn't he?'

Sheila Sutton stared at her for a while, as if she'd asked her something in Greek. Then she made a show of consulting the register.

'Yes, Mr Pearce,' she said.

She stared again. Rachel pointed at the stairs.

'Which room?'

Sheila Sutton's mouth fell open with shock.

'I'm afraid we do *not* allow our guests to host *women* in their rooms.'

She said *women* the way someone in 2013 would say *pigs*.

'Could you call him then?'

'And *whom* shall I say is calling?'

Again with the implied disgust. Rachel felt her fingers itching to slap her.

'Tell him Miss Hines is here to talk to him. Miss Rachel Hines.'

'Wait through there. In the guest bar.'

The young old woman stuck her nose in the air and let it lead her to the stairs. It looked like an invisible farmer was pulling her to market.

Once she was alone, Rachel gazed at the keys hanging behind the tiny reception desk. Only one was missing. She turned the register and read Danny's signature, checked the dates. He was the only guest in the hotel.

She wandered through to the guest bar, which looked like someone's front room: a sofa, a few easy chairs, a couple of coffee tables and a ghastly stand up cocktail bar in one corner: the type people bought at junk shops when they wanted their home to have a kitsch ironic feel.

She wondered why anyone would come to stay at a hotel like this, in Moseley, and choose to drink here instead of any of the pubs in the village.

Someone who's hiding.

'I wondered when you'd show up.'

Danny looked every bit the 1930s chap, even down to the hungry, haunted look she'd seen on most of the men this morning. He looked like he hadn't slept much. Like he was on the run. Like he wanted to look over his shoulder every few seconds.

'I was going to say the same,' she said. 'Except I saw you arrive.'

'Are you sure you didn't follow me here? You seem to do that a lot.'

'It's not all about you, Danny. I was here first. Then you showed up. Then everything started to go wrong. As usual.'

He smirked and went to the window, peered out.

'Isn't that strange. How people who have it in for you always think *they're* the victims?'

'I *am* the victim, Danny. I lost everything. Because of *you*.'

He chuckled. 'You seem to be quite happy. You and your friend Charlie. Quite *busy*. Quite relentless in your attempts to poke your noses into *my* business.'

'I'm trying to get my life back, Danny.'

'And I suppose that means ending Amy's life?'

He turned and looked at her now, leaning back against the window sill, trying to look casual. But his eyes were furtive and couldn't focus on her for long.

'If I'd wanted to kill Amy I could have done it long ago, you idiot. Or her daughter.'

Rachel felt her throat constrict. She remembered swooning in the hospital in 1966 when Amy Parker was lying dying. Amy's daughter, Maddy, who looked so much like her mother, had just told Rachel that Danny was the father of her child. Rachel felt the physical sensation of it again: like being at sea and wanting to fall on deck. Danny seemed so blithely unconcerned that he'd fathered a child with Maddy. If he could choose where he travelled, why wasn't he back in 1966 with Maddy and his daughter? Why was he here with the grandmother?

'What's more interesting is why you're *here*,' said Rachel. 'I mean here *now*.'

'That's none of your business,' he said.

The door blew open and a few sheets of paper danced around the reception. The young/old woman rushed to gather them.

'I know why you're here,' Rachel whispered.

He fixed his eyes on her again, surprised.

'It's obvious what you're up to, Danny.'

'Do tell.'

'The concert is going to happen,' she said. 'I don't care how many hate mails you write or wreaths you buy or how many Blackshirts you stir up. It's going to happen and you'll never stop it.'

He laughed. 'I think you've really gone and lost your marbles, Rachel.'

'I won't let you stop it. And Mrs Hudson certainly won't. You'll see.'

His smile soured.

'Get out,' he said. 'Get out and leave me alone. I won't be bullied by you or that jumped up old bag.'

'You've been warned,' she said, stabbing a finger at him.

She flounced out through a swarm of paper flying around reception, slamming the door behind her.

Strangely, it was totally calm outside.

— 27 —

Danny stomped up the stairs to his room and threw everything he had into his suitcase.

So Rachel was trying to stop him. She was against him and she had the cabal behind her. Fenwick had warned him they would interfere, and he was right. Wherever he went, whatever year he ran to, they hunted him down.

And who were they to do that? He had as much right to use his talent as any of them. To use it in any way he pleased.

If time was not linear. If all time was simultaneous, Danny in 2013 was happening at the exact same moment as Danny saving Amy Parker in 1912, and Danny being arrested as a spy in 1940, and Danny giving Amy's daughter a fortune in 1966.

If all time was simultaneous, who were *they* to police it and tell him he couldn't get involved in other times?

He *was* other times.

He slipped his Kindle into its secret pocket in the briefcase. They would come looking for him now. Rachel would tell them where he was. He had to get out.

Hide somewhere else. Being on the street was risky but staying put was no option.

He stopped and thought for a moment. Why not time travel to another decade? Why not go back to 2013 and then come back again to 1934 for the concert?

No. He'd arrived a week early this time and he'd been concentrating solely on this coming Saturday night. He couldn't be sure he wouldn't arrive two weeks too early. Or a year early. He was here now. So close. He simply had to hide away for a day.

He snapped his suitcase shut, reached for his hat and double checked he'd left nothing at all incriminating in his room.

The receptionist seemed surprised when he told her he was checking out.

'I've been called away on business. Urgently.'

'I'm afraid we can't refund the charge for tonight, as you've stayed here past midday.'

She was trying to wring out a few pathetic coins from him. These petty people, squabbling over their small change that was worth nothing in his time.

'I'll need a forwarding address,' she said.

'Why?'

'Because it's customary.'

'I don't care about that.'

'Sir. What if something should arrive for you? What if you've left something—'

'I don't give a damn.'

Her stupid mouth opened in an O. She had no pearls but clutched them all the same.

'Nothing's arriving for me and I haven't left anything.'

He signed out and handed his keys and tipped his hat. His hand was on the brass door handle to the outside world when she said:

'Is it because of the band?'

He turned. 'The what?'

'Are you leaving because of the band?'

What the hell was she talking about?

'I'm sorry. I could tell them to stay in their rooms, if you like?'

'Why would you do that?'

'Because they're coloured.'

Was this some sort of test? Was she working with the cabal? Had she been spying on him, watching him, reporting to them? Of course. She'd told Rachel he was here. She was one of them.

'We've never had coloured guests before,' she said.

'Why would I care about that?'

'Some guests would take exception. We have to be very conscious of the feelings of our guests.'

'I don't care,' he said.

He turned the handle and fled, out into the street, a sudden fierce breeze slamming the door behind him.

He wondered for a wild moment if he should go to Amy again. No. He'd almost been arrested. He needed to keep out of sight, wait for the concert. That was the only moment he had left.

There were other hotels. There were two on Wake Green Road, he remembered. Or perhaps Kings Heath? They wouldn't find him there. Moseley truly was a village. In Kings Heath he could get lost. The high street was the longest in Birmingham. It was a busy urban centre, teeming with life. He should have stayed there in the first place.

He saw a tram climbing the hill towards him. He ran across the road to catch it. A fierce gust of wind almost took his hat off his head as he stepped on board and headed for Kings Heath.

— 28 —

Sheila Sutton checked the room after he'd gone but he'd left nothing. It was a shame to lose a proper guest by accepting the coloureds but she was already calculating the profit it would mean.

He'd been the only guest in the hotel anyway, and she could now give the coloured band a room each instead of having two of them double up. She would add a surcharge for the late inconvenience. The woman who'd booked them on the telephone had sounded American, and she could tell money was no object. She had a nose for these things.

Strange. The woman who'd called on Mr Pearce had sounded American too. As had Mr Pearce. But only sometimes. The odd word that was mispronounced or used inappropriately. It was all the fault of those Hollywood movies that were on at the cinemas every day.

The postman trudged up the path towards her, smiling his impertinent smile. Who did he think he was to presume to smile at her?

'Afternoon, Miss Sutton,' he sang. He slapped something down on her reception counter. Not a letter, but a handbill announcing Benny Orphan playing at the Moseley Institute. 'What do you think of that, then?'

He was a cheeky oaf. A common labouring ruffian with ideas above his station.

'I've heard all about that,' she said. 'As a matter of fact, I have the band staying at my hotel.'

'Staying here, eh?' He whistled. 'A coloured band. Very exotic.'

'I don't know what you're implying, Fred Foster, but I won't stand for it.'

'Well, how about you come along to this here concert, then?'

'I beg your pardon?'

'With me, like.'

He was actually asking her out. The impertinence of it. How *dare* he?

'Fred Foster. I wouldn't go to that concert with you if you were the last man on earth.'

She couldn't hide the smile of triumph as she said it, but it annoyed her that he only laughed and shrugged his shoulders.

'Ah, all right. There's another girl I'm thinking to ask. Vivian Hunter. I bet she'd like a dance.'

'I'm sure she's more your sort.'

Fred Foster laughed again. He really didn't seem to understand that he was a common ruffian who had no place talking to the likes of her. He and Vivian Hunter would be well suited.

'Well,' she said. 'I take it you haven't come to deliver *that*.'

He smiled his insolent smile and took a letter from his sack.

'Letter. Not for you, though.'

She took the manila envelope and read the address with sudden interest. *To Mr D. Pearce. c/o The Alcester Lodge Hotel.*

Fred Foster tipped his cap and walked out with a cheery 'Afternoon then.'

She could hear him whistling some awful dance tune half way up the street as she flipped the envelope over and read the return address, scratched into a neat corner. *Miss Amy Parker. Newport Road.* Now this was interesting. Amy Parker was the woman whose father had gone mad and tried to kill her. Everyone knew about that. Died in Winson Green Insane Asylum. *Syphilis*, people had whispered.

Amy Parker carried the mark of shame with her and swanned around Moseley as if she were a respectable member of society. And here she was writing letters to mysterious men in hotels.

She tried to peek through the tiny gap of envelope that was ungummed, but could see nothing inside. It was possible, of course, that Mr Pearce would call back for it, so she would have to leave it intact. Although she should, by rights, return to sender.

But first she went to the kitchen to put the kettle on.

It looked like an easy envelope to steam open.

— 29 —

Kath Bright rang the bell and waited on the iron landing. A hot day in summer. She had been working all day at the gleaming new library in Centenary Square. They had abandoned the old concrete monolith that had been the Central Library since the 1960s and shifted the books over all summer, before opening the doors with a great media fanfare.

Many people hated the *brutalist* architecture of the old library, and she did too. But she felt a strange fondness for it, now that it was going, and would be torn down. It was where she'd spent her youth, borrowing fiction from the first floor and then later the second, and then music from the Music Library on the third floor, taking albums home to copy. She'd discovered folk music there, and jazz and classical. Then she'd moved up to the History floor, and later Local Studies, devouring and marvelling at the resources they had. It had seemed inevitable that she would go and work there in the end. Its brutal concrete floors had represented the strata of her learning.

And in a short while it would be gone.

Everyone loved the new library. Everyone except the people who'd always used the library. And the librarians. The regular library customers couldn't find anything, because it was laid out like a department store, not a library. And the staff were all depressed because they had to work under a phalanx of Council-hired commissars whose sole purpose seemed to be to make sure nothing worked properly and no one enjoyed the place. Staff morale was at rock bottom. She wasn't sure she would stay there much longer.

'You're late.'

Mrs Hudson threw in a smile to convince her she was joking, but she was annoyed, nervous, scared. Kath could tell. Here was something threatening her life, her existence. She could be unmade, and the sudden space she left in the world would ripple through time and unleash a tornado that would rip the neighbourhood to pieces.

Mitch was on the sofa drinking luminous orange water, his skin still shockingly pale, setting off his handlebar moustache.

Mrs Hudson poured Kath a cup of tea. She put her bag down and joined Mitch on the sofa, patting his knee.

'You look better,' she lied.

Mrs Hudson was gazing up at the poster for Benny Orphan, and Kath noticed a framed sepia studio portrait of a young 1930s couple right next to it.

'Your parents?' she asked.

Mrs Hudson nodded.

'I've wanted to go back there many times,' she said. 'To see the moment they fell in love, had their first dance. A lot of people joked about it for years afterwards, apparently: how Benny Orphan's visit to Moseley had caused a population boom. There were so many people who traced their parents' romance to that night.'

She had a faraway look. Kath and Mitch both watched her, not wanting to disturb her. Kath took a sip of tea and spilled some on her saucer.

Mrs Hudson came to. She gave Kath a sour look.

'Sorry,' said Kath.

Mrs Hudson continued, 'I suppose we're here to talk about this Jez person though and what's going to happen at Newport Road. Though I still believe it can't be as vital as the dance centre.'

'This Jez doesn't seem harmful,' said Mitch. 'I mean, he doesn't know what he's doing, so there's no intention on his part. He visits this old man once a week; he sees his dead wife in the house.'

'Sees her here, or travels back in time?'

'He's travelling, of course, but he doesn't know it. So he thinks he sees her ghost in the house as it is. Sometimes he thinks he's been teleported back into the past. He's entirely passive in the process.'

'He won't be for long,' warned Mrs Hudson. 'They all start out thinking they've seen a ghost or suffered a timeslip. Then they learn how to control it. Then they start to exploit it, like Danny Pearce.'

Kath felt a sudden urge to defend him. 'I don't think he's—' She stopped herself.

'Travelling to the past to sting half the bookmakers in the city? Getting his face in the papers for it? Delivering the winnings to the daughter of this Amy Parker woman so she could have her face on television? I'd call that exploitation.'

Kath stared into her teacup and felt her blood boil. She was always beating her down when it came to expressing her own opinion on anything. It was starting to annoy her. She sat here judging every new person who discovered their time talent. She practically drove them into Fenwick's arms with her hostility. If she hadn't done that, Kath might have saved Danny. She'd sensed in 1966 that he only wanted to do what he felt was right and was far from evil. No one was evil.

She felt a tight thrill in her belly. Tomorrow she would see him again. She imagined getting to him before the others, convincing him to come clean about his intentions — convince Mrs Hudson that he wasn't there to stop her parents falling in love.

But what was he there for?

She felt the cold blade of malice chill her heart at the thought of Amy Parker. Why was he so fascinated by her? She knew it was jealousy. She knew she'd fallen for Danny a long time ago.

'If it's worthy of your attention, Katherine?'

She looked up into Mrs Hudson's glare. 'I'm sorry?'

'Is all this preparation boring you? Would you prefer to storm right in there and mess it all up?'

Kath placed her teacup down on the side table. She wanted to slam it but was afraid it would break.

'I don't have to listen to this,' she said, getting up.

Mitch reached for her. 'It's all right, Kath. She didn't mean—'

'I'm sick of the implication that I'm new to this and I mess things up.'

'I didn't mean that, Katherine,' said Mrs Hudson, trying to hide the irritation in her voice. 'Please sit down.'

'I didn't storm in there in 1966 and mess things up. I followed your instructions to the letter and things got out of hand. It was not my fault.'

'I know, I know,' said Mrs Hudson, more kindly now. 'I do apologise. I'm terribly irritable over this and I meant no harm. I was simply suggesting that we might all mess this up if we weren't prepared.'

Kath hovered, dearly wanting to flounce out and slam the door behind her. She'd been on the verge of blurting out that Rachel too was plotting her own sting on the bookies, so it wasn't as if Danny was the only one.

She swallowed it and sat down.

Mrs Hudson apologised again and continued with the meeting. They discussed the possible harm that Jez might be causing and how that might connect with the concert, running through their plan of action for the next day.

Kath heard the words, but inside her burned a bright coal of resentment. She would definitely get to Danny before them. She would warn him, plead with him, bring him into their fold. She was a better judge of character than Mrs Hudson. She'd show her.

— 30 —

As the tram sailed into Kings Heath High Street, Danny felt panic coursing through him like the crackle of the electric cable above them.

He hadn't researched Kings Heath and was going there blind. He liked to go prepared, knowing his options: where to stay, where to eat and drink, where to make money. Going off the map disturbed him. He had no idea what hotels and guest houses there were in Kings Heath.

He peered at the surroundings. The left side familiar, the right side all new, except for the library. Wait. The Station pub they'd just passed. The sign said *Station Hotel*.

He got off at the Parade, the row of shops set back from the road with the Kingsway cinema all gleaming and new and bustling with life. In 2012 someone had set fire to it, leaving the black rafters exposed like a burnt skeleton, the rest boarded up and covered in posters. And mysteriously, someone had scrawled in bright orange paint on the hoardings outside: *'Who Burnt Me Down?'*

A place to hide, he thought.

He looked up and down the road, a busy high street crowded with shoppers. He could walk south into the heart of it, but he decided to go back to what he knew. He walked north.

There was a man selling newspapers outside the train station entrance. A sudden sickening lurch of déjà vu. Something about the station there. Something bad. Something that had already happened. He couldn't quite picture it, but he didn't lose the qualm of nausea until he'd walked on past it and was at the door of the Station Hotel.

All his life he'd seen pubs that had the word *hotel* or *inn* in their name but did not rent rooms, but it was different here. The Station Hotel really would be a hotel. A handful of rooms above a pub, but a place to stay and hide.

A fat man with a walrus moustache showed him to a tiny but presentable room above the bar. The décor was still Edwardian. He thanked him and paid for two nights in advance and took a meal at a table downstairs at the rear of the bar. Boiled beef and cabbage.

He hid in his room the rest of the day, photo-reading Hinton's thoughts on the fourth dimension, till the walls seemed to close in on him and he craved escape.

He pulled his hat low over his face, hunched his shoulders and walked quickly to the Kingsway, paid a bored ticket girl a shilling and slumped into shadows in the upper circle.

A not very funny comedy called *Turn Back the Clock* was already running. It was about an unhappily married man who wakes up back in his earlier life, relives it all and discovers in the end that he wouldn't have changed anything after all.

Then Betty Boop had a crazy Hallowe'en party. Jack Frost was flying around in an aeroplane spraying the fields with frost, and a scarecrow was being blown by fierce winds that blew Betty's invitation right into his scarecrow hand.

Then they showed a clip of some crooner sitting on a piano and warbling through *The Very Thought of You*. He looked like an old uncle with crooked teeth, but some of the women around the cinema were gasping like he was a matinee idol.

Then a Pathé newsreel showed grainy pictures of the world's biggest ship, British, arriving in the world's biggest graving dock, also British. Then it was The Invisible Man, an exciting new feature film with never before seen special effects.

He let it wash over him with growing wonder.

This was their TV, their gogglebox, their smartphone. You could sit here and stare at the screen and let its images wash over you all day long.

The air was thick with cigarette and cigar smoke and it swirled in the beam of light that emanated from a lion's mouth behind them and filled the screen with giant portraits of Hollywood gods in silver.

He imagined meeting Amy Parker here, sitting with his arm around her, like the man over there with his arm around his girl, who was hiding her face in his chest at the scary parts.

Nothing about the film was scary. It was the kind of movie you might catch playing on afternoon TV in 2013. He wondered at how their notions of what was scary were so different. They were like children here. What had happened in the intervening years to make humanity grow up? The war, perhaps. It was coming and it was going to destroy their innocence.

His nausea grew, a dizziness fogged his whole head, a lurching in the pit of his stomach, he felt the whole row swaying like he was sitting on a ferry.

He pushed himself up from his seat, hands gripping the velvet arms of the chair so tightly he couldn't let go.

A woman came walking up the aisle, head down, checking her footsteps in the darkness. She halted, frozen. He was gazing into Amy's eyes again, as if he'd summoned her here through his thoughts, the way he'd transported himself to a place and time in history where he knew she would be, purely by thinking about her.

He fell back into his seat, the whole world lurching violently around him, and reached out a hand to her. And that was when a hurricane began to roar through the cinema.

Women shrieked, people jumped from their seats and scrambled for the exits, the wind whipped the clouds of cigarette smoke into violent coiling demons.

Danny tried to stand but could only sit and stare in wonder at his hands, because the hurricane seemed to be coming from his fingertips.

— 31 —

Rachel had worked hard on the concert throughout the day, only occasionally wondering what she would say to Mrs Hudson, Mitch and Kath when they finally showed up. She'd done everything she could to make sure the concert happened but they would have to deal with Danny when they arrived. She had no idea what he might do to sabotage the night, but they would surely have an idea of what precautions to take.

By the evening, after they'd eaten soup with the returning men and all enjoyed another free pint, they'd stayed in the pub to celebrate. Everything was in place and it was now pretty much up to the concert to run itself.

Posters and handbills were everywhere and many people reported a real buzz about the night whistling around the city.

They toasted each other in the main bar with a whisky, paid for, and Henry crowed 'You just see. We'll be turning them away tomorrow night.'

They were shattered but blissfully happy.

'I hope so, Henry,' said Charlie. 'It would be a kick in the teeth if no one came.'

He gave Rachel a searching look, as if she might know the answer, but she shrugged. It wasn't in the history books.

The two men groaned as Sid Haye walked into the bar.

'Evening, comrades,' he sneered. 'How's the bourgeois music business going?'

'Very well, thanks,' said Charlie. 'How's the fight against the National Government today? Any closer to toppling it?'

'The revolution is merely a few square meals away, comrade. And giving out free soup and beer to the starving workers might delay it, but it won't stop it, you mark my words.'

'Yes,' said Henry. 'You have clearly exposed our counter-revolutionary intent.'

'There's never been any doubt as to that, my friend. And you'll find out tomorrow that the workers of this particular parish will be much more interested in a discussion on the real issues facing the proletariat than some crooner feeding sentimental dross to the masses to keep them oppressed.'

Rachel stared aghast at Sid Haye's smug face. She had seen comedians on TV and in films spouting nonsense like this for comic effect but this was shockingly real because he was utterly sincere. He actually thought he was talking truth.

'I'm sorry,' she said. 'But are you telling us you actually think that Benny Orphan's music is oppressing the masses?'

All three men looked at her with surprise and she sensed their opinions had rarely been checked by a female.

Sid gave her a withering look, sort of eyes half closed, as if she were only worthy of half his attention.

'I'm telling it to you because it happens to be the truth.'

'I'm sorry but you're talking rubbish.'

Sid laughed. But it was an empty laugh. 'And why don't you explain it all to me, missy, so we can benefit from your wisdom?'

Rage swelled up inside her like milk coming to the boil but she didn't let it spill over. She'd seen this tactic before in the school debating society: say something outrageous, get people worked up, then force them to explain their opposition, and watch quietly as they tied themselves up in knots trying to articulate their outrage.

Instead, she took a deep breath and smiled and said, 'Why don't *you* tell us how you think a music hall singer can oppress the workers?'

Sid looked her in the eye for a moment, knowing his tactic had failed.

'Well, missy—'

'And don't call me *missy*. It's demeaning and disrespectful. Carry on, *comrade*.'

Sid gave a little laugh that was half a choke. She could tell that no woman had ever spoken to him like this before.

'As I was about to say… It is a well known fact that popular songs are written by government departments with the sole aim of drugging the proletariat with simple emotions like love, devotion, duty, longing. They act as a narcotic, clouding the workers' minds with false emotions. It's even rumoured that they're not even written by people, but turned out by a machine that is programmed to trigger sentimental claptrap.'

'Really?' she said, unable to hide her smile. She could see Charlie and Henry both smiling into their whisky glasses now. 'Love songs are written by a government machine? I suppose Benny Orphan is a government agent as well?'

'Benny Orphan is a cheap pedlar of sticky, sugary sentimental candy that rots the souls of the proletariat.'

'So you're against love songs?' she asked.

'If I was in power I'd ban them all!'

Sid's face was reddening now. He was losing the argument, making a fool of himself and he sensed it. A few people nearby were listening in and openly laughing at him.

'And you'd replace them with what? Marching songs?'

'I'd replace them with songs about the workers and their struggle. Songs about the revolution. Songs against capitalism!'

'So hate songs?' she said simply. As Sid's voice had risen, she had deliberately lowered hers.

'I didn't say that!'

'That's what it sounded like,' said Charlie.

'That's what I heard,' said Henry.

'You'd ban love songs and force us all to sing hate songs,' said Rachel. 'And you wonder why the Institute will be full tomorrow night and your meeting will be empty.'

'We'll bloody well see about that,' Sid growled.

He turned his red face away and crept to a tight knot of Communist Party members occupying their usual spot at the end of the bar known as Commies' Corner.

'I think I love you, Rachel,' said Charlie.

Henry hugged her. 'I've never seen anyone make Sid Haye walk away from an argument.'

The gaggle of customers who'd listened in applauded and laughed. Some of them patted Rachel on the back with cries of 'Well done,' 'Insufferable idiot,' and 'You showed him!'

Henry knocked back his whisky, slammed his glass on the bar and announced, 'Well, I feel an urgent desire to lose myself in the counter-revolutionary bourgeois distraction of cheap cinema.'

'A movie? After today?' said Charlie. 'I'd be asleep in minutes.'

'A movie's just the thing after a day like today,' said Henry. 'Just sit in the dark and be entertained. I fancy this Invisible Man film. It's supposed to have the most amazing special effects.'

'Can we go to the cinema, Charlie?' said Rachel, with sudden excitement. 'I've never been.'

Henry looked puzzled. 'You're American and you've never been to a cinema?'

'I mean here,' she said, stopping herself from adding *in the past*.

'Kingsway Picture Theatre,' said Henry, checking the clock above the bar. 'In twenty minutes.'

'Do you think we should?' said Charlie. 'Have we done everything for tomorrow?'

Henry slapped him on the back. 'We've done more than enough. And we deserve it.'

Rachel and Charlie downed their whiskies and they left the bar in high spirits, walking down towards the village to the tram stop in the centre.

None of them saw the lone figure walking behind them, listening to their eager talk of whether they would catch the opening or not. The man slowed down and listened, and passed them without looking back when they stopped for the tram.

Harold Ogborne recognised them from the fight outside the Fighting Cocks the other night. They were the Jew boy and his friends, the ones who were putting on the concert with the Yid singer and the darkie band that everyone wanted him to take Little Amy to. Well, he didn't bloody care if he took Little Amy there or not. Not after her loopy performance last Sunday. He didn't care if the Institute burned to the bloody ground.

He quickened his step as he saw the corner door of the Fighting Cocks. His drinking mates in the B.U.F. would be particularly interested to know the whereabouts of the Yid and his friends, that was certain.

— 32 —

'Would you like some popcorn?' Amy Parker asked Little Amy as they entered the Kingsway.

The foyer was crammed with people eager for a spot of Friday night escapism and the queue for popcorn was so long she rather hoped Little Amy would refuse.

'I'm fine, thank you, Auntie Amy.'

Little Amy was staring all around at the red velvet curtains with gold braid, the bright orange and green painted walls, the large oil paintings of King Charles. The glamour of it all. Amy thought the colour had certainly returned to her cheeks. She had even talked enthusiastically about seeing Benny Orphan tomorrow.

'Come on then, we'll get our seats and perhaps pop out later when the queue's died down.'

They were about to approach the curtained off inner sanctum when a surprised voice said 'Oh, hallo, Amy.'

They turned to see Harold, his mouth open.

'Miss Parker,' he added.

Amy knew enough about men to know she was looking at one who felt he'd been caught out. She wondered if he was here with another girl, but then he put on a false smile, stuck his hands in his pockets and affected an air of nonchalance.

'Hello Harold,' said Little Amy. 'Are you here for the Invisible Man?'

Harold looked confused for a moment and Amy could tell he had no idea what she was talking about. His eyes flashed around the foyer and he must have seen the display for the film.

'Arr! The Invisible Man. That's right. Heard it's a cracker.'

Amy saw a group of Blackshirts walking through the foyer towards them. It made her uneasy because they seemed to be heading directly for them. Then Harold shook his head and switched on his smile again to Little Amy. The Blackshirts walked right past them. Amy felt sure he'd just told them not to approach him. What was he up to?

'Are you looking forward to the concert tomorrow night, Harold?'

Again a moment of surprise before he caught himself and smiled 'Oh arr, very much so. You still want to go then, Amy.'

Little Amy blushed and looked at her feet.

'Yes, I really do.'

'Then I'd be honoured if you'd go with me, like.'

Amy wanted to look away.

'And, if you don't mind,' he looked at Amy now. 'I could sit and watch the film with you?'

Little Amy looked at Amy.

'Certainly,' said Amy. 'Why not?'

'Arr, that's grand, that is.'

Harold held out the crook of his arm and Little Amy took it. They walked on ahead with Amy following, the dowdy chaperone; the old woman left on the shelf; the spinster whose one romantic possibility had ignored her letter.

Harold seemed to look for ages for the right seats and eventually insisted on the middle of row B in the circle behind two men and a woman in the front row. The woman turned round and Amy could see she was a girl just like Little Amy. She stared at Amy for a few moments and Amy wondered if she knew her. She couldn't recall her face but there was something naggingly familiar about her. She didn't look again but leaned in close to the man next to her and whispered in his ear. Amy dismissed it as paranoia. She was used to the sensation that everyone was talking about her.

*

Harold left it ten minutes while some cartoon nonsense was showing before he made his excuses and nipped to the Gents. He signalled Clifford as he stalked up the aisle and saw him get up to follow.

He turned along the rear aisle and, just before turning into the Gents, spotted a bloke sitting in the back row. He recognised him straight off. It was that dodgy geezer who'd turned up banging on Amy's next door. He'd told PC Davies about him. Right wrong un.

He got a proper look at him, made sure about it, then walked into the Gents. Some bloke was washing his hands and he left the echoing space as Clifford came in. They were alone.

'What's going on, Harold? Thought you were in on this tonight?'

'Bumped into someone I know. Girl I'm keen on, if you must know.'

'You bottling off, Harold?'

'I ain't scared. Don't you worry about that.'

'That's not what it looks like.'

Harold thought about lamping him one right here. Clifford was soft as. Most of the Blackshirts were useless in a fight unless they were outnumbering a bunch of schoolgirls. A few quick punches and la-di-dah Clifford would be lying on the floor spitting his teeth out.

'Don't you worry what it looks like,' said Harold, jabbing Clifford in the chest. 'I've told you where they are, and I've brought you here. Now you're gonna have to take care of them yourself.'

Harold left him standing there, his face reddening at the prods in his chest.

'We were expecting more from you, Harold,' he said, but his voice was weak.

'Well, you're not bloody well gonna get it.'

He stalked out of the Gents and went back to Little Amy, wishing his next door neighbour, Amy Bloody Nosey Parker, wasn't there to interfere.

*

Rachel loved the interior of the cinema. It felt like stepping into a dark palace. She could see how everyone walked a little taller and realised for the first time the allure of the movies. This was why older people were so wistful about it — people who'd not stepped foot in one for decades and never seen a 3D blockbuster. To them cinema meant glamour, and it was the only shred of glamour in their drab, recession-hit lives. She understood now too the lure of the music for them all and what it truly meant to bring Benny Orphan to a place like this.

The glamour was dissipated by the wall of smoke that hit her when they entered the circle and took seats on the front row, overlooking the stalls.

It seemed that almost everyone was smoking: men and women. A few men were even smoking pipes.

Blue white stripes of light flickered in the air through grey clouds.

She couldn't stop looking around at everyone, fascinated by the communal awe of it.

A man and two women came and sat right behind them and she thought for a moment how they had matched up: three men, three women. Her smile faded when she recognised one of the women as Amy Parker.

She stared and Amy Parker looked right back at her.

It was definitely her. She had talked to her in 1940 and seen her die in 1966, when she'd looked through her photographs and even taken some of her dresses. She knew Amy wouldn't know her though. That was all in the future for her. She'd never seen Rachel in 1912. They would only meet again properly in 1940.

She leaned close to Charlie and whispered in his ear, taking in the pleasant scent of aftershave and an indefinable male odour that reminded her of her dad and felt comforting.

'The woman behind us is Amy Parker. The woman Danny saved. I think she's the reason he's come here.'

Charlie nodded and patted her knee.

Then they heard the young girl who was with them talking excitedly about the concert tomorrow. Henry grinned and nudged Charlie. Rachel smiled proudly and hoped the darkness hid the shadow of worry.

*

Harold returned and took his seat on the other side of Little Amy. Amy guessed it was her job to make sure he didn't try any funny business. She would have to keep one eye on his hands and make sure he wasn't attempting to touch her.

But what did it matter? Tomorrow he would take her in his arms and dance with her, his body pressed against hers. It didn't matter at all that they held hands in a cinema. But tongues would wag at one and not the other. She hated society and its absurd morality.

Harold hadn't returned with popcorn, nor even asked if the ladies wanted any, so Amy took her purse and whispered to Little Amy that she would be back in a minute.

She raised herself, edged along the row, made a conscious effort not to look at the strange girl in the front row who'd stared at her so keenly, though she could see the white blur of her face out of the corner of her eye, watching her, judging her.

She found the aisle and edged up it, careful not to trip on the steps, and she was almost at the top when she saw Danny Pearce.

And from his imagining meeting Amy Parker there, sitting with his arm around her, like the man over there with his arm around his girl, who was hiding her face in his chest at the scary parts, he had conjured her here to him.

He must be a god.

And the nausea that grew, the dizziness that fogged his whole head, the lurching in the pit of his stomach, was all the awesome power that coursed through him.

He could only be a god.

He pushed himself up from his seat, hands gripping the velvet arms of the chair so tightly he couldn't let go. Amy's eyes.

He had summoned her here. His mind, all powerful, the mighty whirlwind of history flowing through him.

He was a god.

He reached out his hand to her and a hurricane began to roar through the cinema.

Women shrieked, people jumped from their seats and scrambled for the exits, the wind whipped the clouds of cigarette smoke into violent coiling demons.

And Amy stood, unaffected, frozen in his mighty gaze, her hair whipping gently about her face, as if she were the eye of the hurricane that roared from his fingertips.

For a moment he doubted himself, doubted the mighty power that coursed through him, from him.

Amy was hit by the wave of bodies surging for the exits. It carried her away like a river. The mass of humanity became a single force of nature, a flood of people surging for the exit, down the stairs and out through the foyer, screaming people trampled underfoot.

Danny staggered to his feet as the last of the cinemagoers scattered. Some were still cowering in their seats or lying in the aisles. Others were dashing up the side aisles.

The smoke demons eddying around him began to slow. The wind abated, calmed and soon there were only the groans of the injured filling the air.

A woman walked up the steps towards him. She seemed calm, unlike everyone else. His eyes met hers.

It was Rachel.

He wondered for a moment if he had summoned her too.

There was fire in her eyes. A silent fury. He stared into them, curiously, almost entranced, as if she were a cobra, hypnotising him.

Then she pounced in a flash. A shock of electricity jolted through his bone marrow. A tang of singed hair.

The floor lurched underneath him and he was sucked into a black hole.

*

Cinema ushers and attendants were seeing to the handful of people who lay injured on the stairs and in the foyer.

Rachel felt herself propelled from the cinema as if the tornado were carrying her and it was only when they spilled out into the cold night air that she realised Charlie was gripping her arm so tightly.

A giant crowd buzzed outside and they pushed through it. She could hear the cries of:

'What on earth was that?'

'Well if that was them new special effects, you can keep em!'

'It was a repeat of that tornado from three years ago, I'm telling ya!'

'But it's totally calm out here.'

'Must have been a freak tornado. A small one. It'll have passed on and done some damage, I'll say.'

They pushed through the crowd till they were on the high street pavement. Most of the people were staying, as if someone might walk out of the cinema and offer an explanation. Some on the edge of the crowd had begun to drift away, walking south down the high street, or north to the station and to Moseley beyond it.

'Did you see it?' said Rachel.

Charlie nodded and said nothing, but she could see the shock written across his face. He'd seen Danny cause a tornado in a cinema, then he'd disappeared in a flash of blue light, leaving nothing but a scent of fire.

'Szélkirály,' said Henry.

There was a film of sweat across his forehead and his eyes were still staring in wonder at the cinema.

'What was that, Henry?' said Charlie.

'Szélkirály,' he said again.

'Sail Key Rai?'

'He was Szélkirály.' Henry seemed to realise where he was and to whom he was talking. 'Old Hungarian legend. My grandmother told me. The Wind King.'

He stared at Rachel now with renewed suspicion.

'You know him? You know this man, Rachel. What's going on? Who are you really?'

'Henry, leave her alone.'

'Who are you, Rachel?'

'I know him,' she said. 'He's here to cause trouble. I think he's trying to prevent the concert from happening. At least, I did. Now I'm not so sure.'

Henry looked at Charlie. 'She made him disappear. You saw it too?'

Rachel looked with alarm at Charlie's face.

'I don't know. It was dark.'

'Charlie, who is she? *What* is she?"

Charlie put a protective arm around Rachel. 'She's our friend, Henry. I trust her. Totally and utterly.'

It seemed to be enough for Henry. He took out a handkerchief and dabbed his forehead, nodded and smiled again. It was a forced smile, but it was clear that if Charlie trusted Rachel, then he would too.

'Let's call it a night,' he said. 'Long day tomorrow.'

He shook Charlie's hand, then turned to Rachel and stared at her for a few moments before pulling her close to him and whispering in her ear something that sounded like *'See ya, daily bob.'*

She wondered what it meant. Was it another Hungarian phrase or had she just misheard him?

Henry walked off south up the high street. Rachel and Charlie watched him go until he turned left at the first street.

'Come on,' said Charlie. 'I think we should go home and you can tell me what just happened.'

*

Danny blinked his eyes open and for a while found himself examining the ornate ceiling of the Kingsway. It was colder than it had been a moment ago, and there was a cloying air of damp that hadn't been there. He felt sick and his body ached all over, like he'd been hit by a car. He had to get up. He tried, a sharp pain shooting through his chest. What had she done to him?

Rachel. She'd tasered him, surely? He could still smell the faint tinge of singed hair and wondered if it was his own.

He'd not noticed the taser in her hand as she'd walked up to him. A nasty weapon. Did it mean he was still attached to the gun and she might still send a few more volts through him? He tried to peer around.

The silence was sheer. No one was there. He couldn't even hear the crowd that had run for the exits in panic. Perhaps he'd been unconscious for a while.

He turned over and tried to push himself up, gasping, his knees shrieking as they took his weight.

There was a crackling sound.

He pushed himself to his feet, staggered for a moment, swayed, gripped a velvet covered seat, steadied himself.

The cinema was empty. He peered around, trying to make it all out in the dark. His eyes must be getting used to it because there was a glow of light. It looked older, shabbier, neglected, cobwebs and dust everywhere.

He'd travelled, he realised. He wasn't in the Kingsway cinema in 1934 anymore. He'd flitted to another time. Had Rachel done this to him? There was no taser, he realised. She had sent him back through time. How had she done that?

He turned and almost fell over again as he recoiled in shock at what was behind him.

The back row was on fire, flames leaping high and licking the ceiling. It crackled angrily.

He staggered back down the stairs, realising with horror that he was in 2012, the night the Kingsway had burned down. And he knew now that it was Rachel who'd started the fire.

Panic flooded his senses for a moment. He was going to burn to death in the Kingsway picture house. He retreated down the rake of steps till he came to the balcony. The fire was raging now at the back of the cinema, the velvet seats a perfect kindling. It was going to roar down the bank of seats towards him in no time.

He glanced back at the drop to the stalls. Could he do it? It was break his legs or burn to death. And if he broke his legs he wouldn't be able to crawl out of there.

The back two rows were a wall of flame now.

Calm, he thought. *You can travel.*

He took a deep, long breath and closed his eyes, trying to ignore the crackle of flame. He thought of Amy Parker. Amy Parker in her ball gown. The photo. He tore it from his inside breast pocket. Amy at the concert, her eyes on the crooner. Amy on 21 January, 1934. Be with her. Go back to her.

The light faded and he looked up at the wall of fire advancing towards him. It was paler, waning, its angry roar receding.

A light breeze wafted over him, cool, refreshing, and he found himself standing in a dark alley.

There was a hubbub of voices ahead.

He walked up the alley, dirt creaking under his shoes, and he came out onto the Parade at night, a crowd of people gathered outside the cinema.

He was back.

He pulled his collar up and put his head down, shoved his hands into his pockets and walked north quickly, not looking back till he reached the door of the Station Hotel.

*

It was Julie Hickman who spotted Henry Curtis leaving the cinema. Clifford and the other Blackshirts had been among the first to flee the cinema and had skirted the edge of the crowd, worried that their prey might escape.

Julie had spotted the unmistakable outline of Jew Henry over by the roadside. He was chatting with two others: the man he was organising the concert with, and a girl. She looked pretty. Henry hugged her and Julie felt a sudden rage flame inside her.

Jew Henry, who'd thought he was the bee's knees at school and taken that joke of a valentine seriously. As if she'd ever be attracted to an ugly Jew like him. And turned her down too. As if he was something special.

She called Clifford and signalled, pointing over to where Henry was departing, turning from his friends and walking up the high street, disappearing behind the first building.

She ran to the pavement and looked up the street but he was nowhere to be seen. He must have turned left up Poplar Road. She ran again to Lashford's, the butcher's on the corner. All closed up but the unmistakable stale odour of dead meat and sawdust.

There. Half way up Poplar Road, his shuffling bulk under a streetlamp and fading again into the darkness.

Clifford and the others caught up with her.

'There,' she pointed.

They ran on ahead, swiftly but softly so their footsteps didn't sound and warn him. She followed in their wake, her heart beating madly.

They were on him before she realised. It was absurdly quiet for a beating. At first they seemed to be running and then they were gathered in a scrum and kicking at something on the ground between them. No one cried out or said anything, and Henry hadn't made a sound other than grunting as their boots stomped him.

Then there was a cracking sound as his skull bounced off the pavement. She could see a dark pool of ink blooming from under his head. His hat lay crumpled to the side.

Clifford gave him another kick and something snapped inside him. She thought it must be one of his ribs.

The men were already fleeing up the road.

She leaned down to take a closer look. Henry stared, didn't seem to see her.

'I told you, Jew Henry,' she whispered. 'I told you about the storm.'

Clifford came back and yanked her away and she found herself running into the dark with him, cackling hysterically.

— 33 —

Charlie held his elbow out and Rachel hooked her hand there as she walked and thought of how no man in 2013 could do that without irony. Here it was perfectly serious and natural.

They left the clamour of the Parade behind them and strolled towards Moseley, passing the library on the opposite side. She noticed the Hope Chapel squeezed into the tiny space beside it, and the police station. It all seemed so quaint with none of the ugly new buildings that would one day ruin the high street, and every shop had an old-world charm: Harry Legg, corn dealer, Nellie Bright, confectioner; the Premier Cycle Company; a woollen drapers; a ladies' outfitter called *Claude*; a milliner, another ladies' outfitter, a boot repairer. They walked on in silence past the Station Hotel, its windows frosted and curtained, the hubbub of life inside.

She saw the entrance to the train station opposite and shuddered, remembering 1959. Charlie must have felt it because he pulled her a little closer to him and smiled.

It felt like such a romantic moment, and he must have felt it too because he looked at her and smiled as they prepared to cross the foot of Valentine Road. She saw the sign for the street and almost laughed. A romantic moment on Valentine Road.

A cluster of footsteps slapping the pavement. A woman shrieking. Rachel felt momentary alarm. Charlie gripped her closer.

Shadows exploded from the side street and were on them before they could react. They ran all around them, nearly knocking them over, and straight into the street like a herd of startled gazelle.

She had only a moment to see their shadowy forms sprint into the park across the road, swallowed by the blackness.

She recognised them immediately.

'Dear god,' said Charlie. 'Did you see that?'

He still gripped her tightly.

'Wasn't that—?'

Charlie peered into the black mass of the park even though they were long gone.

'I think it was,' he said.

He was fearful suddenly.

'I don't like this.'

He looked back up the high street. The cinema crowd was still dispersing. People were filing into the train station. She could see his mind working out the way Henry had turned and how they might have circled round the block.

'It's Henry. I'm sure of it.'

He took her hand.

'Come.'

They trotted up the slope of Valentine Road, passing cosy suburban villas with quiet gardens, and came to the five-way crossroads with its tiny island, the giant Methodist church looming over them, imposing and eerie in terracotta gloom.

They doubled back down Poplar Road. The side street dark and foreboding with only the faint glow of the high street at its end.

He halted and stared hard down the straight line of Woodville Road to their left.

'He lives down there. Can't see him though.'

They crossed to the corner to get a closer look, straining their eyes down the dark street to make out his outline shuffling home. Rachel looked behind her, suddenly scared.

'Oh God.'

Charlie turned. Rachel pointed.

Through the gloom they could see the strange art deco house set back from the road and a dark shape lying in its forecourt.

Charlie ran.

By the time she caught up, Charlie was on his knees and lifting Henry's head up. It flopped back and his mouth fell open just like his eyes. Ink oozed from his skull.

Charlie slapped his face, shook him.

'Come on, Henry. Wake up. Wake up, now, chap.'

Rachel leaned down and took his wrist, feeling desperately for a pulse. But there wasn't one.

'Charlie,' she said. 'He's dead.'

— 34 —

Charlie ran to the high street to find a police officer while Rachel stayed with Henry.

She stroked his face and whispered a lullaby and felt her tears falling on him. The street was black and silent and suddenly very cold and the whole world was asleep.

'I'm so sorry, Henry. If I'd known about this I could have stopped it.'

She heard a faint whistle from somewhere down the street. Eventually, footsteps padded towards her out of the gloom. It was Charlie with a policeman who looked absurdly young — a schoolboy dressed in a policeman's uniform for the school play — his eyes widening when he saw Henry and the pool of blood.

'My colleague is coming,' he said, his voice breaking. 'He's calling an ambulance.'

They knelt around Henry and just stared. There was nothing they could do. Rachel noticed that the art deco building she'd always thought must have been a coffee house or stylish café, was actually a tripe dressers.

A small crowd gathered. People from the cinema. They must have seen the commotion as Charlie summoned the police and come to see what was happening.

An ambulance arrived. It looked old fashioned and amateurish, like an ambulance from a silent comedy film. One of the paramedics was smoking a cigarette and she wanted to slap it from his mouth. But she realised he wasn't even a paramedic. There was no such word as *paramedic*. He was just a driver.

They put Henry on a stretcher and covered his face with a blanket and heaved him into the back of the ambulance like a pallet of meat for delivery.

Charlie asked if they could come along in the ambulance.

'Not much point, fellah,' said the smoking driver.

The schoolboy constable asked them to come to the station to make a statement.

They walked, down to the high street, a crowd following. She saw that Charlie's face had the look of a bomb blast survivor: dazed and livid. She knew her own must look the same.

The small crowd walked them to the police station door and stood outside. It was a quaint little building where you couldn't imagine murder ever being discussed.

They were invited to sit in the waiting room. They waited for a long time. She slipped her hand into Charlie's and squeezed his fingers, then noticed both their hands were red with Henry's blood. His trousers and her skirt were both stained wine red too.

It made her feel like a murderer caught in the act.

For a long time they waited and nothing happened but the occasional drunk being frogmarched in and processed to the cells.

Eventually, the schoolboy constable came back and took them to an office and took a statement, his fountain pen poised over a sheet of pristine white paper.

He took Charlie's name and address. Rachel said she was an American citizen visiting on vacation. He didn't ask to see her passport. She didn't care. If he wanted her papers she would have to say she would return with them and just disappear back to her own time.

It didn't matter.

Charlie insisted that he had seen a group of Blackshirts running from the scene of the crime.

'Running along Poplar Road, sir?'

'No. They ran across us at the bottom of Valentine Road. Into the park.'

The schoolboy constable frowned. 'So you didn't see them on Poplar Road?'

'No, but that was where they were running from.'

'You didn't see them within the vicinity of the deceased?'

'Look, they were in the cinema. They saw us leave. They followed Henry up Poplar Road, murdered him, and ran on, circling round and down Valentine Road.'

'But you didn't see them on Poplar Road?'

'No.'

Rachel butted in. 'Henry was attacked by the same group last Sunday. At New Street Station.'

'Oh really?'

The schoolboy constable was frowning but he didn't write it down.

'He came to my flat straight afterwards,' said Charlie. 'He still had the boot print on his coat.'

'And did he report this attack to the police?'

Charlie sighed. 'I don't know. I don't think so. He laughed it off.'

'So in your words, he was attacked and kicked, but he didn't take it seriously?'

'That's not what I said. He just wasn't the sort to let it worry him. And now he's dead.'

The schoolboy policeman stared, wanting more, fountain pen poised.

'Henry got into a fight with the same group on Wednesday evening,' said Rachel. 'The police have a report on that.'

'So these Blackshirts attacked him on Wednesday evening too?'

'That's correct,' said Charlie.

'And they were arrested?'

'No. Henry and I were arrested.'

The schoolboy constable put his pen down. Rachel could see Charlie visibly deflate, the hope leaking from him. It was all useless. Nothing would be done about it.

When they had finished making the statement, he informed them that he would be calling on them again to make further enquiries.

They emerged from the station at two in the morning. Charlie lit a cigarette and blew angry smoke at the indifferent night air.

'We'll have to cancel the concert,' he said. 'I'll telephone Benny Orphan's agent first thing in the morning. And Lester Johnson's. We can't go ahead with it now.'

'But Charlie—'

'There's no point,' he said. 'It's over.'

He walked off, heading for Moseley and didn't seem bothered if she followed or not.

— 35 —

For a few moments Rachel felt the excitement she'd imagined she would feel that morning, with the delicious anticipation of the concert ahead of them.

Then it all flooded back — Henry lying in his own blood — and doused the feeling, leaving a frail wisp of smoke and the acrid taste of despair.

One by one all the plans she'd had in her mind died quietly: going to the Prince to see the men off for their last morning of leafleting; arranging the drivers to collect Benny Orphan and Lester Johnson's band and take them to their separate hotels; heading to the Institute to dress up the hall; making sure Manny Singer's security team arrived; hooking up with Mrs Hudson, Mitch and Kath; preventing time from being altered.

She pushed herself out of bed and strip-washed in cold water in the cramped bathroom, shivering, reluctant.

Charlie was sitting in the armchair staring into space, the gramophone crooning *It's All Forgotten Now*. She put a hand to his shoulder and he seemed to wake up. Had he been sitting there like that all night? He tried to smile. She stroked his hair.

'You know, I've always found Benny Orphan a bit too sad and sentimental for me. Always preferred happier tunes. But right now he really is hitting exactly the right note. When you really listen to him, there's such an ocean of loss behind every line, isn't there?'

He snorted a half laugh, bitter. 'I wonder if you have to experience the death of someone close to you to hear it.'

'I'm so sorry,' she said.

'In a way, it's a pity he won't be coming today to sing to us.'

The record finished. He got up, searched through his giant stack of 78s for another, put it on. *Be Still, My Heart*.

She knew all these records, had listened to them alone in her flat in 2012, and had never guessed they would be linked to a morning as awful as this.

'I have to go to the hospital. I'm not sure why. There's nothing to see. I suppose I'd better ring the agents first though.'

He went to get his coat and hat.

She had failed. How could she face Mrs Hudson? How could she tell her that the concert would never happen now? Mrs Hudson would accuse Danny of meddling, but surely Danny had had nothing to do with this? Surely even he wouldn't sink that low?

She had almost forgotten the Kingsway incident. What was it Henry had called him? Szélkirály. The Wind God. Whatever it was Danny had done last night, it was nothing to do with getting the concert cancelled; nothing to do with Henry being murdered.

And yet the concert was cancelled. And Henry was dead.

Charlie was out in hallway, opening the front door. She rushed out and stopped him.

'Charlie. No.'

He looked at her hand on his and when he lifted his face to her, there were tears in his eyes.

'Charlie. It's what they want. It's what they've been trying to achieve. We can't let them win. We have to go ahead and put the concert on. We have to. For Henry.'

'It's no use,' he said. 'I can't face it.'

'What would Henry have done?'

'He'd do what I'm doing.'

'You know he wouldn't. You know he'd say *stuff them*. He'd go right ahead and stage that concert. With bells on.'

Charlie couldn't stop a smile breaking through his face. He sniffed, wiped his nose, tried to find a handkerchief.

He took his hand from the latch, nodding, blowing his nose.

'Yes, with bells on,' he said. He looked at Rachel: 'And more security.'

— 36 —

Rachel squeezed into the red phone booth on Victoria Parade with Charlie. It was the first time they'd pressed this close to each other since they'd danced to the Wayne Shorter tune playing on the Dansette in the Lickey Hills, the day England won the World Cup.

No, he'd taken her in his arms in 1959. A brief respite from her nightmare on the station at the end of time.

All of that was to come for him. All of that was over for her.

He got through to Manny Singer's number at the social club above the fish and chip shop on Hurst Street and told him the news.

There seemed no time for emotion. So many facts to impart — how it had happened, the Blackshirts, the police dismissing everything, how to inform his family — but she couldn't hear how Manny was taking it.

'I wanted to cancel the concert,' said Charlie. 'But—'

Whatever it was Manny said, and she could only hear the light squeak of a voice, she knew he was saying no: the show must go on.

She smiled.

Charlie was about to hang up.

'Give me the phone.' She grabbed the receiver from him. 'Manny? It's Rachel.'

'Hello girl. What terrible news.'

'I'm so sorry for your loss,' she said. 'I just had an idea. The friend you mentioned, who works in the factory with Harold?'

'Jimmy Connor, yes.'

'Could you get a message to him this morning? Could he find out what they plan to do today? The fascists?'

Silence on the line. She wondered if he'd broken down in tears. But his voice came back firm, determined.

'That's a good idea, Rachel. He'll be at work. I'll drive over there right away.'

Of course, she thought. Everyone still worked on Saturdays.

She explained her idea to Manny and he chuckled.

'And we're going to need a lot more than ten men on the door,' she said.

'Don't you worry,' said Manny. 'I'll round up the biggest gang of commie Jew agitators they've ever seen. And this is for free.'

When she hung up, Charlie was looking at her like she was a different person.

'I'd no idea you could be so ruthless,' he said.

'Trust me, Charlie. You can't reason or negotiate with Nazis. If you do, they will ride right over your skull and crush it like a tank.'

He considered her sudden vehemence. 'It was something I might have laughed off only yesterday,' he said. 'But that was before I had to wash my best friend's blood off my hands. I guess you're right. The storm has arrived.'

They made a few more calls, putting various allies into action, and walked to the Prince.

Mr Hollis was surprised to see them so early but knew something was wrong by the grim expressions. Charlie explained everything and the old man slumped into a chair.

'Oh dear. Oh my Lord. I'm so sorry. What a terrible tragedy.'

They explained all the things they'd have to do today and he suggested they use the upstairs parlour and its telephone so they could communicate with Manny's base.

'Give this number to everyone involved today. This is your office.'

Rachel hugged him and smiled and rushed off to tell Mrs Hollis, who was preparing soup for the men.

Before they arrived, Rachel told Mr Hollis they'd decided to keep Henry's death a secret from the performers. It was best they didn't know the concert was being threatened. They would deal with the threat quietly and well away from the performers, who would be protected by bodyguards at every stage.

Once the men had eaten and been given their last batch of handbills, Rachel suggested she leave Charlie here and go to town to meet the performers as they arrived.

He protested that he couldn't possibly let her out of his sight today, with so much danger. She laughed and said 'Charlie. You forget I've met you in the future. If anything terrible happened to me today, I'm sure you'd have told me about it.'

He frowned and didn't seem convinced, but gave in, exasperated.

'I suppose I might have,' he said.

She kissed him and he stepped back with surprise, and she was gone, stepping onto the first tram into town. It was a calm, sunny day and you would only guess it was January because of the chill in the air. *Please let the sun be the omen,* she thought, *and not the chill.*

— 37 —

She thrilled as she came to New Street Station and found a giant glass-vaulted Victorian pod of a building. It was black and dirty but its glass ceiling looked magnificent arching over the city. She realised the Selfridges building was not the first to do this.

She found a way in and down to platform 2 where the train from London was arriving. She pushed through crowds to reach the end of the platform where she presumed the first class carriages would alight, and marvelled at the clouds of steam hissing from the engines.

She found a chap holding a cardboard sign with the name MR SINGER scrawled on it and recognised him as one of the card players at Manny's social club. Henry had suggested days ago that holding up a sign in New Street Station announcing the arrival of Benny Orphan might cause a riot, but only now did it seem much more necessary to keep it all clandestine.

'Hello there,' she said. 'I'm Rachel. Concert organiser.'

The man tipped his cap. 'Hello, miss. I'm Abe.'

He crooked his thumb behind him to indicate a cluster of young men smoking at the edge of the platform. They looked nonchalant and you might pass them without a second thought, and only if you stopped and took a second look would you notice that they were being very attentive to every person on the platform.

'Don't you worry,' said Abe. 'Our guest is in safe hands. Benacre Street Boxing Club.'

There was also a small cluster of girls nearby, talking excitedly.

'Henry said to bring them along,' said Ben. 'They've been told to stay quiet.'

The doors opened and passengers stepped through the great clouds of steam. A man in a blue suit, white shoes and an overcoat over his shoulders stepped down. He was one of the only men on the platform not wearing a hat of some sort.

Abe held the sign high. The Benacre Street Boxing Club had already moved in to crowd around the guest. It was impossible for anyone to reach him.

Benny Orphan stepped towards the sign, smiling brightly. Rachel could sense the sheen of fame on him. It was something indefinable, it seemed like a little man inside of him was burning a bright light that sort of shone through his translucent skin.

'Hello, Mr Orphan,' said Rachel, stepping forward to hold out a hand. 'Welcome to Birmingham.'

'Well hello there, dearie,' he said, planting a kiss on the back of her hand. 'What a sight you are for sore eyes after a long journey.'

'We'll be taking you to your hotel, where you can relax for a few hours before the concert tonight. It's very close.'

'That's a relief, my dear,' he beamed. 'Well, this is quite a welcoming committee, I must say.'

All the boys of the Benacre Street Boxing Club were smiling the sort of smiles people smiled when meeting someone very famous. The girls were giggling to themselves and whispering.

'We'll have plenty of time for introductions later,' said Rachel. 'Let's get you out of here.'

'Hold on,' said Benny Orphan. 'Here's my faithful sidekick.'

A man struggled off the train with a large suitcase, his face red with the effort. He straightened his hat and eyed the group with suspicion.

'Hey, Arthur, they've provided me with an entourage. Maybe I don't need you after all?'

Arthur walked forward and raised his hat. 'Who's in charge here?'

'I am,' said Rachel.

Arthur looked surprised. 'Oh,' he stammered. 'You're a girl.'

'Yes,' said Rachel. 'Very observant.'

Benny Orphan cackled and slapped Arthur on the back.

'Now, please let's move on,' she said. 'This way.'

'Follow her, Arthur,' said Benny Orphan with a cackle. 'She's in charge.'

They bustled off the platform, the boys forming a protective circle around Benny Orphan, Rachel and Abe as they marched through the station, the girls behind.

No one really noticed. They were just a part of the crowd.

They emerged at the foot of what she recognised as Navigation Hill and went straight to a coach that was parked up, *Keller's Coaches* painted on the side. They all piled on, Benny Orphan in the middle, and the driver set off.

Two minutes later they pulled up outside the Grand Hotel on Colmore Row and the gang crowded into the foyer.

The concierge seemed surprised to see so many people. Rachel greeted him warmly, turning her American accent up a notch, and informed him that Mr Orphan had arrived, was booked as Mr Singer for safety's sake, and would be taking his room for the afternoon with his entourage who would be providing security.

The concierge nodded and bowed, telling her he'd received instructions already from Mr Curtis and had informed only the most senior of his staff members and warned them that the strictest secrecy must be maintained.

The assistant manager was ready to show Mr Orphan straight to his suite. He led him to the lift, and three of the Benacre boxers squeezed in with them. The rest began to tramp up the plush carpeted stairs. Arthur viewed them with despair.

'Now, miss, I'd better tell you about arrangements for the raffle,' he said.

'Oh yes, the big prize.'

'I'll be running it. So I'll need a table at the entrance where I can personally hand every lady a ticket.'

'Can't we just get the box office person to hand them out.'

'Certainly not,' he said. 'We've done this at concert halls up and down the land and I don't see why this place will be any exception.'

'Okay,' she said. 'I'll sort it.'

He looked puzzled, or annoyed. She couldn't work out which.

He was too out of breath to complain by the time they had climbed to the suite. Two of the men were already guarding the door, and inside they found Benny Orphan in cheerful mood, calling for extra glasses so everyone could share the champagne with him. The girls had already formed a now openly adulatory circle around him.

'Well, I have to be going,' said Rachel.

'Surely not, dearie. We're just getting started.'

'I'm afraid I have to go and meet the band now,' she said.

'Ah, the band. Coloured players I've heard?'

'That's right,' she said, wondering if this might suddenly become a problem. 'We've heard great things about them.'

'As long as they can play sweet as well as hot. I sang with Duke Ellington's boys one night, you know, in New York. Man, that's a band that knows how to play it sweet when they want to. Gorgeous boys. Really lift a singer up, they do.'

'I'm very much looking forward to seeing you perform tonight.'

'As the actress said to the bishop.'

The girls giggled. Benny Orphan cackled, feeding off their adoration.

Rachel smiled politely and left with Abe. She realised now why it was such a good idea to bring the girls along. Something told her Benny Orphan wouldn't find a few hours in the company of the Benacre Street Boxing Club nearly so appealing. Poor Henry really had thought of everything.

— 38 —

Abe drove the charabanc back to New Street Station where they waited half an hour. Another ten boys from the Benacre Street Boxing Club shuffled onto the platform and hung around. She recognised two of them from her evening at the social club with Henry.

Again the shudder every time she thought of him.

Poor Henry was lying on a hospital mortuary slab somewhere.

When the steam engine rolled in and deposited its passengers, Lester Johnson and his band were easy to spot. Everyone on the platform looked twice.

How strange, she thought, that it was still a time where you would see a black man and find it unusual. These people would go home tonight and say to their family, *you'll never guess what I saw today*. And yet she knew from her studies that black people had lived in Britain in significant numbers for centuries.

She pushed forward and greeted Lester Johnson with a smile. He was tall, lean, handsome, and had a confident smile. They were all dressed in sharp suits with kipper ties and homburg hats, and she thought of the newsreels she'd seen of the Empire Windrush.

'Hello there,' she said. 'You must be Lester. I'm Rachel. Welcome to Birmingham.'

He shook her hand and bowed. 'Good day, ma'am. We're honoured to be here.'

She realised her pretence of being American might unravel and reminded herself to tell Charlie not to mention it later.

Lester was courteous and leonine and carried an air of authority that seemed to cow everyone around him. The boxing club boys gathered as the rest of the band spilled onto the platform, humping their instrument cases and overnight bags. A couple of them helped with the larger bags, but the rest were still furtively checking the human traffic on the platform. Rachel realised they wanted to keep their fists free.

'Oh, there's something I have to tell you, ma'am,' said Lester.

Abe butted in. 'Can it wait for a while? We need to get you out of here and onto the coach. Parking restrictions, I'm afraid.'

They filed out of the station and piled onto the coach. It set off down the back streets of Digbeth on the three-minute journey to Hurst Street.

'What was it you wanted to tell me, Lester?'

'Oh, yes. I'm afraid our pianist has fallen ill. Can you find a replacement?

Rachel couldn't hide the shock in her face. How was she going to find a replacement pianist now?

'But they won't know your music.'

Lester patted his briefcase.

'I have all the sheet music here. He won't need to improvise, just accompany. We'll be playing sweet, not hot.'

'I'll see what I can do,' she said.

The coach pulled up outside the fish and chip shop and they climbed the steps to the social club.

Manny greeted them warmly, shaking the hand of every band member and ushering them to tables where they were offered drink and food.

The band looked pleased with the gig, their bright smiles lighting the room. A large crowd had turned up to see them and they were overwhelmed with curious conversation.

Rachel took Lester to one side and explained the band would be here for a few hours, just to relax and then they'd be taken to their hotel in Moseley where they could check in, and then straight to the hall for a couple of hours before the concert.

No one mentioned Henry's murder, and if Lester found the arrangements and the presence of so much muscle suspicious, he said nothing.

Manny pointed her to his office where she could use the phone. Charlie's number at the Prince was pinned on the wall. She wondered how the hell people organised anything in the past without cell phones.

She dialled the heavy apparatus, finding it difficult to push the numbers round with her fingertip, and then feeling increasing impatience having to watch the dial wind all the back after each one. Eventually, she heard Charlie's voice through the fuzz at the other end.

'Benny Orphan's at the Grand. The band are at the social club. All safe. Just one problem.'

'I knew there'd be at least one.'

'Lester's pianist is ill. What are we going to do?'

There was silence on the other end.

'Hello? Charlie?'

'I know a local pianist,' he said. 'Lives in Kings Heath. Don't think he's ever played jazz before, though.'

'They've got sheet music here.'

'Hmmm. He's more of a classical chap. I think he knows his way around popular song. He can probably tinkle his way through a foxtrot.'

'Will he be good enough?'

'He'll have to be. I'll go and get him. Good work, Rachel. You're quite amazing.'

She felt her heart flutter as he hung up and sudden music erupted from the next room. The band had taken out their instruments and launched into *Blue Minor*.

Manny came in with a big smile on his face. 'Just wanted to say. Our friend at a certain factory in Moseley. He should be hearing all about today's schedule round about now.'

'Good,' said Rachel. 'Let's hope it works.'

— 39 —

The band played an impromptu concert and it seemed that half of the Jewish quarter had climbed the stairs to see it.

Then they ate fish and chips and knocked back a few pints. The band members were all beaming, feeling like royalty. Only Lester looked worried, checking his pocket watch.

'We'll be going soon,' said Rachel, trying to smile away his worry.

'Oh, don't mind me, miss. I'm never quite comfortable until we're playing the first tune to the audience.'

Rachel looked across with surprise when one of the old Jewish gentlemen approached her. She'd seen him playing chess earlier. He walked up to her and stared.

'Hello?' she said.

'You were a friend of Henryk Kertész,' he said. 'You were there when he died?'

She nodded and choked back sudden tears. 'Yes. Just after.'

He gripped her hand and squeezed it. A tear fell from his face onto her wrist.

'Such a tragedia. I was just now told the news. Such a great man. We are from the same town. Debrecen.'

Rachel placed her other hand over the old man's. 'I didn't know him long,' she said. 'But I already miss him a great deal.'

The old man smiled and nodded. 'He had that effect on people. Such a tragedia.'

He shook his head some more and shrugged and let go of her hand.

'You're Hungarian too?' she asked.

'Igen,' he said.

'He said something to me I didn't understand. It was the last thing he said, actually. I think it was Hungarian.'

'What it was?'

'It sounded like *see ya, daily bab*. I think that was what it was, anyway.'

The old man stroked his chin. '*Délibáb*,' he whispered. 'Strange.'

'What does it mean?'

'Well, *szia*, means *goodbye*, or even *see you*. But *délibáb* is a... oh, what it is? Like when you are in the desert and you see things that are not there?'

'A mirage?'

'Igen! The mirage. I don't know why he would say that to you. Perhaps he think you are not real?'

She nodded and tried to smile. 'Perhaps I misheard him.'

'Oh, *Délibáb* is also a character. From the mythologia. She was a mortal girl. The Wind King loved her but she didn't love him. She loved his brother, the Sun King.'

'The Wind King?' she said. '*Szélkirály?*'

His eyes lit up with delight. 'You know Hungarian?'

She shook her head. 'Henry said this word to me. He told me about the Wind King.'

'Ah. So he joke that you are *Délibáb*. He was always the joker. Now it makes sense.'

The old man nodded, squeezed her hand once more and then walked away.

It was late afternoon before they all got back in the coach with the ten bodyguards from the boxing club and another ten to bulk the numbers. She told Lester they were just getting a lift to the venue ahead of time, and the bandleader nodded, as if nothing was unusual.

The coach rattled south to Moseley. Everywhere they drove, pedestrians did a double take at the sight of so many black men in a coach. Coming up Alcester Road through Balsall Heath a group of girls waved and laughed excitedly.

Abe drove straight through Moseley village and parked up outside the Alcester Lodge Hotel. They got the band inside quickly, the bodyguards checking up and down the street, but everything was quiet. Rachel couldn't hide her worry. The band in Hurst Street surrounded by bodyguards was safe. Here it felt more out in the open.

The band checked into their rooms. Sheila Sutton on reception recognised Rachel and blushed, no longer acting the snob now that she realised Rachel was the person filling her hotel for the night.

She remembered confronting Danny in the bar. She scanned the guest book as the band members signed in and noted Danny had left yesterday morning.

She remembered the strange gust of wind that had blown through reception, papers scattering. *He is Szélkirály.* Where was he now? What was his plan? What was he going to do tonight?

The thought of a tornado sweeping across the Institute dance floor made her shudder. She must tell Mrs Hudson. If only they would show up.

Once they'd checked in and deposited overnight bags in their rooms, she rushed the band back to the coach and they drove back through Moseley village, on past the Prince and down the hill to the Institute, right next to the tram depot.

They climbed the steps and went straight in through the open door. She was about to tell one of the bodyguards to stand guard on the door but as soon as the band were inside, they closed it and slid the bolt across.

The giant hall was lit dimly and seemed like an enormous warm cave. The band walked across the dance floor to the stage, their two-tone shoes clacking on the parquet.

A man was slumped in a chair, feet up, reading a book. Rachel walked over to him and it seemed he didn't hear her till she was standing right over him. He jumped up and closed the book. Sherlock Holmes.

'Oh, hello there,' he said, rising and holding out a hand. 'I'm Tony. Tony Pratt. The pianist.'

He filled out a tweed suit and wore jam jar bottom glasses. She'd have put him at fifty but knew he was probably more likely thirty.

'Do apologise,' he said. 'Can't put it down. I do so love a good murder mystery. Don't you?'

She cringed, thought of Henry. Smiled. Nodded.

'Conan Doyle. He lived in Birmingham, you know. Worked as a doctor in Aston 35 years ago. Fascinating, eh?'

'Have you played jazz before?'

'Ah,' he said. 'Not your actual jazz, no. More of a classical man, myself. But I hear you've got sheet music so I can just play the notes, eh?'

Lester Johnson came over and introduced himself.

'We should go through a few numbers. Give you a feel for it?'

'Righto,' said Tony, following them to the stage. 'I have to say, this is a turn up for the books. Didn't expect this to be happening today.'

Tony Pratt climbed the stage and shook the hand of every band member. He sat at the upright piano and ran through some scales. Lester handed him the scores.

'*Stompy Jones*,' he said.

The band kicked in. A fast swinger. Tony's hands were a blur on the keys and sweat began to dot his forehead. He looked like a man running for a bus just at the point he realises he's not going to catch it.

When they finished, Tony took his jacket off and mopped his brow with a handkerchief.

'Goodness me. That was rather fast.'

'Let's try *Doin' the Uptown Lowdown*.'

Tony scrambled for the right pages and the band started without him. He joined in as soon as he could. It was even faster than the last one.

Rachel watched aghast, but Lester caught her eye and winked. She realised he was testing him out. They stormed through it without vocal.

Tony reached for his handkerchief again.

'I say, are they all going to be this fast?'

'You're doing great, Tony,' said Lester. 'We'll be much slower for the concert. Just blowing off the cobwebs, that's all. Now, let's try *Stars Fell on Alabama.*'

Tony found the music.

'Ah. *Slowly*. Very good.'

Rachel checked her watch and signalled Abe. It was time to take care of the Blackshirts.

— 40 —

Clifford waited opposite the gates of Braddock's and thought about how he was going to kill Julie Hickman. It was night already and yet still afternoon. He crushed another cigarette under his boot and resisted the urge to light a third. He ought to cut down. The adverts said they were good for you, scientists said so, but the Führer didn't smoke and he had to admit they made him short of breath.

He felt excitement stirring deep inside.

If only his police mole had been able to tell him earlier that they wouldn't be pursued for the murder, Julie Hickman would still be here in Birmingham.

Her initial excitement over the event had turned sour and paranoid. The giddy sexual glee as they'd run through the park, much to his disappointment, had turned to terror once they'd reached his house. They had all cowered behind his curtains for a few hours, expecting every knock at the door, every footfall in the street to be the police.

He had wanted Julie to stay, but she had paced his parlour saying *Oh God, what have I done?* again and again and rushed home before dawn, packed a case and caught the first train to her aunt's in London.

She was going to do something stupid. Something like return and confess everything to a policeman. He wondered if arsenic might work. Perhaps too slow. She might confess before she croaked. Perhaps he should simply strangle her. Hang her. Make it look like a suicide.

It had to be done quickly, though. He ought to go to London and find her. Just as soon as this business was over. He would catch a train from New Street this evening.

First, though, he had to deal with Benny Orphan. He was determined to see it through. If these reds thought they could bring a Jew warbler and some darkie minstrels to Moseley, they had another think coming.

He heard the hoot of the klaxon inside and saw the men come filing out, quickstepping their way to their weekend with smiles on their faces.

Harold saw him as he crossed the road but didn't stop. Clifford walked alongside, trying not to skip.

'What do you want? I've told yer all I know.'

'You know what I want, Harold. It's time to show what you're made of.'

'Haven't got time. Got to get changed and out on a date.'

'There isn't going to be any concert, Harold. Or haven't you worked that out yet?'

'I know that, Einstein. But there's *supposed* to be a bloody concert, and I'm supposed to be taking my future wife to the bloody thing, so what's it gonna look like if I don't bother going because I knew the singer was gonna get crippled?'

Clifford risked a chortle. 'Always an excuse from you when it comes to the crunch.'

Harold stopped and turned. The threatening jab in the chest again.

'Any more of your lip, *Clifford*, and you'll find out what a crunch feels like. I ain't scared of no one. Now I've told ya where they're gonna be, and this is the second time I've done ya this service. So why don't you run along and do what you're supposed to be best at, eh?'

Clifford stopped and watched Harold stalk up Newport Road. He stamped his foot and marched up the steep slope of Church Road, cursing every step. By the time he reached the top he was huffing and puffing.

Needed to do exercise more. Perhaps send off for one of those Charles Atlas chest expanders. The coming storm needed its foot soldiers.

He walked along Woodbridge Road, past the station, and on past Lukers, trying not to stare too hard. A few girls were hanging around outside, giggling, clutching autograph books. Evidently, Harold Ogborne had blabbed to more than just his Blackshirt friends. Clifford walked on, fists clenched, wanting to punch someone.

The others were waiting in the Fighting Cocks in their usual corner of the bar. Thankfully no one was wearing their Blackshirt uniform. There were a few of them you wouldn't put it past, they were so stupid.

They looked nervous, sweating, and he realised it wasn't the coming action that worried them.

'Don't you worry about last night,' he said. 'Our friend in Her Majesty's constabulary will be along in a minute to put your mind at rest on that.'

He ordered a round of cheap brandies for them all and by the time the barman brought it to their table on a tray, their police mole had entered.

The men looked up to him, desperate for solace, and they found it in his smile.

Constable Davies didn't look the same in normal clothes. You would never recognise him.

'Tell them,' said Clifford.

'No evidence,' said Davies. 'They're not even going to investigate the witness statement. No proof it was you lot.'

Grins broke out and they all knocked back their brandies. Clifford gulped his down, felt it sting his throat and the heat bloom through his limbs.

Davies plonked a sack on the seat. Clifford delved in and pulled out a truncheon. He snatched it out and hid it in his inside pocket before anyone in the pub could see it. The delighted men did the same.

They waited for a signal from Clifford and then scrambled out, their boots tramping the pavement, marching, hurriedly now. Clifford led them. This was what it must feel like to march alongside Hitler. Marching to glory. Marching to war.

They passed the girls waiting with their autograph books, ducked down the side alley, running now.

He could barely see five yards in front of his hand, the alley was so dark. Should have brought torches. An army should be able to see where it's striking. There it was: the service dock, just like Harold had said. Waist high, a set of wooden steps leading up to it. The secret back entrance. Hop up onto the bay where they off-load the bread, down a short hallway and into the back room bakery where Benny Orphan was giving a private singalong to the Jewish bakers.

Clifford took the steps two at a time and was first onto the dock. The men rushed up behind him, truncheons drawn.

They stormed into the dark hall and the floor echoed with their boot steps. He saw the outline of a table lamp in the gloom. A sideboard. Some chairs stacked up.

There was something not quite right about it.

It was the floor. It was wooden.

They didn't break through the dark hallway to the bakery beyond it. There was no bakery beyond it. It wasn't, in fact, a hallway.

He looked back, too late, as a metal shutter came down. He saw only the silhouette of the man that trapped them inside before everything went black.

The floor shuddered with life — roared, in fact — and then the earth lurched underneath them as if an earthquake had struck.

He struggled to keep his feet. But Davies crashed into him and they both fell.

He had a moment to think it was a repeat of the tornado that had seemingly blown through the cinema last night, before he realised they weren't in Luker's at all.

They were in a furniture removals van.

— 41 —

Rachel and Charlie laughed all the way from the Prince back to Charlie's flat. Passersby gave them funny looks but couldn't help smiling, catching their infectious merriment.

Joshua Goldman would drive the Blackshirts to a very isolated scrap yard owned by a respected member of the Singer's Hill synagogue, making sure to hit every bump in the road. He would leave the van there overnight, sure in the knowledge that no one would hear any Blackshirt cries and shouts, and head to the concert with everyone else.

In the morning, they would be rescued from their ordeal and attended to by a reception committee comprising several star members of the Benacre Street Boxing Club.

They climbed the iron steps to the flat and burst into the parlour, still giggling at their triumph. Charlie put a kettle on the hob straight away. Before it had boiled they had lapsed into sullen silence, remembering Henry.

The angry whistle startled them.

'I'll get ready,' she said.

She checked the clock on the wall. They had a little less than an hour before they had to be at the Institute. An hour after that the doors would open.

'Oh. I got you something,' he said.

He went to the sideboard and pulled out a crêpe paper wrapped present, handed it to her shyly. She unwrapped it and held a tiny bottle that bore the label *Soir de Paris — Bourjois*. Perfume. He'd bought her perfume.

'I got it with the winnings,' he said, scratching the back of his neck.

'Oh Charlie, it's lovely. Thank you.'

She leaned forward and kissed his cheek. He blushed and looked at the carpet.

'I'll put some music on,' he said.

She left him rooting through his stack of 78s, and took the kettle of hot water to the washstand in her bedroom, stripping naked and soaping herself down, the faint lament of *Gee Oh Gosh I'm Grateful* drifting up the stairs to her.

She applied a cloud of *Bourjois* and made her face up in what she hoped looked tasteful and refined for an average 1930s girl.

From her wardrobe she took the slimline blue ball gown with silver brocade that had come from Amy Parker's storage chest after she'd died. There was a tear at the seam by the collar and she wondered when that had happened. It looked like it had never been worn. She should have stitched it. Perhaps no one would notice in the dim light of the ballroom.

There was a sound behind her, a pop of air, as if a light bulb had blown.

'Hello, Rachel.'

She wheeled round, catching her breath.

Kath Bright was standing over by the safe. Her red hair looked wild as if charged with static, and her eyes were rimmed with shadow. There was something eerie about her.

'What the hell are you doing here?'

Kath smiled. 'This is our base, Rachel. You know that.'

Rachel put a hand to her chest. Her heart was beating like mad. It was fine, she told herself. They were supposed to be coming tonight. She'd been waiting for this.

'Sorry. I didn't expect you here. How come Charlie lives here now?'

'He's renting it. Maybe you told him to?'

'I don't think so. This is the first time I've met him.'

'Maybe I'll go back to 1931 or something and suggest it to him? Who knows? We're all cogs in Mrs Hudson's grand plan.'

There was something about her manner that wasn't quite right. She had a smile at her lips, as if she knew something funny and didn't want to share it.

'Aren't you supposed to be at Newport Road?'

Kath checked her watch. 'Yes. I think we're there round about now.' She saw Rachel's confusion. 'I'm coming from a different time. Not 2013. Much later. I've managed to free myself of using my own little touchstone — the Dovecote. It's rather liberating. You're going to love it when you get the hang of it.'

Rachel glanced at the door. Would Charlie hear her talking to someone and come up to investigate?

'Tell me everything's going to be all right tonight.'

'Don't worry,' said Kath. 'You've done a wonderful job so far.'

'So far?'

'Things could change. That's the problem with time.'

'But you're coming from later. You know what's happened tonight.'

Kath giggled. 'Thing is, if I tell you too much, it might change things yet again.'

'What's Danny going to do?'

A shadow fell across Kath's face. 'I'd ignore Danny if I were you. Just leave him to me tonight.'

'What's happened to him? That thing, with the tornado?'

'It happens.'

'What do you mean, it happens? Things like that don't just happen.'

'Like time travel?' said Kath. Her smile was a sneer now. 'There's a reason Moseley and Kings Heath keep getting hit by tornados and it's nothing to do with meteorology. Problem is, it's impossible to know when it's going to happen.'

'What are you saying?'

'You change time in 1934 — affect time in a really bad way — and a time wind wreaks havoc in, say, 1931. A girl's whole existence is wiped out in 2011 and a tornado destroys half the neighbourhood in 2005.'

'What? That tornado was because of *me*?'

'Who knows?' Kath giggled again. 'If I were you I'd forget all about tonight. You want your life back and nothing you do here is going to help you. You know that. You need to go to 1980. You should do it now and leave tonight to me.'

Rachel found herself shaking her head. This wasn't right. She wasn't going to leave now, just before the concert. Just disappear and leave Charlie on his own.

'Danny needs to be stopped,' Rachel said. 'He's not normal. What if he does tonight what he did last night? Someone could get killed.'

'Just watch out it isn't you.'

The shadow on Kath's face became murderous. She lunged at her. Rachel shrank back, covering her face, falling to the floor. Water slopped from the enamel wash basin. Kath was no longer in the room.

It had felt like an electric shock. There was a smell of singed hair in the room. It was as if Kath were a moth that had hit a light bulb.

'Are you all right?'

Charlie's voice from the bottom of the stairs.

'Yes,' she called. 'Everything's fine.'

But she knew everything wasn't fine. Kath, or some Future Kath, had turned against her, tried to kill her. And, if Kath had been the moth, it meant that Rachel was the flame that had burned her.

She'd thought Danny had disappeared in the cinema. Flitted to another time in a flash of flame. But now she wondered if she'd done it. Just like with Future Kath. It looked like she had.

But she had no idea how.

— 42 —

Kath Bright knew that things weren't going to plan. It was in Mitch's sullen demeanour that was something beyond his Time Flu, and in Mrs Hudson's frosty impatience.

They waited at the foot of Newport Road by the telephone box, which was the only place you could loiter on a quiet neighbourhood street like this without drawing immediate attention.

'Someone coming out,' said Kath.

Mitch put his opera glasses to his face.

'Neighbour,' he said. 'Woman.'

'What's she wearing?' asked Mrs Hudson.

'Ball gown.'

'Well, what a surprise.'

Kath hated this. The tension was unbearable.

They had come through together. It was easy when she travelled with Mrs Hudson and Mitch. She sort of closed her eyes and hung onto their coat tails and they took care of it. Perhaps that wasn't how it was and she did all the work, but it helped her to think of it like that. No needing to walk up to the Moseley Hall hospital grounds, climb the fence and walk up the wooden steps of the Dovecote.

Mrs Hudson checked her watch and tutted.

'Anything yet?'

'No one's emerging,' said Mitch.

'I meant your feelings,' she snapped. 'Are you feeling anything?'

Mitch shuffled uncomfortably.

'I don't know why it is. It's just… not the same as I felt last time. It was off the charts then.'

'And now?'

'Nothing. Not a sausage.'

Kath spotted activity far up the road.

'Hold on,' she said.

Mitch peered through his opera glasses again.

'Looks like the whole family coming out. Hefty mother, ferret-faced teenage son, looking rather self important, and younger teenage daughter. They're all dressed to the nines.'

'Well, is it obvious now?' snapped Mrs Hudson. 'Everyone is off to the concert and nothing is going to happen here.'

'I don't know why I don't feel anything,' said Mitch. 'Strange.'

'Shall we go, then, and do what we should have been doing all along?'

There was nothing more to do. Mrs Hudson had been right. They had to head for the concert.

'Let's go,' said Kath, patting Mitch on the arm.

As they walked up Newport Road she was wondering how she could get away from them and somehow get to Danny before they saw him. If she did that she might be able to help him. Surely she could pull him back from the brink, make Mrs Hudson see that he was all right? She had sensed it so much sharing the flat with him in 1966. They didn't know him like she did.

They walked past the house, from which Mitch still sensed nothing.

'Shouldn't we contact Rachel?' she said. 'I mean, we sent her off to organise the concert, so we should maybe give her some support?'

Mrs Hudson looked at Mitch.

'Let's check the venue first,' he said. 'Hopefully she'll be there.'

'Along with everyone else,' said Mrs Hudson.

— 43 —

Sid Haye arranged his papers on the head table in neat configurations. They had to be just so.

Agenda paper.

Sheaf of notes outlining his speech (five pages).

Fountain pen.

Handbill for concert poster (to be used as a prop for when he came to the part of his speech where he dismissed the bourgeois social democratic approach to anti-imperialism).

Glass of vodka.

He took his fountain pen and scribbled a note in his speech: *joke about Benny Orphan being just like Trotsky?*

He rearranged the desk again. It didn't seem right.

He mentally went through his speech one last time and calculated the order of each prop, left to right.

Leonard, to his right coughed, sucked on his pipe and said, 'Sounds nice and busy down there.'

The hubbub from the pub below promised a great crowd. Sid looked out at the rows of empty wooden chairs and imagined them full to heaving. Imagined his words flying out above their heads, whipping them into revolutionary frenzy. Lenin at the Finland Station.

He took a deep breath.

'Let's open the doors, shall we, comrade?'

Leonard nodded, blew out tobacco smoke and jumped off the low stage. His footsteps clattered as he made his way across the empty function room.

Sid could see the faces of the first few through the glazed doors, knowing they would be queued right down the stairs and out of the pub to the rear yard.

Leonard opened the door with some ceremony and the first few piled in, making for the front row seats. He nodded to familiar faces: long-serving party members, one or two old faces who hadn't been so active of late (a few stern reminders of revolutionary duties in order), a man he'd never seen before (undercover policeman?). They took their seats, scattered here and there in the acre of chairs.

No one else. Had Leonard opened the side door downstairs? He must have. Where were the rest?

Leonard stood at the open door, peered down the stairs, shook his head.

Sid felt the blood rush from his face. He scanned the faces and counted them. Fourteen in all.

What was going on? Where was everyone?

He stared at his desk and his eyes fell on the handbill and Benny Orphan's smiling face.

— 44 —

Amy Parker knocked the door to the Dowds. It seemed like a lifetime ago she'd knocked the same door, to call on Little Amy and ask her about her ghost. She had been fraught then, thinking herself crazy, but now she knew her own ghost was real.

Still, he won't come, she thought. Her letter to him had gone unanswered. Her eyes had fallen to the doormat every morning, and every afternoon returning from work, but no letter had come.

Had she written the wrong words?

I do wish to see you. But it is not safe for you to call on me at my home. Too many prying eyes. But your suggestion to meet at the concert meets with my approval.

Was it too cold, impersonal? Too suggestive? Was he disgusted with her? She didn't think he would be. But she didn't really know him. Three, four brief encounters in 1912, and now another couple, 22 years later, in which they'd barely exchanged a word. She didn't know him at all.

The door opened and Little Amy smiled proudly.

Amy took her in. She looked absolutely divine in a floor length silver ball gown, fake fur stole, her hair permed tightly in a bob. Harold Ogborne did not deserve her.

'You look wonderful,' she said.

'I feel like a princess!'

'And you shall go to the ball,' said Amy, thinking *only to kiss a frog after all.*

She followed her inside to the front parlour. Mrs Dowd had on her Sunday dress and a little make-up. It was the first time Amy had seen her with make-up.

'My, don't we all look the bee's knees,' said Mrs Dowd, lighting a cigarette and taking the ceremonial bottle of sherry from the glass cabinet.

She poured a thimble full into two tiny crystal glasses and caught Little Amy's hopeful glance.

'I suppose you think you should have a tot too, Little Amy?'

'I don't think I want to be called Little Amy anymore. I'm grown up now.'

Mrs Dowd exchanged an amused glance with the older Amy and frowned. Amy could tell she was thinking *But if we call you 'Amy', we'll have to call Amy 'Old Amy'.*

'You're a long way off twenty-one, young madam,' said her mother, pouring a third tot. 'But I guess you'll be a woman soon enough, arr.'

They all sipped and practised looking sophisticated.

'I still can't believe I'm actually going to see Benny Orphan,' said Little Amy. 'I mean, really *him.*'

Mrs Dowd chuckled. 'I think Harold might get jealous tonight.'

'Oh, mum.'

Little Amy tried not to blush, but it made her face go even more crimson.

Someone rapped at the door.

'Talk of the devil,' said Mrs Dowd.

She pushed herself up, groaned as her knees creaked, and shuffled up the hallway.

'I'm not sure how I feel about Harold,' said Little Amy. 'I'm not sure I want to go and live in that house after…'

Amy stared with surprise. Little Amy's lips were pursed with sudden determination, as if she'd been thinking it over for a long time.

'Why don't we not think about that tonight,' Amy said softly. 'Let's go and dance. With real men. Not ghosts.'

Little Amy nodded.

The Ogborne family's footsteps came tramping up the hall.

Little Amy stood up, took in a deep breath and put on a fake smile.

— 45 —

The Moseley and Balsall Heath Institute ballroom was laid out much as Rachel remembered it from her first nights out drinking. For her it had been the Moseley Dance Centre, hosting Friday and Saturday night soul and disco nights. An ironic retro treat that had run for twenty years or more and been the Moseley drinker's weekend last resort until late licensing had finished it off.

She had been old enough to catch the tail end of its fame on some of her earliest nights out drinking. In 2013 it was closed up and left forlorn, hosting only stage school day classes.

She walked around the dance floor and surveyed her work. The same arrangement of tables down each side, leaving a huge dance floor space down the middle. The bar to the right of the entrance. The stage at the far end, guarded by giant scarlet curtains. Bunting hung from the rafters.

Charlie came to her side.

'Looks grand. You've done a great job, Rachel.'

'We,' she said.

He checked his wristwatch. 'Time to start.'

The band were on stage and already playing a gentle waltz. Manny's tuxedoed bouncers were clustered in the entrance hall. The first people were entering, the buzz of excitement around them. Benny Orphan's manager was situated firmly at the entrance to the hall, dispensing raffle tickets to every lady.

Mr and Mrs Hollis arrived, both dressed up to the nines and looking all about them with wonder.

'What a lovely evening,' he said. 'You must be very proud, Charles.'

'Thank you for your help,' said Charlie.

'We couldn't have done it without you,' Rachel added.

'Nonsense,' he said. 'You'd have found a way. It was my pleasure to help it along a little.'

They watched him get a table and take his wife's coat, sit her down. An old couple, still very much in love.

'Thank you,' Charlie whispered to Rachel.

'What for?'

'For persuading me we should do this. It's the right thing.'

She took his hand and squeezed for encouragement, interlaced her fingers with his and squeezed again.

'Here we go,' she said. 'Let's just make it worthy of Henry.'

The first groups came through, having deposited coats in the cloak room and rushed for the best tables. Rachel and Charlie went to the entrance to check on things there. Manny's men were running things smoothly, discreetly; a presence that wasn't intimidating but was ready for any eventuality.

The punters streamed through, chattering excitedly, all freshly soaped and gleaming in their evening wear. It was a pale imitation of the sophisticated Mayfair crowd, the men wearing their Sunday suits not tuxedoes, with ties instead of bow-ties, the women in evening gowns that had been run up on sewing machines, with imitation jewellery. But to these people it represented the height of sophistication.

Rachel gazed in wonder as they filed through and paid for their tickets. This was how the great working mass of the city had found their entertainment: a single night of glamour, once a week in a place where you could forget the Depression, and the world outside sliding towards war.

After they'd secured their tables and their drinks, a great many of them gravitated to the dance floor, but no one danced. They crowded to the stage to peer at the band in wonder.

She knew from her History studies that black people had been present in the city for a hundred years or more, but this crowd acted like they'd never seen a non-white person in their lives.

Lester and his band played *Moonglow* and she felt it flow through her like sweet wine. The kind of song that made you feel every drop of joy in the world and all its sadness at the same time. The crowd just stared and talked. She heard their comments from the fringe of the crowd.

'A coloured band.'

'Have you ever seen anything like it?'

'They play just like a white band.'

'Who'd have thought?'

'It's jazz, Phyllis. I think you'll find they invented it.'

'I know, but still. A coloured band.'

She recognised Sheila Sutton from the hotel, who was crowing to all within earshot. 'Of course, they're staying at my hotel. The whole band. Perfect gentlemen. Quite civilised.'

Rachel scanned the crowd, wondering what her purpose was now. The concert was on. She had succeeded. Somewhere in this crowd were Mrs Hudson's parents-to-be. They would fall in love tonight and any attempt to wipe out Mrs Hudson's existence would be scotched.

Would Danny come? She felt more certain now that he was here for Amy Parker and it was nothing to do with Mrs Hudson. But what of Kath Bright? What was she up to? She shuddered at the memory of Future Kath. What had happened to her — what was going to happen to her — to make her so unhinged in 2014? Would it be something that happened tonight? And what of this other matter they were investigating: the more important thing that had something to do with a house on Newport Road — would that have anything to do with tonight?

The band ended the song and the crowd applauded enthusiastically. Charlie was by her side, hands clapping twice as hard as anyone else, as if he were applauding for Henry too.

'In a way,' he said. 'I wish those Blackshirts were here now to see this. It would kill them to see a band of coloured musicians being welcomed so warmly.'

'Did you ever doubt it?' she asked.

'I don't know. I suppose I did. There's so much hate around, it overwhelms you, makes you despair.'

She thought about it and tried to find the words to explain it to him. She remembered a debate in History class at school. Her teacher had marked her down for making vague platitudes that had no basis in research but she remembered it now and knew it to be true.

'We get a rough ride,' said Rachel, 'but I've always felt that British people, as a whole, are very tolerant and open to new cultures. And we don't really do extremism the way other European nations do. We're far too sensible to get whipped up by nonsense. We see through it. That's why fascism can take off in Germany and Italy and Spain and in plenty of other places, but it will never thrive in Britain. There'll always be a minority of idiots who whip up fear and hate. They'll never go away. But they *will* lose.'

He looked at her curiously. 'What future do you live in, Rachel?'

She smiled and wondered if she should tell him. She was about to say something about 'multicultural Britain' and wondered if the word would confuse him, Could she tell him that the Moseley village she knew had half a dozen Indian restaurants, a Caribbean, a Chinese takeaway, an Italian, a Moroccan, a French café, a tapas bar and three fish and chip shops that also sold Indian food and pizzas. Did anyone in this dance hall even know what a pizza was, let alone a samosa? The Blackshirts would lose, be swept aside as an irrelevance, and Britain's cultural life would be immeasurably improved after the war by so many alien cultures.

She was trying to formulate an explanation that he might understand when she saw Harold Ogborne walking across the dance floor.

He had a teenage girl on his arm and was followed by four other women.

Sudden fear gripped her and she clutched Charlie's arm. He followed her eyeline.

'Don't worry,' said Charlie. 'I'll tell the boys to keep an eye on him. If he's with the Blackshirts, he's the only one of them here.'

But it wasn't Harold she was afraid of. It was another woman in their party: Amy Parker. And the fact that they were wearing the same dress.

Of course they were. She'd taken it from Amy Parker. It was in the trunk of her clothes after she'd died in 1966. Stupid, stupid, stupid. They weren't just wearing the same copy of a dress — it was the exact same dress.

She ducked behind a crowd of women who were standing close by, using them as a wall to screen her from Amy Parker.

She remembered with growing horror that Amy had made the dress herself. In the trunk of her old clothes was the *Du Barry* pattern from Woolworths. What were the odds of making your own dress for a night out and seeing another woman wearing the exact same design? She looked around the room and saw that every dress on every woman was unique.

She peeked through the wall of women and saw that Amy's party had found a table close to the stage and were making a great fuss about taking seats from the next table and who would sit next to whom.

'That's *her*. Amy Parker's her name.'

The women between them were all talking about Amy Parker, Rachel realised. She couldn't help hearing what they said.

'Wasn't she the one whose father went doolally and died in the loony bin?'

'Winson Green, arr. You know what it was sent him mad and all?'

It was Sheila Sutton from the hotel, whispering viciously with a gaggle of friends. They lowered their voices for certain words and she couldn't catch them, but the general tenor of the conversation was clear enough.

'She's here to meet a fancy man — I won't call him a gentleman — in secret. I read her letter to him, clear as day, the filthy slut. Had to, like, as he was one of my guests and had moved on without leaving a forwarding address.'

'Well, it's no wonder with the likes of her.'

'Always said she was a wrong un.'

'You watch her. She's here for that fancy man of hers. You'll see.'

It must be Danny, Rachel thought. He'd been at the hotel and had moved out. Amy Parker had got in touch with him. But what were they meeting for?

— 46 —

She had to hide. She gripped Charlie's arm and hissed 'Come with me.'

She marched through the crowd of people craning their necks to stare at the band, using them as a screen, and scooted up the wooden steps at the side of the stage, hiding behind the curtain with Charlie.

'What is it?' he asked.

'Amy Parker. She's here. And Danny will be coming too.'

He peered through the peep-hole. 'She's with Harold Ogborne's party as well. You don't think?'

Rachel shook her head. 'I'm sure she's nothing to do with that. And Danny. No, it's something else.'

She wondered what it could be. Mitch had been certain that the time anomaly was concentrated at Harold's house and it involved a stranger travelling there from 2013. And here was Amy Parker, somehow connected with Harold Ogborne. But Mrs Hudson had been certain that it was the concert that was important. And here they both were. And Danny was, of course, somehow involved.

She knew there was something they were all missing.

'You don't think Danny's going to do what he did in the cinema last night, do you?' asked Charlie.

'You think he did that?'

She knew the answer; was only surprised that he thought it too.

'Henry seemed certain. And you do too. I can tell.'

She nodded and linked arms with him, pulling him closer to her, resting her head on his shoulder, wanting him to hug her suddenly.

'Now, now. Keep it clean!'

They jumped apart. Benny Orphan grinned and winked, rubbing his hands together in glee. His bodyguards were behind him, walking him to the stage.

'It's normally after I've started singing that the canoodling starts.'

Charlie blushed and looked at his feet. Benny Orphan cackled. He stared out at the band, who were skipping through *Oceans of Time*.

'Great band you've lined up here. Pianist looks a bit out of place,' he laughed.

'Last minute replacement,' said Charlie. 'Local lad.'

'He's no Duke Ellington,' said Benny. 'But he'll do, all right.'

Lester Johnson, leading his band on stage, noticed Benny standing in the wings and nodded to him. Benny Orphan saluted and turned back sharply.

'Now, how do I look?'

'You look perfect—' stammered Charlie.

'Not you!' Benny Orphan smiled at Rachel. 'How do I look to the ladies?'

She straightened his bow tie, brushed a fleck of lint from his white tuxedo jacket.

'You look a million dollars,' she said.

Benny Orphan's face lit up like a Christmas tree. 'Now that's what a man wants to hear!' He turned to Charlie. 'You just get out on that dance floor and get ready to catch the ladies when they faint. After you've introduced me, of course.'

Charlie looked scared suddenly. He hadn't thought of taking the stage.

The song came to a close and Lester Johnson looked expectant as the crowd applauded.

'Go on, Charlie,' Rachel whispered.

She gave him an encouraging pat on the arm that was also a gentle shove, and he was onstage and walking to the microphone.

'Er...Hello. Good evening,' he said. 'Ladies and gentlemen.'

'He's not done this before, has he?' quipped Benny Orphan.

'Welcome to our... to our concert. And a very warm welcome to our special guest band, Mister Lester Johnson and his Coloured Jazz Orchestra!'

The crowd applauded enthusiastically. We won, Rachel thought.

'And also featuring a local boy guesting on piano tonight. He's stepped in at very short notice. Mr Anthony Pratt!'

As the applause continued, Charlie's smile widened and his confidence bloomed.

'And now, without further ado. Please welcome tonight's star billing. The legendary Mr Benny Orphan!'

Charlie walked backwards off the stage, applauding with the crowd, as if blown off stage by the wave of acclaim. Benny Orphan skipped over to the microphone, arms aloft, accepting their love.

Rachel was taken aback by the noise. Some women were actually shrieking. It wasn't a Beatles scream. Their grandchildren would do that. It was the sound of decorum being abandoned as women, young and old, shrieked with sheer disbelief at seeing an idol in the flesh for the first time.

Charlie was by her side, his hand resting gently on her waist.

The band kicked into *What a Difference a Day Made* and she saw the dance floor suddenly become a spinning, swirling mass of couples quick-stepping. A band of women stuck doggedly to the edge of the stage, gazing in adoration, but they were gradually picked off one by one as gentlemen asked them to dance.

Out on the dance floor, the heads of couples bobbed and weaved. It was a river of dancers, swirling and eddying. Every man was looking at his woman, and every woman was looking over his shoulder at Benny Orphan.

She watched him with growing excitement. He closed his eyes as he crooned, as if dreaming of a certain sweetheart lost to him forever. Benny Orphan the joker had been replaced by a sensitive romantic. She felt her knees go slightly weak.

They stood watching from the secret seclusion of the side stage. A few of the Benacre Street Boxing Club guys watched too, but the girls they had with them dragged them to the dance floor, leaving only a couple on guard.

She felt Charlie pressed against her, acutely aware of his touch, the rhythm of his breathing, wishing he would pull him to her and kiss her. There was something about Benny Orphan's singing that made you long for a deep, long kiss.

He crooned through *True, That's Me Without You* and *The First Time I Saw You*. Arthur, his manager, seemed to have abandoned the raffle idea and come onto the stage with a large box camera. He stood behind Benny Orphan and took a picture. Rachel wondered why and then realised he wanted the audience in the background. Benny Orphan crooning to his fans. She couldn't see the corner of the dance floor but realised it would be the table where Amy Parker was sitting.

Benny Orphan opened his eyes and announced he was going to sing *Let's Fall in Love for the Last Time*. A roar of delight came from the dance floor.

'Miss Hines? Would you care to dance?' said Charlie.

She wasn't sure she should. If she ventured out onto the dance floor, Amy Parker would see her and her dress. But she desperately wanted to dance.

She nodded and Charlie took her hand, led her down the wooden steps at the side of the stage and walked her to the other side of the dance floor, far away from Amy Parker's table. A hand to her waist, the other holding her hand out, his chest pressed to hers. He moved suddenly and she realised she knew no dance steps. It seemed to be some kind of waltz, luckily, a very slow waltz. She stumbled at first, then worked out the one-two-two, one-two-two rhythm of the steps and kept up with him.

Then she remembered the song. Deirdre Foster, her maternal grandmother, in the café in 1959, telling her this was the song her parents fell in love to. This song. She scanned the sea of couples dancing, caught up in the romance of the moment. Here, somewhere, surely, her maternal grandmother's parents were falling in love for the first time. Fred Foster was possibly meeting Vivian Hunter and having their first dance.

It seemed that so many people were coming together for the first time tonight, as if the band and Benny Orphan's performance was the epicentre of love.

The song ended.

Charlie stepped away from her and applauded politely.

She remembered all the things that might go wrong tonight. She had been swept up in the romance of the moment and forgotten that she had a mission.

She checked her wristwatch.

Where were Mrs Hudson, Mitch and Kath? Would they come?

She shuddered at the memory of Future Kath, lunging at her with hate in her eyes.

— 47 —

Mrs Hudson was almost running ahead of them, a youthful spring in her step, drawn by the small crowd outside the Moseley and Balsall Heath Institute.

Kath tried to keep up with her, aware that Mitch was slowing down behind her, wheezing as he walked.

'Hurry up, Mitch,' she called back.

Mrs Hudson climbed the steps and disappeared inside. Kath wondered why there were a group of men outside holding placards but she had no time to examine them.

'She was right,' said Mitch. 'The vibration is much stronger here. I don't know how I got it so wrong before.'

'Don't worry,' said Kath, holding his arm. 'We're here now.'

'He's not here yet. Jez. But there's something here that's really bad.'

Kath climbed the steps, holding onto him. She'd never seen him this weak. A phalanx of tough looking men in tuxedoes manned the door and waved them through. She wondered if the heavy presence was due to the men with placards. Had someone tried to stop the concert? Maybe Mrs Hudson had been right about everything.

They pushed through, ignoring the cloakroom, and found themselves at the edge of a giant dance floor. An all-black jazz orchestra played on the stage at the far end and she could make out the white crooner, who must have been the infamous Benny Orphan.

Mrs Hudson was standing staring at the dance floor, a smile on her face. She followed her gaze. She seemed to be looking at a table visible through the swirling dancers. A young man, his skinny neck protruding from his too-big suit, stealing glances at a teenage girl squirming, her legs and arms in knots. Between them a much older couple looking at the proceedings with an air of disapproval.

Kath could just about recognise them as the couple from the photograph on Mrs Hudson's wall.

'Dear lord,' said Mrs Hudson, all her irritation now gone. 'They look so young. I thought I'd never see them again.'

Her eyes were misting over and Kath wondered why she'd not used her gift to visit her dead parents as often as she liked. It seemed stupid to possess such a gift and to go on missing people you loved simply because of a technicality like death; a technicality that was easily sidestepped. She felt a sudden surge of irritation — as if Mrs Hudson had transferred her mood to her — and wanted to be free of the old lady.

She backed away into the crowd, leaving the old lady there, staring at her teenage parents.

'Where are you going?'

Mitch grabbed hold of her arm.

'I'm going to have a look around,' she said, pulling her arm free. 'We can't all three of us stare at them like weirdoes.'

Mitch nodded and tried to smile. 'You're right. I'm just worried is all. She might be getting caught up in the moment too much — getting personal. We have to stay detached at all times.'

Kath nodded and left him there. She began to skirt the edge of the dance floor, looking for Danny. She had a chance now, she thought, to catch him before the others.

But it was Rachel she saw.

The girl was wearing a blue ball gown and looked quite stunning. She was staring at her with something like fear. What was wrong with her?

'Rachel,' Kath smiled. 'Here you are. How are you?'

Rachel let her tug at her hand but there was something in her face — it was as if she didn't know her. Kath thought for a wild moment she might be meeting a different Rachel, an earlier one who'd never met her, or perhaps her great-grandmother, and she panicked for a moment.

'Rachel?'

'Yes. Kath!' said the girl suddenly, smiling. 'I was wondering when you'd arrive.'

'Mrs Hudson's over there, with Mitch. She's found her parents and everything seems to be normal so far. But look at this.' Kath waved an arm at the ballroom. 'You've done so well. Mrs Hudson is very pleased.'

'It was touch and go,' said Rachel. 'But it's happening at last.'

'Now. Have you seen Danny?'

Again the fear in her face. Was it suspicion? What had happened to make her like this? Kath knew she'd gone out of her way to make Rachel trust her.

'No,' said Rachel. 'Is he coming then?'

'We think he is.'

'I knew it. He can't resist Amy Parker. But it's awful. The damned letter. Everyone's talking about it. He's totally compromised her.'

Kath nodded, pretending to understand. 'Listen. Is there a side room, a dressing room? With a key?'

Rachel looked puzzled. 'The performers' rooms are backstage, but we can't access them. I've got a key to the backstage area, though.'

Rachel indicated a door in the dark corner of the ballroom, hidden behind a giant pot plant.

'Give me the key.'

'Why?'

Again the mistrust. Why was she making things so difficult?

'Because when he turns up I want to distract him. Get him out of harm's way.'

Rachel had a faraway look in her eyes, as if remembering something particularly frightening. She nodded and reached into her purse, pulling out a brass key.

'Thank you. If you see him, don't attempt to approach him. Leave him to me.'

'Don't worry,' said Rachel. 'I won't.'

She marched off and was lost in the crowd, leaving Kath to wonder why Rachel had actually shuddered at the thought.

— 48 —

Danny had tried to control the tornado emanating from him ever since Friday night. He'd cowered in fear in his room at the Station Hotel. When he'd thought back, he'd realised it had been there all the time, growing and growing.

He'd wondered if it was like a super power. Could he control it? It had seemed to increase whenever he'd thought about Amy, he knew that. He'd tried to meditate. To clear his head. Then had let the thought of her drop into his consciousness. The breeze would increase. Just a murmur. He would empty his mind. For hours he'd done this, allowing himself to think more about her each time; taming the zephyr around him to nothing but a light breeze.

By the time he walked to the Moseley and Balsall Heath Institute he was serene and in total control of it.

There seemed to be some sort of demonstration outside; men and women waving placards. It worried him for a second. Demonstrations meant fights, and fights usually ended up with Danny in a police cell.

He paused and read the slogans. *Down with Mosley's Blackshirts! Fight the Forces of Fascism! Unite Against Capitalism with our Coloured and Jewish Brothers and Sisters!* It seemed to be a demonstration in support of the event, but Danny couldn't work out why it was thought necessary. Most people entering in their best clothes were frowning at its peculiarity as much as him. The demonstrators continued chanting and waving their placards. They didn't seem to care. As if it were enough that they were simply seen to be there.

He breezed up the steps, paid his money and sauntered into the ballroom.

He felt detached from it all, as if it was happening to someone else. He had to, in case he created another tornado. He knew that if he maintained serenity and allowed no emotions to build inside him, he could control it.

He stood for a while, watching the dancers, then began a circuit of the floor. Before he'd reached the stage he was surprised to find himself looking into the eyes of Kath Bright.

Fenwick had warned him about her. She was the enemy. He stilled the surge of surprise, fear, suspicion peaking inside him. She was smiling. She could do him no harm. He remembered waking up with her on a sunny morning in 1966. A good thought. A calm thought.

She came to him, still smiling that warm smile, the stage lights glinting on her red hair.

'Danny,' she said, as if to an old friend. 'Long time no see.'

'Haven't seen you since thirty years from now,' he said.

She laughed. She couldn't be the enemy. He could read the warmth in her eyes and he knew that it was genuine.

'You're looking for Amy, aren't you?' she said.

'How did you know?'

A sudden stab of fear in his chest. Control it, quell it, she means you no harm.

'Thing is, you've made it rather difficult for her. Everyone knows about your letter. You've compromised her.'

'Compromised her?'

'Things are different here,' she said. She placed a comforting hand on his arm. 'She can't meet you here. Too many eyes.'

He nodded. It seemed logical. Yes, they did things differently here. Perhaps he'd been too forward.

'I've got a key for backstage,' she said. 'I'll get her to meet you there in a few minutes.'

She turned and he followed her to the shady corner of the ballroom, behind a giant fern, there was a door. She unlocked it. He peered through. It was a side stage corridor, illuminated by the light from the stage. He wondered if it was a trap of some kind. It didn't matter. He could walk right onto the stage and jump off it if he chose. He suppressed a giggle in his throat at the thought that he could blow the door right off its hinges with a breath. Who could stop him?

'Wait here,' she said. 'I'll bring her along in a minute.'

He walked through. Before she locked the door he asked, 'Why are you doing this for me?'

She thought about it a moment, her smile fading.

'Because I know what it's like to love someone and not be able to have them,' she said.

She closed the door. He heard the key turn in the lock and wondered why she thought she could lock him in. Was it to keep him here or prevent someone else entering? It didn't matter. He waited.

— 49 —

Rachel pushed her way through the crowd, heading for the entrance. She needed air.

She also wanted to get away from Kath Bright.

She was perfectly pleasant and friendly, but Rachel had seen Future Kath and it scared her. Something was going to happen to Kath that would sour her, and that something was quite possibly going to happen tonight.

She was being a coward. She should confront her, perhaps even warn her, and here she was putting as much distance as she could between them.

She saw Mrs Hudson standing at the edge of the dance floor. Mitch was with her.

She could go over now and warn her. *Something's going to happen to Kath, she's going to turn against us, I've seen it.*

But she remembered how Kath had lunged at her and been repelled by something inside her, something inside Rachel that had knocked her back like an electric shock. Could she explain that? She didn't want to. It scared her. It was too much like the thing that was happening to Danny and she wanted nothing to do with it.

She shuddered and pushed through to the entrance, gulping down the fresh night air.

Charlie was standing at the entrance with Manny. He turned to her.

'Rachel, are you all right?'

'I'm fine,' she said, forcing a smile. 'Just needed some air. It's so hot in there.'

'We'll be carrying ladies out soon,' joked Manny. 'I'd better go in and check.'

Charlie took her hand and walked her outside to the top of the steps. She was puzzled to see a crowd of men out there waving placards.

'What's going on?'

'It's Sid Haye,' said Charlie, 'and his Communist Party members.'

'Weren't they holding a meeting tonight?'

'They certainly were.'

She read the anti-fascist slogans on the placards.

'So why are they here supporting this? Wasn't he against it earlier?'

Someone took a photograph with a giant flashbulb that blinded her temporarily.

'This is what they do,' said Charlie bitterly. 'They campaign against something, denounce it as incorrect, tell everyone their way is the correct way. Then when the tide goes against them they don't even say they've changed their mind — they just pretend it was their idea all along and take credit for it.'

The men were chanting about the evils of fascism and posing with their placards for the photographer. One of them was even holding up a poster for the concert. Anyone would think it was their event.

'You see, they'll claim that they were responsible for defeating the Blackshirts. Sid Lowe will tell everyone that it was him and the C.P. who organised the concert. And the worst thing is, in a few years' time he'll actually believe it himself.'

Rachel nodded. 'Four legs good. Two legs better.'

'What does that mean?'

'Nothing,' she said. 'Yet. But it will do soon.'

She took his hand, suddenly aware that they had very little time left together.

'Come inside,' she said. 'Let them pretend all they want.'

— 50 —

No one saw Jez standing across the street staring at the Moseley and Balsall Heath Institute, because he wasn't there. To him, he was still in 2013.

He was in 2013 as he threw his cigarette aside, crossed the road and walked up the steps to the faded Moseley Dance Centre sign and the much newer plastic banner swaying in the breeze announcing a vintage retro night called *Hot Ginger*.

He was still in 2013 as he walked through the entrance.

But somewhere between the threshold and the door to the dance floor, somewhere half way across the foyer, he drifted from 2013 and melted into 1934.

It was the first time he'd deliberately willed himself into the past, and he'd achieved it by refusing to allow his mind to believe it wasn't possible. For a month or more he'd been seeing Amy, the dead wife of Harold, in the old man's dilapidated house, sometimes drifting back to the house's past history as a ghost. It had happened so much he no longer felt he belonged in his own time.

As he walked into the ballroom, the vintage-dressed ghosts of the present day being replaced by the real life 1930s dancers, a wave of music hit him. He strode purposefully across the dance floor. He knew what he was looking for. He knew who. He scanned the tables that skirted the edges of the room, and there she was.

Little Amy, sitting alone in a party dress: awkward, shy, a wallflower. She looked up. He stood above her, holding out his hand. Her eyes met his and he felt no fear. There was only hope and love in their eyes. She rose uncertainly, placing her hand on his, letting him lead her to the dance floor where he stopped and turned. They stood face to face. He eased her closer to him and started to dance to the music. She placed her free hand on his arm and let her cheek brush his and he took in the sweet scent of her and felt her body pressed close to his.

They circled round and she pulled her head back to look him in the eye, unsure of him suddenly — could he really be real? — but she was swept away by his tenderness, swept away on a wave of emotion as he stroked her cheek, and she smiled.

And he thought of her on a photograph that would be taken years from now: the photo that would haunt him.

They swayed together to the hypnotic music. He closed his eyes, trying to hold back the present, the awful future. He gripped her a little closer to him as the music swelled to a brass fanfare climax.

Her face on the photograph, eyes averted, unsmiling.

He stumbled. She stepped back from him. He reached out for her. Her smile was gone now. He reached out for her, desperately, but other dancers were passing between them. Her face receded, lost in the crowd as she backed away.

She turned, casting a glance back over her shoulder and she was gone and he opened his eyes to find himself in 2013, lying on the dance floor at the *Hot Ginger* night, blinking up at a ring of concerned faces. Someone was calling for an ambulance on their cellphone.

— 51 —

When Amy Parker returned to their table she felt sure there had been a fight. The crowd had formed a concerned circle. She fought her way through and found Little Amy lying on the floor, Harold propping her up. Her mother was fanning her face.

'What's happened?' she cried.

'Where is he?' spat Harold. 'I'm gonna knock his block off!'

She looked around and saw a strange man with a handlebar moustache slinking away from the scene.

'He was the one,' she heard one of the women say.

'I'm gonna have him!' shouted Harold.

'No, not the one dancing with her. He was the one who hit him.'

'Hit who?'

'The fellah that was dancing with her.'

'Inappropriately, I might add.'

'The one with the girl's hair. Looked like a right Mary Ann.'

'Had his hands all over her, poor girl.'

'She looked scared.'

'Came over and hit him, he did.'

'He didn't hit him. He just tapped him on the shoulder. I saw it.'

'The bloke just fell down.'

'Where the hell is he?' snarled Harold.

'He just disappeared.'

'Fell on the floor. I saw him!'

'Must have run off.'

'He disappeared, I tell you. Like a ghost. I saw it.'

'Don't be bloody soft. You've had too many sherries.'

Amy knelt by the girl's side and stroked her face. She could smell burning. A familiar smell. No, it was singed hair. She stroked Little Amy's hair. It didn't appear to be burned anywhere but the smell was unmistakable.

'Where the ruddy hell were *you?*' snapped Mrs Dowd. 'You were supposed to be looking after her.'

'I went to the bathroom,' she said. 'I left her with you.'

Harold and Mrs Dowd pulled Little Amy up and sat her in a chair. Amy fanned her face.

'Anyone got smelling salts?'

'She don't need it. She's coming round now.'

Amy stroked the girl's cheek as her eyes fluttered open.

'Are you all right? What happened?'

Little Amy smiled and whispered, 'It was him. It was *him*. I danced with him. He was *real*. Then he disappeared. Like a ghost.'

'Come on,' said Amy. 'We should take you home.'

'*I'll* take her,' barked Mrs Dowd. 'She's *my* daughter.'

She snatched Little Amy away from her, yanked her to her feet. What was wrong? What had she done?

'I thought I'd help, that's all,' she stammered.

'We don't need any more of *your* help, Amy Parker.'

Amy recoiled. She knew that tone. It was the tone of accusation, of disapproval, of scandal. She'd heard it her whole life. She'd thought Mrs Dowd was above all that.

Mrs Dowd dragged Little Amy away and Amy watched them plough through the dancers and fade through the exit. She looked all around. The Ogbornes avoided her gaze. Mrs Ogborne reached for her coat.

'Reckon it's time for us to leave too.'

'Oh, mum!'

'Come on, Judy.'

Harold glared at Amy like she was somehow responsible for it all.

'What a great night this has turned out to be,' he spat, and marched off after his mother and sister.

Amy looked all around and her eyes met Sheila Sutton's. She was staring back with a look of malignant glee.

The letter.

She knew it now. She'd read her letter to Danny Pearce. She'd told everyone. There probably wasn't a person in the dance hall who didn't know about it now.

She looked around for her things. She needed to get out of this place, run away and hide. They were turning their backs to her. A young girl in pigtails was staring at her. Amy reached for her purse and dropped it on the floor. Someone picked it up for her.

'Here you are.'

A friendly voice. She looked up into the smiling face of a young woman. A redhead. There was something about her that didn't quite belong, but then, neither did she. She didn't belong anywhere.

'It's Amy, isn't it? Amy Parker?'

Surprise. Was this the introduction to some fresh humiliation? Would she laugh at her, spit in her face, slap her?

'You don't know me,' said the redhead. 'It's all right. I'm a friend of Danny's.'

She looked all around. No one was watching now, only the girl in pigtails.

'He's waiting for you,' she said.

'Did he not get my letter?'

'Er… Yes. He got it.'

'Then why isn't he here?'

She couldn't hide the despair in her voice, the anger. Why has he abandoned me?

'He thought it would be inappropriate. There are far too many eyes here.'

'It's a little late for that.'

'He's waiting for you. At the village crossroads. If you hurry, you might catch him.'

Could it be true? Could he be waiting there for her? What mystery had prevented him from coming here? Perhaps he knew his letter had been intercepted and he'd thought it best not to appear. He was protecting her. She felt a sudden thrill for him. She should run from here, run from their wagging tongues and vicious whispers and go to him: go to wherever he wanted to take her. She could leave this all behind and start anew with him, somewhere else.

The music had stopped. Someone was on stage calling out a number. She couldn't hear it. All she could do was stare into the eyes of the redhead and see her means of escape.

'Go now,' said the redhead.

'It's her!'

She clutched her purse close to her. She would run now. Run to him.

'It's her. She's got the number!'

They were all turning to look at her. What fresh hell was this? Why didn't they all leave her alone?

The girl with pigtails was pointing at the table and the two raffle tickets still lying there.

'It's her!'

'She's won!'

'Over here!'

'She's got the ticket!'

The girl with pigtails picked up the raffle ticket and pressed it into her hand. What was happening? She had to go now. He was waiting for her.

'It's her!'

'Here! She's got the ticket!'

No, it wasn't her ticket, it was Little Amy's. It was all a mistake. The redhead looked panicked.

'Just go. Now!' she hissed.

But someone pushed Amy towards the stage. Before she could run she was being herded to the steps at the side of the stage.

She heard their whispers as she climbed the steps. Why did it feel like a scaffold? She stepped up into the light, clutching her purse, blinking. No, this wasn't happening.

Benny Orphan's smile dropped when he saw her and she knew instantly that he had expected someone younger, prettier. His manager looked at him and gave a shrug.

The crowd were applauding as she stepped up to his side. But she could hear the whispers too.

Benny Orphan plastered on a fake smile and asked her name.

'Amy. Amy Parker,' she croaked. 'But—'

He nodded to Lester Johnson and the band broke into *Love Me Tonight*.

Benny shoved her onto the stool. He was going to sing to her. She wanted to die. The lights were blinding her; she could only just make out the shadow of the crowd on the dance floor, a many-headed monster that rippled and snaked as Benny Orphan sang to her. He closed his eyes throughout as if he were singing to some imaginary woman. Was it Little Amy he was thinking of? Had he set up the whole thing with his manager? That must be it, she thought. The raffle was all a ruse. The manager would pick a nice looking young girl and they would make sure they drew her ticket. They had chosen Little Amy. She realised suddenly she was saving Little Amy from his paws.

The song came to a close and Benny Orphan went down on one knee to her. She heard laughter from the audience but it was thankfully drowned out by applause. The manager walked on and took the microphone.

'Give her a big hand, ladies and gentlemen. What a lucky lady!'

She wanted to go now. She could get off this stage and run. She could run to him. Danny was waiting for her at Moseley village.

'But that's not all. She also gets to go backstage and have her photograph taken with Benny Orphan himself. In the meantime, we'll leave you in the capable hands of Lester Johnson and his band!'

Benny Orphan was waving to the crowd, blowing kisses. The manager gripped her elbow tightly. She gasped in pain. 'This way,' he hissed. 'Come on.'

He shoved her to the back of the stage. She stumbled down wooden steps, down a dark corridor, and he threw her into a dressing room. Benny Orphan followed them inside, wiping his face with a handkerchief.

'What a bloody shambles!' he shouted.

He pulled her to his side and said 'Smile!' A bright light flashed. The manager had a camera. He walked out and slammed the door.

Benny Orphan took her arms, gripping too tightly.

'Let's have a look at you then,' he said.

'I have to go,' she said. 'Someone's waiting for me.'

'You can't go without your prize, love,' he said.

She didn't like the way he grinned at her, the spark of lust as he ran his eyes over her.

'Nice dress,' he said. 'Get it off, then.'

She recoiled, squirmed out of his grasp. He slapped her across the face. She screamed. She heard the seam tear at her shoulder.

He was pulling her towards him, moaning, grunting like a pig at the trough.

'Get off me!' she cried.

He clamped his sweaty hand over her mouth and pressed her back against the dressing table. She couldn't move, couldn't break free of him.

There were shouts outside. The manager. He was telling someone everything was fine. She tried to cry out again, her voice muffled.

She heard the door fly open, a gust of wind blew in and Benny Orphan slammed against the far wall. He gasped in pain and slumped, his face livid with agony.

A hand grabbed her and pulled her out.

It was Danny Pearce.

He had come to rescue her.

The door was barred. A group of men, alarm in their faces. Danny held out a hand, as if to tell them to halt. But they flew back down the dark corridor towards backstage.

'Come on,' Danny said. 'This way.'

He pulled her with him, turning the opposite way, deeper into the building. They ran down the dark corridor. He pushed against a door and they came out into a yard where a coach was parked. Cold air on her face, fierce wind blowing. He ran across the yard and she flew with him, her feet barely touching the ground. A gate with a lock. The padlock exploded, the chain buckled, the gate blew open with a bang. And they were on the street, Brighton Road, running to her house.

— 52 —

Rachel saw the sudden urgency among the Benacre Street Boxing Club boys, signalling to Manny to come backstage.

For a moment she thought it might be the Blackshirts. Had they finally managed to target Benny Orphan, even this late? She glanced across to Amy Parker's table. No one there. Perhaps it was Harold Ogborne after all. But as she grabbed Charlie and ran through the crowd in Manny's wake, she knew it wasn't him.

She knew it was Amy Parker.

She knew it was Danny.

Lester Johnson's band carried on playing the final few numbers of the night. People were still dancing.

She followed as fast as her heels would allow, down the dark back corridor, trying not to trip, feeling Charlie's hand at the small of her back.

A group of the boys were crowding round the dressing room entrance. She pushed through.

It looked like there had been a fight in there: a chair on its side, a picture tilted, the contents of Benny Orphan's suitcase strewn across the floor.

Arthur was shouting at Manny, his face purple with rage.

'It's a bloody outrage is what it is and you've allowed your star to be attacked. Yes, attacked! Right here in his dressing room!'

Manny's huge presence was calming the air somewhat and he deliberately lowered his voice to soothe the situation.

'Now please calm down and tell me what happened.'

'He's already told you!' shouted Benny Orphan.

'It's scandalous!' Arthur spluttered. 'And you knew something like this was going to happen all along. Don't tell me you didn't!'

'Now that's absurd,' said Manny.

'So why the mob-handed security all day?' Arthur laughed. 'Do you think we're blind? You knew something like this was going to happen. And when it happened you failed to stop it. That makes you liable.'

Charlie stepped forward. 'Now, now, there's no need for that kind of talk. Security here has been well taken care of.'

'And yet your star act has been attacked. How do you explain that?'

Rachel knelt down and picked up Benny Orphan's belongings, placing them back in the suitcase. She stopped at a photo album which had fallen open. Each page featured a young girl in either one or up to four photographs. On every page was written the name of the girl and the venue. She flicked through it. Most of the photographs were innocent enough, every girl posing with Benny Orphan, but she noticed that on some pages the girl was photographed alone, sometimes hiking up her skirt to show her thigh, a few were posing in their underwear, hiding shy smiles, scared eyes.

'Mr Orphan has never been treated like this in all his days. Hundreds of performances up and down the country, day in, day out, and nothing to match this!'

Manny's face was flushed. He turned to his boys crowding the corridor. 'How many were there?'

'Just the one. A man.'

'Just the one?' He looked at Benny and Arthur again, trying to weigh up what was really happening here. 'Is that true? It was just one man?'

'There were more,' said Benny Orphan, rubbing his neck. 'They threw me across the room. One man couldn't have done that!'

'We heard a scream,' said one of the boys. 'It was a woman. We ran to the dressing room, and there was this man, he grabbed the woman and ran out.'

'Hang on,' said Manny. 'You heard a scream?'

'That was probably me,' said Benny Orphan. 'Not a woman. I was being attacked.'

'It was a woman. Definitely. We heard it, boss.'

'He tried to stop us going in,' said one of the boys, pointing at Arthur.

Rachel saw the look that passed between Benny Orphan and his manager. She handed the photo album to Charlie.

'Would this have been the woman who won your raffle?' asked Rachel. 'The raffle you were very keen to run yourself?'

Charlie looked up from the pages of the album, showed it to Manny. Rachel saw his jaw tighten.

'I don't know what you're implying, young madam,' said Arthur, wagging his finger in her face. 'But you'd better be very careful.'

'So *you* pick out the girl,' she said, pointing at Arthur, 'and he gives her the prize, is that it?'

'You watch your mouth, missy.'

It was Benny Orphan wagging a finger at her now. Charlie pushed him back. Arthur leapt forward. Manny's giant hand shoved him back. He held up the photo album.

'Is this what you do; up and down the land; day in, day out?'

'Those are just harmless photographs,' said Arthur.

'Some of those don't look harmless,' said Charlie. 'In fact some of those girls look positively scared.'

'Was the woman who was in here scared?' asked Manny. 'Did she put up a fight?'

'She wanted it!' spluttered Benny.

'You animal,' said Rachel.

She stepped forward, hand raised to slap him. Benny Orphan shrank back, eyes bloated with alarm. Manny caught her hand, mid-air, and edged between them. Rachel backed away, folding her arms, tears of rage springing to her eyes.

'My boys have provided you with protection all day,' said Manny, towering over Benny and his manager. He seemed to be growing another inch with every word, filling the room with a menacing presence. 'But protecting a man who's forcing his attentions on a woman — that's where our protection ends.'

Arthur tried to speak but Manny prodded him in the chest and he looked at his feet.

'Now, I'm going to call a cab and they're going to drive you back to your hotel and you're going to shut your mouths. We're all going to forget about this. But I'll tell you this now. If I ever hear of you performing anywhere in this country and staging this raffle of yours again: you're going to be hearing from me. And you don't want to be hearing from me ever again. Is that understood?'

Neither of them answered. They couldn't even raise their heads. Arthur reached for the photo album. Manny snatched it away.

'We'll be keeping this. And the camera. Just in case we hear any more tales of innocent girls crying out for help.'

'You bloody great big—' Benny Orphan started at him, fists clenched.

Arthur pushed him back. 'Shut up, Benny. It's over. We've all seen enough. Let's go.'

Manny nodded towards one of his men. Arthur picked up Benny's case and they shuffled out of the room. The Benacre Street Boxing Club boys parted to let them through. Both men seemed to shrink, becoming smaller and smaller, as they walked out.

Charlie took Rachel's arms. 'I'm so very sorry,' he said.

'What for?'

'That you had to see that. That I booked that man to come and perform here.'

She wanted to hug him. He was so young and innocent, such a boy still. She unfolded her arms and stroked his cheek. He almost recoiled with surprise.

'Charlie, don't ever apologise for him. You weren't to know what he was. None of us knew.'

Manny nodded. 'She's right. Not your fault. Not anyone's. And at least we've put a stop to it.'

They all realised the band were still playing onstage.

'Let's go and enjoy the band,' said Rachel. 'It's nearly over.'

Charlie nodded.

They filed out of the room towards the sound of sweet music.

— 53 —

The dance floor still teemed with life as Lester Johnson's band swayed through *Let's Stop the Clock*.

'Are you dancing?' asked Charlie.

Her heart thrilled. 'Are you asking?'

She laughed. And then she saw Mrs Hudson across the floor. The old woman summoned her.

'Just a minute,' said Rachel. 'I have to talk to those people over there.'

Charlie followed her gaze. 'Do you know them?'

'They're from… where I come from.'

'Oh,' he said. 'Are they going to take you away from me?'

He laughed a little but it didn't seem funny. She felt miserable. This was the end of it all.

'I think they are, Charlie.'

She squeezed his hand and made her way to them, slaloming through the dancing couples.

Mrs Hudson was smiling. Mitch looked ill. Kath seemed annoyed about something.

'Rachel,' said Mrs Hudson. 'Well done, girl. You did everything asked of you, and from what I hear it involved a great deal of hard work.'

'Did we win?'

'I rather think we did,' said the old woman. 'My parents had their first dance after all and love seemed very much in the air.'

She leaned in and hugged her, whispering in her ear, 'Thank you for letting me see them again.'

'What about the other thing? The man on Newport Road?'

They all looked at Mitch.

'He arrived here. We missed him enter. He was dancing with a woman before I could send him back to his own time. Job done, I think.'

'But what about Danny Pearce?'

Rachel noticed Kath scowl at this.

'What about him?' asked Mrs Hudson.

'Where is he?'

'We don't know that he ever arrived.'

'He did. I saw him.'

Mrs Hudson looked at Mitch. Kath looked at the dancers.

'Well,' said Mrs Hudson. 'He didn't interfere in any way. The concert went ahead. All is well.'

'But—'

'It's all right. Mission accomplished. Let's go.'

'I have to wind things up here.'

Mrs Hudson suddenly seemed stern. 'We have to go. Right this minute.'

'I'm not going yet.'

'Rachel. I can't have you disobeying a direct order like this. We have finished our work here and we are going.'

Rachel thought of Charlie, still waiting for his dance. She had to give him the list of dates when she would meet him. It had happened. If she left now, it wouldn't happen. She looked at Kath but Kath didn't seem to be listening to any of it. Was this the moment she unmoored herself and floated away into the darkness?

'It's not right,' said Rachel, firmly. 'I can't just disappear. There are things to do, people to say goodbye to.'

'Nonsense. We don't belong here.'

'But we *are* here. And we owe it to the people we interact with to behave properly — not just get what we want and disappear. It's not right.'

'Very well,' said Mrs Hudson. 'But do not stay the night and do not do anything to affect the future.'

'Okay,' said Rachel.

She wasn't at all sure she wouldn't do both.

Mrs Hudson turned and walked out.

Mitch smiled wearily. 'Good work, Rachel. Very special evening.' He winked and followed Mrs Hudson out.

Kath stayed a moment. She said nothing. It wasn't exactly a look that would kill, more a look that wondered what it might be like to kill, one day, if the fancy took her. She walked out and Rachel knew for certain that the Kath she knew before this night was now much closer to the Future Kath she'd encountered.

She sighed and felt suddenly weary.

Charlie was still standing at the edge of the dance floor. He asked with his eyes if she was fine. She gave him a smile and rushed to him, suddenly so eager to be in his arms.

'I want that dance now, Charlie Eckersley.'

He took her in his arms, just as the band finished the song.

Everyone stopped and applauded. Lester Johnson came to the front of the stage and took a bow. The band all stood and did the same. The applause rang out all around them. Some men whistled and cheered. Surely it wasn't over?

Lester nodded to his men and said something to the pianist. They put their horns to their mouths. Another song. She would get her dance with Charlie.

But they launched into *God Save the King*. She thought it was a joke. Even more so when all those sitting down suddenly rose to their feet. For a second she looked around and giggled. Then saw that Charlie was standing erect and singing along with everyone else. She realised this was what they did here: they ended the night standing for the national anthem, standing for the king, without irony, without scepticism.

The national anthem ended.

The band took their last bows and filed backstage. People started heading for the doors. It was over.

She looked at Charlie. He shrugged an apology.

'Never mind,' she said. 'We can put a record on later and dance to that.'

Mrs Hudson's words about not staying the night echoed in her head. But it was the faint echo of a song, and she wasn't sure she liked the tune anymore.

— 54 —

Danny had checked behind them as they ran down Brighton Road. No one had followed. He kept on running with her, slowing his pace a little, calming himself.

It seemed he'd been able to control it. Use it. Almost as if it were a special power he could unleash when he chose.

They passed under the dank shadow of the railway bridge and walked. She was breathing heavily. Amy Parker. Holding his hand. Still distraught at her ordeal. Too distraught to wonder at this turn of events: that Danny was taking her home.

He tried to take his mind off it. Stay calm. Be remote. Float above the situation.

They turned up Kingswood Road and he checked back. No one following. They were safe.

He thought about Fenwick's words. There was no touchstone. This was a talent. It was a skill he possessed. And now this. The ability to unleash a tornado. It was almost as if he was becoming superhuman. Perhaps this had been his destiny all his life. *As we watch Hinton in this struggle, we seem sometimes to be conscious of a prophet who is caught up from the Earth in a whirlwind he cannot control, and borne away in a chariot we cannot follow.* He was a superhero. He could do anything.

They turned into Newport Road and he caught her looking up into his face. Was it adoration he saw? Was it awe? Perhaps she thought he was her movie hero. She could only think of it in terms of him being dashing. What could she know about the awesome power he possessed?

They came to her house and she opened the waist-high gate quietly, as if not to disturb the neighbours, closing it after him so it didn't click, like a burglar. Stealing into her own house.

He wondered if he should speak out. Make some kind of excuse to enter with her. He said nothing.

A light was on in the parlour next door.

Amy slid the key into the lock and stole inside, motioning him to follow quickly. Once he was beside her in the narrow, dark hallway, she shut the door and sighed with relief.

She stood with her palm to the door for a few moments. He watched her, nothing but a shadow in the dark. The sound of their breathing. Alone together. What was she thinking?

She came alive again, as if she'd drifted away to another time or place for a moment. She came back to her body and squeezed past him. Should he take her in his arms? Kiss her?

He followed her down the hall, past the mahogany coat stand, through to the middle room. A couple of armchairs, a sideboard, a dining table with wooden chairs. A door to the kitchen. Another door on the inner wall, open, revealing the stairs to her bedroom. She drew the curtains to the back yard and turned on a lamp. Golden glow. Secretive.

Finally, she looked at him. They stared across the expanse of the room. Amy Parker and Danny Pearce. Alone together.

'You don't look much older,' she said. 'It's as if you're a ghost.'

'I'm not a ghost.'

'But you're not real either.'

'I'm real.'

An owl hooted out the back somewhere. She suddenly seemed uncomfortable in herself, hugged herself. Did she want him to do that?

'You're not like other men,' she said.

He said nothing. What could he say? It was true.

'I knew it,' she said. 'Even back then I knew it. Even before the thing with my father.'

'He was going to kill you.'

'I know.' She looked at him again. 'I've just never known how you knew that.'

He tried to imagine it from her perspective. He'd appeared to her when she was a teenage girl; a stranger trying to spirit her away from her mad father. A stranger who'd saved her life when her father had tried to murder her. And then he'd disappeared. And here he was again, hardly changed, back in her life after twenty years.

She must have sensed what he was thinking because she said, 'Where have you been all these years?'

He shrugged, smiled. How could he answer that? He'd been in her future.

'You wanted to take me away,' she said. 'Do you remember? You wanted me to run away with you.'

'I still do,' he said.

She seemed surprised, and relieved. 'Where would we go?'

He thought of the touchstone. When he'd asked her, back in 1912, to run away with him, he'd thought he could take her to St Mary's church yard, touch the stone and take her to 2012 with him. But now he knew that couldn't work. She could never travel through time with him. He could only ever travel through time to visit her life. He couldn't take her from this time, but he could take her from this place.

'We could go anywhere,' he said. 'Do anything.'

'You're so sure of everything. When you're here it always seems so simple. So right. But then you disappear and I don't know what to think anymore. Are you going to leave me again?'

He took a step towards her. 'No. I want to stay with you.'

She looked scared. He walked the five steps across the room to her, which felt like five miles. Would she tell him to go? Would she fight him off, like she'd tried to fight off Benny Orphan? Her eyes questioned him. There was pain in her eyes, and doubt and disbelief and also a terrible longing: for answers, for respite, for love.

He put his hands to her arms. She shuddered. He pulled her close to him. His lips sought hers. She didn't push him away. She didn't struggle. He tasted her lips at long last and melted into her kiss.

— 55 —

Rachel and Charlie went backstage and made sure everyone got paid for the night. They congratulated the band and Manny's army of heavies. Tony Pratt, the guest pianist was mopping his brow, wiping his glasses, red-faced but excited.

'That was rather spiffing,' he said. 'Thank you for asking me, Charlie.'

Lester Johnson came over and shook his hand. 'You did well, sir. Thank you for standing in. It was a pleasure playing with you.'

The other band members slapped him on the back and he blushed and took out his Conan Doyle book.

'I say. You couldn't all sign this for me, could you? It's all I have with me, and I'd so like a memento of the night.'

They all took turns with his fountain pen and signed their names on the title page, including Charlie and Rachel.

It was an hour or more before they all piled out into the midnight air. A fierce wind was blowing and they rushed to climb aboard Abe's bus that drove them to Moseley.

He pulled up at the quiet crossroads of Moseley village and they got out, waving to them all. Rachel felt a sudden longing to continue with them, like a girl who can't bear the thought of the holiday being over. The bus drove on up the hill to take the band to the hotel.

No one about. Only the wind singing in the trees.

Charlie took her hand and crossed the road. They walked round the back of Boots to the back yard and up the iron steps.

They cowered inside from the wind. She could hear it howling all around.

Charlie looked for some music, put a slow record on the gramophone. *Midnight, the Stars, and You.* They didn't dance.

'You look sad,' he said.

She nodded, afraid she might cry if she spoke. 'I just thought of Henry.'

He slumped onto the sofa. 'I can't believe I'll never see him again.'

'I'm so sorry, Charlie. When will the funeral be?'

He shrugged. 'I don't know. This week, I imagine. Will you come?'

She shook her head. 'I have to go.'

'When?'

'Tonight.'

Now it was his turn to look sad.

'But I'll see you soon. In 1940, in fact. In the middle of an air raid.'

'An air raid?'

She bit her lip. 'There are a few things I need to tell you about the future. I shouldn't. In fact I've been told not to. But, well... I sort of already have. So now I have to do it.'

A sudden look of realisation lit his face. 'The football,' he said. 'It's Saturday. I didn't place those bets.'

'Don't worry. You're going to make a lot of money. But like I said: try to lose some too. Bernie Powell's going to become a very powerful and very dangerous man. You need to milk people like him gradually. Then you'll have enough money to become a bookie yourself. Don't worry; it'll be legal by 1961.'

'I'm going to become a bookie?'

'Yes, after the war.'

'There's going to be a war?'

She got up suddenly. 'I've got a list of dates to give you. It's in my room.'

She rushed out and up the stairs to the back room. The list was tucked in her jacket pocket. The names of the people he needed to befriend: Amy Parker, and Rachel's ancestors: her grandmother and great-grandmother. There were only two dates: one in 1940 and one in 1966. He would be waiting for her both times. It had already happened.

She wondered if she should include the 1959 encounter? Had it really happened? She wasn't sure of the exact date anyway. No. She would leave it. It had been an accidental meeting.

Her night dress was on the bed. Could she stay the night? Could she stay the night with Charlie? If anything had happened between them, he had never let her know.

The wind was howling at the skylight. The thought of Future Kath made her shiver. She rushed out of the room, like a child afraid of ghosts, and back down the stairs.

He was standing at the window, looking out at the night.

'Here,' she said, holding out the slip of paper.

He took it, read the dates. 'Is that all?'

She shook her head. 'There might be others. Those are the ones I know for now. I'll need clothes both times. Meet me where you first found me.'

He nodded and stared at the dates. This was it, she thought. For him it was the beginning, but for her this was the end. She had done everything she had to do. She would never see him again.

'I need to get my life back,' she said. 'Danny changed something in the past. He saved Amy Parker's life and now I haven't been born. Something in her life has cancelled out mine. If you can help me... well, it's going to mean a lot to me. I can't do it without you.'

'I'll do anything,' he said.

'Thank you.'

She had found herself here in 1934, as if washed up on a strange shore, and he had taken her in, and she'd known this was the time she would set all of this in motion, set him on the long path of helping her for the rest of his life. She would decipher this collision of Amy Parker's descendants and how it would somehow wipe out her existence. But she knew that the answer lay somewhere in 1980. Just like Mrs Hudson's parents tonight, Rachel's parents were supposed to meet at a dance, and Amy Parker's granddaughter, Esther, would get in the way.

She had to go there and stop Esther and get her life back. But surely she could stay here with Charlie just a little while longer?

She had a terrible swelling in her throat.

'Can I stay the night?' she asked.

It was as if someone had said it for her. She hadn't meant to say it at all.

'You can stay as long as you like,' he said.

'Can we have that dance now?'

He smiled. The record had finished. He went to the gramophone and the stack of 78s and searched for another.

He stayed there, kneeling, listening to an orchestral introduction, scared to stand up and face her. She smiled bitterly. Mildred Bailey was singing *Give Me Time*.

This was all the beginning for him, but for her it was the end. He had kissed her before. Kissed her three times. Held her in his arms. Asked her to stay with him forever.

Mrs Hudson had told her not to stay the night.

She could stay the night with him. Would it be such a scandalous thing? Would the sky fall in?

She felt a sudden acid stain seep through her.

Scandal, rumours, gossip. Amy Parker. The bastard child she'd had. A girl called Maddy. The rumour that it was the crooner who was Maddy's father. Benny Orphan?

But it wasn't Benny Orphan. She knew it, suddenly.

Charlie stood and faced her, smiling bravely. His smile fell when he saw her face.

'Rachel? Are you all right?'

She tottered. A wave of nausea swept through her. She knew it now. This was the disturbance Mitch had detected: the time crime, the violation.

The violent wind that had rattled at the window panes suddenly went silent.

She knew with absolute certainty that it had disappeared, sucked through a vortex, to wreak its havoc in 1931.

It wasn't Benny Orphan at all, even though they would gossip about it for years.

It was... Oh God.

'Rachel? What's wrong?'

Oh God. It was the worst thing that could happen. It was...

Charlie's face was fading. The room disappearing, crumbling, melting. She reached out for him. *Hold me. Keep me here.* But she knew it wasn't Charlie disappearing. It was her.

Charlie lunged across the room and reached for her but she never felt his touch.

She felt a blast of wind hit her face. Like the first gust of a tornado, cool on her skin, which was burning up.

Then the floor fell away from under her and Mildred Bailey wasn't singing *Give Me Time* anymore.

— 56 —

Danny woke on the floor, his neck stiff, his shoulder aching. The putrid smell of damp ash made him choke. He gagged and sat up, blinking.

His pin-striped suit was creased. He shivered inside it, huddled himself up to stay warm. Blew on his hands. A spot of rain on his face.

He looked up at a grey sky. Charred rafters a net enclosing. He was in the Kingsway again. After the fire. He looked around him at the charred shell of a building and leapt to his feet with sudden panic.

His legs were still asleep. He nearly fell. Pins and needles swarming down his left leg. He steadied himself, bent double, trying not to vomit.

He had been in Amy Parker's bed. Woken in the morning with her. The blissful intimacy of first love. Excited talk about running away together. Getting married somewhere. The whole future before them. He would stay in 1934 with her. They could live out their lives together.

She had gone downstairs, singing a love song, and he'd listened to her preparing breakfast in the kitchen as he'd dressed and smiled at himself in the mirror. His mission finally accomplished. Knotting his tie, slipping his jacket on, wondering if it was too formal for breakfast. He must go back to the Station Hotel and get his suitcase. His Kindle hidden in the lining.

Smiling at his own face in the mirror. You've done it, mate. They all tried to stop you, but you've beaten them.

Then he had fallen through.

Fallen through decades and landed on a carpet of sodden charcoal.

He stood up and breathed slowly, trying to think himself back to her. He could do this. He could go back to her bedroom and be there before she'd even realised he'd gone. Go back to that exact moment.

Nothing happened.

The photograph. The photograph still in his pocket.

He shoved his hand into his inside breast pocket, pulled out the photograph and handbill for the concert. Amy's face a beacon in the dim light of the dance hall, just beyond Benny Orphan's right shoulder, gazing out at him with a face of rapt wonder.

He thought himself back to her. Back to that morning. Back to her house on Newport Road.

Nothing happened.

He cried out, his scream echoing off the burnt walls. She was lost to him. He would never get back to her. He'd abandoned her just at the moment he'd promised to marry her. She would greet him years later with the wounded suspicion of the abandoned woman, and that bitterness would curdle into outright hate. There was nothing he could do about it.

A surge of vomit assaulted his throat and he fell to his knees, spewing it out, choking, gagging, retching out bitter bile.

By the time it subsided, his tears were falling onto the burnt carpet.

He lurched to his feet and clambered through the scorched and blackened debris, stumbling through to the old foyer. The walls were painted with soot but most of it was intact. Slashes of daylight through the slats across the doors.

He had to get out of here. Either smash through the boarded up entrance or find a side door.

The first door he found opened to a store cupboard. A broom, an old telephone, a paint pot and brush. The paint was orange. He stared at it and his heart sank. He smiled bitterly, the victim of a practical joke.

He knew now who'd burnt the cinema down. The moment Rachel had tasered him into the present. She'd ignited the fire.

And he knew now who'd written that cryptic message on the hoardings outside. It was him.

He took the paint pot and brush and kicked the front doors open, then pushed his way through the boards nailed across the entrance, emerging onto the Parade, gulping in fresh air.

A few cars parked, but no one around. Early morning. Just after dawn.

He prised the paint pot open, giggling to himself, sploshing the brush into the gloopy orange paint and daubing his message across the white hoarding in giant letters.

WHO BURNT ME DOWN?

He dipped the brush in again, to write *Rachel Hines* in the space below, staggered for a second, dizzy, swooning, orange dripping onto the tarmac.

He was flitting again. Would he find himself back with Amy? He somehow knew he wouldn't.

With a sudden cry of hate, he stabbed at the hoarding with the brush.

No. Let me stay another few seconds. Let me tell the world it was Rachel.

He lurched forward but the brush fell from his hand, and he had disappeared before it hit the tarmac.

— 57 —

Rachel opened one eye and swam to the surface of the room, air and light flooding into her. There was a hum of traffic from somewhere below. She was staring at a field of red and gold twine.

The rug. The rug in her flat.

She was home. She knew she was back in the flat above the village crossroads in 2013, before she'd even staggered to the window. Rain flecked the lead latticed panes. Moseley village out there, just as it had been in 2013.

A double decker bus sailed past, pausing right there, and a man in a tracksuit and baseball cap, jabbering on a cellphone, looked right at her, surprised to see a face so close.

She shrank back and flopped on the sofa. The apartment, just as she'd left it, the morning she'd taken her case and met Kath Bright at the door. Charlie's apartment.

Charlie, shocked, reaching out for her, too late, as she disappeared before his bewildered eyes. Eighty years ago, in the flat across the road.

The moment surged inside her like milk coming to the boil, spilling over in a cascade of sobs.

Danny had conceived a child with Amy Parker and disappeared from her life again. She would call that child Maddy.

And in 1966, Maddy Parker, all grown up, would tell Rachel her big secret: that Danny was the father of her child, Esther.

Oh God.

Danny had fathered a child with his own daughter.

She sprang up from the sofa in sudden panic, rushing out and down the corridor to the toilet, only just making it as she threw up.

He can't have known.

She wiped her mouth and saw her pale face in the mirror.

He can't have known.

She ran through the dates in her head. Maddy had a child who was six in 1966. Little Esther. So she was conceived in 1960?

No. She knew it now. 1959. While Rachel was trapped in a nightmare on the station at the end of time. Danny had probably been lost in his own UnTime. He probably didn't even remember it. That's when he'd slept with Maddy. Before he'd even known she was his daughter.

She retched some more, until nothing more would come, then drifted back to the lounge, hugging herself, passing the framed photograph on the wall: Charlie and Rachel sharing a picnic in 1966. The day England won the World Cup. The day they'd buried Amy Parker. The day Charlie had sort of proposed to her.

It was gone, she realised. It was over. She'd never see Charlie again.

She kneeled down before the giant stack of vinyl records stored in the sideboard, ran her fingers along the spines, pulled out a 78 and placed it on the Dansette. It spun and crackled.

Kath's words came to her again. *Go to 1980. That's where you'll find answers. That's where you'll get your life back.*

She had to do that.

She would go to 1980. Soon. But first she would listen to *Remember Me* and think about love.

— EPILOGUE —

Mitch sat in his car, twenty yards from the house on Newport Road. This was the end, he could sense it.

He recognised Jez walking up the street towards the house.

He'd followed him for a few days. Last night he'd watched Jez strolling through the park with his girlfriend. They had argued. Not so much argued. The talk had been intense. But she had taken his face in her hands and kissed him, then walked on ahead, laughing, sunlight dancing in her hair.

Mitch had sensed the love between them. It was a new thing. A recovered love. They hadn't been in love for a long time. Of course they hadn't. Jez had been in love with a woman who had died years ago. He had seen her in that house, visited its past, even taken a trip to the concert and danced with her.

But it was about to end.

He could feel the vibration receding.

Jez came to the house and waited, sitting on the low brick wall.

An ambulance pulled up and two paramedics jumped out. Jez shook their hands. They took an old man out of the back in a wheelchair and wheeled him to the front door.

This was the husband, thought Mitch. The old man whose memories Jez was feeding off.

Jez unlocked the padlock on the front door. The old man stood up and supported himself with his walking stick, tongue sticking out with the effort. The paramedics looked up at the crumbling house with shock. They retreated and Jez took the old man inside.

Mitch closed his eyes and tried to sense what was happening in there. He had wanted to approach Jez. Recruit him to their group. But Mrs Hudson had vetoed it. *Too soon. Watch him, observe; see if it develops.*

He thought now she might have been right. This was the end of it, he could feel it.

Jez emerged five minutes later, without his bag. He was going to the shop round the corner.

Mitch started the car and pulled out. He slid down to the T-junction and parked again. He could see right down the side road. Jez walked down and entered the off-licence.

Mitch waited, feeling sleepy. When this was over he would sleep for a week. He felt a jolt, a static charge, a shock.

She was there.

In the street. Seeing him. Seeing Jez through decades. As she always had, time and again, her whole life in that house, seeing this man from the future she thought was a ghost.

He sensed her terror, how unhinged she was. But also a calm acceptance. Resolution. And he knew, this was the moment she was going to end her life.

He saw it clearly. Her bully of a husband was retiring from his job at the factory around the corner. He was coming home to be with her day upon day. She was buying a bottle of brandy, walking back home, walking upstairs, sitting on their marriage bed, swallowing the bottle of tablets one by one.

And Jez had seen it too.

Mitch gasped, clutching his heart. He felt her sad and lonely death. He struggled for breath, feeling it recede. Relief.

Jez came out of the shop. He ran back to the house. Yes, there was something wrong. It had gone now. The vibration from the house had quite disappeared.

Jez shouldered the rickety front door open and rushed inside.

Mitch felt it now, taking air deep into his lungs, like a man who'd almost drowned.

The old man had died.

His memories were fading. And with it his dead wife and Jez's link to her.

It was over.

No. There she was again. In the house. Staring at Jez. Seeing him as a young woman, not long after she'd moved in there. She was a new bride. What was her name? He tried to feel the shape of it in his mind. Lilian. No, Little Anne? Little Amy!

She was seeing Jez in her house. It was 1939. He was a ghost to her. He was seeing her now at the moment her husband had finally died.

And then she was gone.

Mitch felt tears on his face, running into his mouth. Sweet, salty tears. He felt their pain. Little Amy's, Jez's, even the old man's: Harold. His name was Harold. Even his.

Mitch wiped his eyes and felt the emotional torrent recede.

It was over. Jez would never travel back into her past again. His one emotional link with the past had gone now. Mrs Hudson had been right all along. He would be no use to them.

He started the car. It stalled. The third time he turned the ignition the engine hummed.

The vibration was quite gone now. They had solved the mystery of Newport Road.

But there was something else there. A distant undercurrent; like a faint scent of perfume when a woman has left the room. What was it?

Something else.

He pulled the car around and drove away down the street.

He had a terrible feeling they had missed something.

* * *

Thank you...

... for buying and reading *Touchstone 5: Let's Fall in Love for the Last Time*. If you enjoyed it, please do give it a review on Amazon. Reviews help promote the series and ensure future Touchstone books.

The story will conclude in a night club in 1980 in the sixth and final part of Touchstone's first season, to be published early 2014.

Make sure you know when it's out, and take part in my regular free book giveaway, by joining the mailing list at **www.andyconway.net**

If you enjoyed the sub-plot of Jez's time travelling jaunts to Little Amy, you can read the full story in the timeslip ghost story novella **The Very Thought of You...**

What happens when you fall in love with a woman who died before you were born? Community visitor Jez becomes obsessed with Amy, the dead wife of an old man he visits. Harold is a cantankerous old codger who takes a venomous delight in confrontation and lives in a house that is falling down around him. But when Jez starts to see Amy's ghost and finds himself propelled into the house's secret past, his obsession with her threatens his hold on the present. A moving, evocative meditation on love and betrayal and the persistence of memory.

"Suspense, mystery, intrigue and supernatural... this delivers on all aspects... Couldn't put it down! Finished it in almost one sitting."

Available in ebook. Buy it at andyconway.net
Also available in French, translated by Fabien Cathelin

Also by Andy Conway

Touchstone (1. The Sins of the Fathers). One touch and you're who knows when?

Rachel: the dirt poor girl brought up by her single parent father. Danny: the arrogant rich kid who has everything his wealthy parents can afford. Two History students who wouldn't normally mix, but whose lives become entwined when an old gravestone catapults them back in time. In 1912, they explore their city's dark past, a gritty, violent, gaslit world of real danger, and try to prevent the murder of a teenage girl at the hands of her abusive, syphilitic father. But they find that every action has an unforeseen consequence that can ripple through generations.

"A brilliant teenage time travel drama that manages to be both intelligent and action-packed. Leads to a climax that takes your breath away…"

"A really cool concept that rattles along like an express train. It's never too long before something interesting happens, so it's turn, turn, turn. Ideal for mobile devices like Kindle…"

Touchstone parts 1 and 2 are also available in a single volume paperback edition. Buy it at andyconway.net

Touchstone (2. Family at War). Dealing with the catastrophic fallout of their previous encounter with Amy Parker in 1912, they now race to locate Amy during the 1940 Blitz and become caught up in the nightly German bombings of Birmingham and their chilling aftermath.

"I enjoyed this book. I have read a few time travel books but this one really got to me. I thought it was going to be a typical teenage romance but it certainly wasn't. I had to buy the second book and can't wait for the third. Absolutely gripping …"

"Although the Touchstone books may have been written for a younger audience, I assure you; if you are a true fan of timeslip reads these will not disappoint! Each went by far too fast and I find myself waiting in anticipation for the next installment…"

Touchstone parts 1 and 2 are also available in a single volume paperback edition. Buy it at andyconway.net

Touchstone (3. All the Time in the World). Rachel, lost and alone in 2012, travels back to 1966 to repair her lost timeline with the help of Charlie, now 50 years old but still in love with her. The Swinging Sixties are in full flow, Birmingham is being rebuilt and England are hosting the football World Cup. The temptation to stay there and live with Charlie is overwhelming, but Danny is there too, and the World Cup betting sting he's carrying out on the city's bookies brings them all to the attention of a local gangster, a corrupt politician, a cop with a grudge and a cabal of mysterious time travellers who are determined to prevent the past being changed. In the end it's hard to care about correcting the past when you're in danger of becoming the foundations for a new high rise.

"Great continuation of the series. He turned my preconceptions of the swinging sixties upside down a couple of times. ..."

Available in ebook and paperback editions. Buy it at andyconway.net

Touchstone (4. Station at the End of Time). A haunted train station in 1959, a freight train with a mysterious cargo and a young woman determined to throw herself in front of it… Rachel miraculously finds herself back at home in the present with her father but suffering a recurring nightmare of being trapped on Kings Heath station in 1959, trying to prevent her maternal grandmother, Deirdre Foster, committing suicide. As more and more characters from her time-travelling past intrude on both her too perfect waking world and her nightmares, she begins to wonder which world is real… leading to a terrifying battle to hold onto her own sanity.

This edition also contains bonus short story *The Reluctant Time-Traveller*, a creepy, spine-tingling investigation into the truth behind the Touchstone stories.

"An eerie ghost story with a couple of great twists to keep you on your toes once you think you've worked it out. It oozes atmosphere, reminiscent of old TV shows like Sapphire and Steel or the Twilight Zone… a cracking read which never really stops for breath…'

Available in ebook and paperback editions. Buy it at andyconway.net

ANDY CONWAY

GHOSTS ON THE MOOR

Three women spend Christmas in a remote cottage on Dartmoor to escape problems at home, but their long hike across the moor turns tragic as old ghosts return for vengeance…

"Dartmoor at Christmastime. What a spine-tinglingly perfect setting for a ghost story. The three women with a complicated past could take the book into a dreary (for me) chicklit direction, but it actually gives the ghost story its bite. It might arguably be described as a present-day M.R. James as thoroughly malevolent ghosts wreak havoc on our heroines… It's a cracking little ghost story."

"Glad I read this in the morning — at least I got my sleep in first. I shall think twice about going to Devon again."

Available in ebook. Buy it at andyconway.net

The Budapest Breakfast Club. Ten years ago, a group of students fell in love with each other and had their perfect moment. Now screenwriter Nathan Beck is back in Budapest to shoot a movie about it. But his return stirs up memories for the old Breakfast Club survivors trying to cope in this city now their perfect moment is over. And his secret affair with movie star Judy Carter threatens her marriage and career, with two muckraking Hungarian journalists digging up all the dirt they can find.

"Packed with extraordinary characters, wonderful comedy and some breathtakingly poignant moments. Conway's writing… picks you up and almost physically drags you through the ups and downs of an utterly believable and thoroughly irrepressible bunch of friends, each with their own story, and each with their own perfect moment. The way Conway weaves them seamlessly together is, in itself, close to perfection. Highly recommended."

Available in ebook and paperback editions. Buy it at andyconway.net

Can your love live up to the most romantic city in the world? Five couples try to find the answer on New Year's Eve in the French capital. By morning they'll know...

Lovers in Paris is a delightfully romantic collection of short stories that intertwine in a hearstopping climax.

"I'm not into romance books or short stories in any way, shape, or form but I really liked this story. It was pleasant, nice, and very touching. The description of the streets and surroundings made me feel like I was there again. Kudos. A fine read. Highly recommend this one."

"Funny, witty, with characters you want to root for. And if you've ever been to Paris and stayed near the Gare du Nord and Montmarte then you will enjoy this book even more. Good book and good writing…"

Available in ebook and paperback editions. Buy it at andyconway.net

Get a life. Get the girl. Get to Wembley. **The Striker's Fear of the Open Goal** is a desperate, comic look at how a football team can be the most depressing thing in a man's life... and the only thing worth living for. Ewan Glumie was born on the day Man City last won a trophy, and for 35 years it's been failure for both of them. But success might be on the horizon. City are heading for an FA Cup final and Ewan knows he has to get a ticket, get a career and get a girl before it happens or forever accept that *he's* the jinx, and that the gloating *35 Years* banner at Old Trafford is more about him than City.

"A wonderful encapsulation of the lows, highs and utter life affirming joy of our journey over the last 35 years supporting City."
   "I was in floods of tears with the Cup Final bit."
   "Just bought your book on itunes and didn't draw breath til the final whistle of the semi... Brilliant. Utterly Brilliant."

Available in ebook and paperback editions. Buy it at andyconway.net

The Girl with the Bomb Inside. Set in 1981, in the aftershock of Joy Division singer Ian Curtis's suicide, this 16,000-word novelette explodes with all the filth and fury of a three-minute punk song, hammering at the bars of its teenage prison with a foul-mouthed and brutal depiction of a schoolboy's attempt to deal with his girlfriend's pregnancy and write a novel about it.

"Get this book now. Andy Conway has absolutely nailed the uncontrollable insanity of being a teenage boy."

"Takes you on a journey that will stay with you long after you have finished reading."

"Delivered in such a punchy, gritty style it's hard to set aside."

Available in ebook. Buy it at andyconway.net

Coming soon by Andy Conway

Touchstone 6

Long Dead Road — a thriller

Relationship Status

Cinema Purgatorio

Learn to Croon

Autumn Leaving

For up-to-the-minute publication updates see
www.andyconway.net

Printed in Great Britain
by Amazon.co.uk, Ltd.,
Marston Gate.